ALMOST LOST

IF SHE SAW (Book #2)
IF SHE RAN (Book #3)
IF SHE HID (Book #4)
IF SHE FLED (Book #5)
IF SHE FEARED (Book #6)
IF SHE HEARD (Book #7)

THE MAKING OF RILEY PAIGE SERIES
WATCHING (Book #1)
WAITING (Book #2)
LURING (Book #3)
TAKING (Book #4)
STALKING (Book #5)

RILEY PAIGE MYSTERY SERIES
ONCE GONE (Book #1)
ONCE TAKEN (Book #2)
ONCE CRAVED (Book #3)
ONCE LURED (Book #4)
ONCE HUNTED (Book #5)
ONCE PINED (Book #6)
ONCE FORSAKEN (Book #7)
ONCE COLD (Book #8)
ONCE STALKED (Book #9)
ONCE LOST (Book #10)
ONCE BURIED (Book #11)
ONCE BOUND (Book #12)
ONCE TRAPPED (Book #13)
ONCE DORMANT (Book #14)
ONCE SHUNNED (Book #15)
ONCE MISSED (Book #16)
ONCE CHOSEN (Book #17)

MACKENZIE WHITE MYSTERY SERIES
BEFORE HE KILLS (Book #1)

ALMOST LOST

(The Au Pair-Book Two)

BLAKE PIERCE

BLAKE PIERCE

B lake Pierce is the USA Today bestselling author of the RILEY PAGE mystery series, which includes sixteen books (and counting). Blake Pierce is also the author of the MACKENZIE WHITE mystery series, comprising thirteen books (and counting); of the AVERY BLACK mystery series, comprising six books; of the KERI LOCKE mystery series, comprising five books; of the MAKING OF RILEY PAIGE mystery series, comprising five books (and counting); of the KATE WISE mystery series, comprising six books (and counting); of the CHLOE FINE psychological suspense mystery, comprising five books (and counting); of the JESSE HUNT psychological suspense thriller series, comprising five books (and counting); of the AU PAIR psychological suspense thriller series, comprising two books (and counting); and of the ZOE PRIME mystery series, comprising two books (and counting).

ONCE GONE (a Riley Paige Mystery--Book #1), BEFORE HE KILLS (A Mackenzie White Mystery—Book 1), CAUSE TO KILL (An Avery Black Mystery—Book 1), A TRACE OF DEATH (A Keri Locke Mystery—Book 1), and WATCHING (The Making of Riley Paige—Book 1) are each available as a free download on Amazon!

An avid reader and lifelong fan of the mystery and thriller genres, Blake loves to hear from you, so please feel free to visit www.blakepierce-author.com to learn more and stay in touch.

TABLE OF CONTENTS

AUTHOR NOTE:

You may have noticed that this book was first published with the author name "Ophelia Night." Occasionally I like to experiment and try new genres, and when doing so, I might use a pen name to keep it separate and prevent confusion for my fans. I initially published this book with the Ophelia Night pen name. Soon after publishing it, I was happily surprised by the reception and reader feedback, and I realized that this book and series would indeed be a good fit for all Blake Pierce fans. So I've changed the author name back to Blake Pierce. If this is your first time reading one of my books, welcome to the Blake Pierce universe! Feel free to discover my other series. I have made the first books—and audiobooks-in most of my series free to enjoy!

CHAPTER ONE

Cassandra Vale stood in the long, slow-moving queue for the London Eye. After half an hour's wait, she was close enough to see the giant wheel looming above her, its steel span arching into the overcast sky. The aerial view of London was a major attraction even on this gloomy November day.

She was on her own, although it seemed everyone else was here with friends or family. In front of her was a nervous blonde woman who looked to be in her mid-twenties, about Cassie's age. She was in charge of three unruly, dark-haired boys. Bored with the wait, they had started shouting and squabbling, jostling each other and breaking away from the line. They were causing such a disruption that people were starting to complain. The elderly man ahead of her turned and glared.

"Could you please tell your boys to be quiet?" he asked the blonde in exasperated, upper-class British tones.

"I'm so sorry. I'll try," the young woman apologized, looking on the point of tears.

Cassie had already identified the stressed blonde woman as an au pair. Watching this confrontation took her straight back to where she'd been a month ago. She knew exactly how helpless the woman felt, trapped between unmanageable children who'd begun acting out, and disapproving onlookers who'd started to criticize. This could only end badly.

Be glad you're not in her situation, Cassie told herself. You have the chance to enjoy your freedom and explore this city.

The problem was that she didn't feel free. She felt exposed and vulnerable.

Her ex-employer was about to stand trial for murder and she was the only person who knew the whole truth about what had happened. Worse still, by now, he would have learned that she'd destroyed some of the evidence he was hoping to use against her.

She felt sick with fear that he would be hunting for her.

Who knew how far the reach of a wealthy, desperate man extended? In a city of millions, she'd thought it would be easy to hide, but the French newspapers were all over the place. Headlines shrieked at her from every corner shop. She was aware of the intensive camera monitoring, especially at tourist attractions—and central London was basically one huge tourist attraction.

Glancing up, Cassie saw a dark-haired man standing on the platform by the wheel. She'd felt his gaze a while ago, and saw he was staring in her direction again. She tried to reassure herself that he was probably a security guard or a plainclothes police officer, but that gave her no comfort. She was doing her best to avoid the police, whether they were plainclothes, or private detectives, or even ex-cops who'd taken up a more lucrative line of work as paid thugs.

Cassie froze as she saw the watching man pick up his phone, or maybe it was a walkie-talkie, and speak urgently into it. The next moment he left the platform and strode purposefully in her direction.

Cassie decided she didn't need to see an aerial view of London today. Never mind she'd already paid the entrance fee—she was getting out. She'd come back another time.

She turned to go, ready to push her way through the line of people as fast as she could, but saw to her horror that two more police officers were approaching from behind.

The teenage girls who'd been standing behind her had also decided to leave. They had already turned and were shoving through the line toward the exit. Cassie followed, grateful that they were clearing the way for her, but panic surged inside her as the officers followed.

"Wait, ma'am! Stop now!" the man behind her shouted.

She wasn't turning around. She wasn't. She'd scream, she'd grab onto the other people in the line, she'd beg and plead and say that they had the wrong person, that she didn't know anything about the suspected murderer Pierre Dubois and had never worked for him. Whatever it took to get away, she would do.

But as she tensed for the fight, the man shouldered past her and grabbed the two teenagers ahead of her.

The teen girls started shouting and struggling just as she'd planned to do. Another two plainclothes police converged, pushing the bystanders aside, grasping the girls' arms while one of the uniformed police opened their bags.

To Cassie's astonishment, she saw the cop take three cell phones and two wallets from the taller girl's neon pink rucksack.

"Pickpockets. Check your purses, ladies and gentlemen. Please inform us if any of your possessions are missing," the officer said.

Cassie grabbed her jacket, relieved to feel her phone safely stashed away in the inside pocket. Then she looked down at her purse and her heart plummeted as she saw the zip was open.

"My wallet's missing," she said. "Someone's stolen it."

Breathless with anxiety, she followed the police out of the line and around the corner to the small security office. The two pickpockets were already waiting there, both in tears, as the police unpacked their bags.

"Are any of these yours, ma'am?" the plainclothes officer asked, pointing to the phones and wallets placed on the counter.

"No, none of them."

Cassie felt like bursting into tears herself. She watched as one of the officers upended the rucksack, hoping she would see her scuffed leather wallet fall out, but the bag was empty.

The officer shook his head, annoyed.

"They pass them down the line, get them out of sight very fast. You were in front of the thieves, so yours was probably taken a while ago."

Cassie turned and stared at the thieves. She hoped that everything she felt and thought about them showed in her face. If the officer hadn't been standing there, she would have sworn at them, asked them what right they had to ruin her life. They weren't starving; she could see their new shoes and brand-name jackets. They must be doing this for cheap thrills, or to buy alcohol or drugs.

"Apologies, ma'am," the police officer continued. "If you don't mind waiting a few minutes, we'll need you to make a statement."

A statement. Cassie knew that wouldn't work for her.

She didn't want to be the focus of any police attention at all. She didn't want to give them her address, or say who she was, or have her details noted down on any official report here in the UK.

"I'm just going to tell my sister that I'm here," she lied to the officer. "No problem."

He turned away, speaking on his walkie-talkie, and Cassie hurried out of the office.

Her wallet was history, it was gone. There was no way she could get it back, even if she wrote a hundred police reports. So she decided to do the next best thing, which was to walk away from the London Eye, and never come back.

What a disaster this outing had been. She'd drawn a lot of cash that morning, and her bank cards were also gone. She couldn't go into a bank to withdraw money because she had no ID with her—her passport was at the guesthouse and there was no time to fetch it, because she'd planned to go straight from the London Eye to join her friend Jess for lunch.

Half an hour later, feeling shaken by the crime, appalled by the amount of money she'd lost, and thoroughly annoyed with London, Cassie walked into the pub where they were meeting. She was ahead of the lunchtime rush, and asked the waitress to reserve a corner table for them while she went to the bathroom.

Staring at herself in the mirror, she smoothed down her wavy auburn hair and tried a cheerful smile. The expression felt unfamiliar. She was sure she'd lost weight since she and Jess had last met, and she thought critically that she looked too pale and too stressed—and this wasn't only due to the trauma she'd been through earlier today.

Exiting the restroom, she was just in time to see Jess walk into the pub.

Jess was wearing the same jacket she'd had on when they'd first met more than a month ago, both on their way to au pair jobs in France. Seeing her brought the memories flooding back. Cassie remembered how she'd felt as she boarded the plane. Frightened, uncertain, and with serious misgivings about the family she'd been assigned to. These had proven to be well founded.

In contrast, Jess had been employed by a lovely, friendly family and Cassie thought she looked very happy.

"It's good to see you," Jess said, hugging Cassie hard. "What fun this is."

"It's so exciting. But I have a crisis on my hands," Cassie confessed. She explained about being pickpocketed earlier.

"No! That's awful. What bad luck that they found other wallets, but not yours."

"Could you loan me some money for lunch and bus fare to get back to my guesthouse? I can't even withdraw cash at a bank without my passport. I'll transfer it back to you as soon as I can get online."

"Of course. It's not a loan, it's a gift. The family I'm working for has come to London for a wedding, and they're all in Winchester with the bride's mother today, so they threw money at me to enjoy London for the day. After this, I'm going to Harrods."

Jess shook back her blonde hair, laughing as she shared the cash with Cassie.

"Hey, shall we take a selfie?" she suggested, but Cassie declined.

"I have absolutely zero makeup on," she explained, and Jess laughed and put her phone away.

The lack of makeup wasn't the real reason, of course; she was trying her best to stay under the radar. The first thing she'd done after arriving in London was to change her social media settings, turning them fully private. Well-meaning friends might say something, and the path could be traced. She didn't want anyone knowing where she was. Not her ex-boyfriend back in the States, and certainly not her ex-employer and his legal team in France.

She had thought she would feel safe once she'd left France, but she hadn't realized how accessible, and interconnected, the whole of Europe was. Going straight back to the States would have been a more sensible choice.

"You're looking amazing—have you lost weight?" Jess asked. "And are things going well with the family who employed you? You said you were worried about them."

"It didn't work out, so I'm no longer with them," she said carefully, glossing over the ugly details that she couldn't bring herself to think about.

"Oh dear. What went wrong?"

"The children moved to the South of France, and the family didn't need an au pair anymore."

Cassie kept it as simple as possible, hoping a dull explanation would prevent any further questions, because she didn't want to have to lie to her friend.

"I guess that happens. It could have been worse. You could have worked for that family everyone's talking about where the husband is standing trial for murdering his fiancée."

Cassie looked down hurriedly, worried that her expression would give her away.

Fortunately they were distracted by the arrival of the wine, and after they'd ordered food, Jess had moved on from that juicy morsel of gossip.

"What are you going to do now?" she asked Cassie.

Cassie felt ashamed by the question, because she had no coherent answer. She wished she could tell Jess that she had a plan and wasn't just living day to day, knowing that she should make the most of her time in Europe, but feeling increasingly uncertain about her situation here.

"I'm not sure. I was thinking of going back to the States, finding work somewhere warmer. Florida, perhaps. It's expensive to stay here."

Jess nodded in understanding.

"I bought a car when I arrived. Someone at the guesthouse was selling it. That took a lot of my cash."

"So you have a car?" Jess asked. "How awesome!"

"It has been wonderful. I've gone on some amazing drives out of the city, but using the car with the gas and everything, and even day-to-day living, is costing more than I expected."

Hemorrhaging money without any prospect of earning income was stressing her out and it was reminding her of the battles she'd gone through when she was younger.

She'd left home at sixteen to escape her violent and abusive father, and ever since then she'd had to look after herself. She'd had no security and no savings and no family to fall back on, because her mother was dead and her older sister, Jacqui, had run away a few years earlier and had never been in touch again.

Living on her own had been a case of month-to-month survival for Cassie. She'd sometimes only made it by the skin of her teeth. Never mind having peanut butter at month's end; it had been her staple diet when times were tough, and she'd gotten into the habit of taking restaurant or bartender work, partly because the jobs came with a free staff meal.

Now she was panicking about living off a dwindling nest egg that was all she possessed in the world, and thanks to the cash that had been stolen today, that nest egg was even smaller.

"You could look for a temporary job to tide you over," Jess advised, as if reading her mind.

"I have. I've approached a few restaurants, and even applied for bartending work at some of the pubs, but I got turned down right away. Everyone here's a stickler for the correct paperwork and all I have is a visitor's visa."

"Restaurant work? Why not au pairing?" Jess asked curiously.

"No," Cassie shot back, before remembering that Jess knew nothing about the circumstances of her previous job. She continued.

"If I can't work I can't work. No visa means no visa, and au pairing is a longer commitment."

"Not necessarily," Jess countered. "It doesn't have to be. And I have personal experience of doing it without a visa."

"You do?"

Cassie knew her mind was made up. She wasn't going to au pair again. All the same, what Jess was saying sounded interesting.

"You see, all the restaurants and pubs get checked regularly. There's no way they can hire anyone without the right visa. But working for a family is different. It's such a gray area. After all, you could be a family friend. Who's to say you're actually working? I stayed with a friend in Devon for a while last year, and ended up doing a few babysitting and temporary childcare jobs for neighbors and people in the area."

"That's good to know," Cassie said, but she didn't have any intention of exploring that option further. Talking to Jess was cementing her decision to head back to the States. If she sold the car, she would have enough money to support herself there until she got back on her feet.

On the other hand, she'd expected to spend much longer traveling. She'd been looking forward to a full year abroad, hoping it would give her the time she needed to move on from her past. This was her chance to make a fresh start in life, and to return as a changed person. Arriving back home so soon after leaving would feel like giving up. Never mind that other people would think she hadn't made a go of it—she would personally believe that she'd failed.

The waiter arrived, bringing plates piled high with nachos. Hungry, because she'd skipped breakfast, Cassie dug into the food.

But Jess paused, frowning, and took her phone out of her purse.

"Talking of part-time jobs, one of the people I worked for called me yesterday to see if I could help him again."

"Really?" Cassie asked, but her attention was focused on the food.

"Ryan Ellis. I worked for him last year. His wife's parents were moving house, and they needed someone to look after the kids while they were away. They were lovely people, and the kids weren't bad either—they have a boy and a girl. We did lots of fun stuff. They live in a beautiful seaside village."

"What is the job?"

"He's looking for somebody for about three weeks, urgently, to live in. Cassie, this could be just what you need. He paid very well, gave me cash, and didn't mind about the visa at all. He said if I had been accepted by an au pair agency I was clearly a trustworthy person. Why not call him and find out more?"

Cassie was tempted by the prospect of cash in her pocket. But another au pair assignment? She didn't feel ready. Perhaps she never would be.

"I'm not sure it's for me."

Jess, however, seemed determined to sort out Cassie's future for her. She tapped keys on her phone.

"Let me send you his number anyway. And I'll message him now and say you might get in touch, and that I recommend you highly. You never know, even if you don't work for him, he might know someone who needs a house sitter. Or a dog walker. Or something."

Cassie couldn't argue with her logic, and a moment later her phone buzzed with the arrival of Jess's message.

"How's your work going?" she asked, once Jess had finished her messaging.

"It couldn't be better." Jess piled guacamole onto a tortilla chip.

"The family is lovely. They're very generous with time off and keep giving me bonuses. The kids can be naughty but they're never nasty and I think they enjoy me, too."

She lowered her voice.

"Last week, with everyone arriving for the wedding, I was introduced to one of the cousins. He's twenty-eight and gorgeous and he runs an IT support business. I think he likes me, and let's just say it's fun to be flirting again."

Even though she was glad for her friend, Cassie couldn't help feeling a pang of envy. This dream job was what she had secretly hoped for. Why had everything gone wrong for her? Had it only been bad luck or was it, in some way, because of the decisions she had made?

Cassie suddenly remembered what Jess had said to her on the plane to France. She'd shared with Cassie that her first assignment hadn't worked out, so she'd ditched it and tried again.

Jess had only gotten lucky on the second try, and that made Cassie wonder if she was giving up too soon.

When they had finished their nachos, Jess checked the time.

"I'd better run. Harrods is waiting," she said. "I'll have to buy gifts for everyone back home, and for the children, and for the gorgeous Jacques. What should I get him? What do you give someone you're having a flirtation with? It may take me a while to decide!"

Cassie hugged Jess goodbye, feeling sad their lunch was over. The friendly chat had been a welcome distraction. Jess seemed so happy, and Cassie could see why. She was needed and valued, she was earning money, she had a purpose in life and was secure.

Jess wasn't drifting around on her own, lonely and jobless and paranoid about being hunted down because a murder trial was starting.

A few weeks in a remote village might be exactly what she needed right now, in more ways than one. And Jess was right. The phone call could lead to other opportunities. She'd never find them if she didn't keep trying.

Cassie headed out of the crowded pub to find a quiet corner, glancing around in case any pickpockets or phone grabbers were passing by.

She took a deep breath, and before she could think too hard about it and lose her nerve, she dialed the number.

CHAPTER TWO

H olding her phone tightly, Cassie moved closer to the wall to shelter
from the drizzle. Now that she'd dialed Ryan Ellis, she was feeling
more and more nervous.

She had to earn money somehow if she wanted to stay in the UK for
longer, but after what she'd been through in France, was au pairing the
right decision? Even if the job sounded ideal, would he be prepared to
accept her with so little experience and no real qualifications?

Cassie imagined gathering her courage to ask if she could take the
job, only to be given a shameful "No" in response.

The call rang for so long she feared it would go to voicemail. At the
last possible moment, a man picked up and answered.

"Ryan speaking," he said.

He sounded out of breath, as if he'd had to run for the phone.

"Hello, is this Ryan Ellis?" Cassie asked.

She cringed at the obviousness of her question, but she didn't know
him at all and it felt wrong to say, "Hi, Ryan."

"Yes, that's me. Who's calling, please?" He didn't sound irritated, but
rather curious.

"My name's Cassie Vale and I got your number from my friend Jess,
who worked for you last year. She mentioned you were looking for someone to help out with your children for a while."

"Jess, Jess, Jess," Ryan repeated, as if trying to place the name, and
then, "Oh, yes, Jess from America! I see she's just sent me a message.
What a lovely lady. Did she recommend you? Is that why you're calling?
I haven't read the message yet."

Cassie hesitated. Was she going to say yes? To do so would be making a commitment, and she wasn't sure she wanted to take that step yet.

"I'd like to know more about the job," she said. "I was au pairing in France but my assignment's ended. I've been thinking of doing something short term, but I'm not sure at this stage."

There was a short silence.

"Let me fill you in. I'm desperate at this moment. I've just been through a divorce, which has left me pretty shell-shocked. The kids won't even speak about what's happened and need someone to cheer them up and have fun with them. On top of it all, I have a massive work project, with a deadline that's taking up all my time."

Cassie was shocked by Ryan's words. She hadn't expected him to be in such a serious predicament. No wonder he was desperate for somebody to help out.

The divorce must have been traumatic if it had affected the children so badly. She guessed if Ryan was looking after them, his wife must have left him, probably for somebody else.

She had no idea what the right response would be.

"That sounds very stressful," she said eventually, to fill the short silence.

"I've been phoning around, because I haven't had a chance to advertise the job, and I'm feeling so muddled I don't think I'd be especially good at screening anybody new. Everyone who's worked for me before has been unavailable. I don't mind telling you, I'm stuck for help. I'm prepared to pay triple the usual rate, and the job will be for maximum three weeks."

"Well—" Cassie began.

She couldn't bring herself to say no. It would be callous when this man was in such dire circumstances. She felt sorry for him and felt it would be selfish to refuse the job outright. They were clearly desperate for help, and the good money, combined with the short timeframe, was tempting.

"Why not come and meet us?" Ryan suggested. "Do you have a car? If not, I can fetch you at the station. I'll pay for your ticket, of course."

"I have a car," Cassie said.

"That makes it very easy and it should take around five hours if traffic cooperates. I'll message you the address now, and refund you for the trip if you don't like us."

"All right. I'll leave tomorrow morning. I should be there by lunch time," Cassie said.

She disconnected, relieved that she would have a chance to spend time with the family before making up her mind. If she liked them, she might have an opportunity to make a real difference in their lives, offering help and support during a difficult time.

When Ryan had told her that he was recently divorced, she hadn't expected to feel so much sympathy for him. Growing up in a home filled with conflict, and losing her mother at a young age, she understood what it was like. This was a situation where she knew she could be valuable to the family.

Leaving home as a desperate, scarred sixteen-year-old, she had been determined to follow in her sister's footsteps and get away from her father's abuse forever. But after escaping from his angry dominance, she'd ended up in a damaging relationship with her toxic boyfriend, Zane. Then, traveling to France to get away from Zane had landed her in the biggest nightmare of all.

Out of town, in a remote coastal village, she'd be safely tucked away and would be able to experience a family environment where she felt needed, which was one of the main reasons she'd wanted to au pair in the first place.

Cassie hoped she could use her time there to heal.

CHAPTER THREE

The trip to Ryan Ellis's house took Cassie longer than she'd expected. It seemed impossible to avoid the heavy traffic that clogged up the highways on the drive south, and there were two sections of road works where she had to take a lengthy detour.

The extra time on the road meant she almost ran out of gas. She had to use the last of the money Jess had loaned her to top up her tank. Worried that Ryan would think she had changed her mind, she messaged him to apologize and say she'd be late. He'd replied immediately saying, "No problem, take your time, drive safe."

Once she'd left the highway and headed into the countryside, the views were idyllic. She craned her neck, staring over the trimmed hedgerows at the sloping vistas of patchwork fields in every shade from deep green to golden brown, scenic farmhouses, and winding rivers. The orderly landscape gave her a sense of peace, although she knew the gathering clouds meant afternoon rain, and she hoped she would reach her destination before it set in.

More than six hours after leaving London, she arrived at the quaint seaside village. Even in the dull light, the village was enchanting. The car rattled over cobbled streets, where gaps in the rows of houses gave her glimpses of the picturesque harbor beyond. Ryan had directed her to drive through the village and along the cliff side road. The house was a couple of miles further, overlooking the sea.

Pulling up outside the open gate, Cassie stared in amazement, because the house beyond was almost too perfect to be true. It felt like a place she'd always dreamed of living in. A simple yet gorgeous home, with sloping lines and wooden detail that blended harmoniously with its surroundings and reminded her of a ship moored in the harbor—only this building was nestled on a cliff, with an incredible view of the ocean beyond. The well-tended yard housed a swing and see-saw. Both were slightly rusty, and Cassie guessed the state of the equipment provided a clue about the children's ages.

Cassie glanced into the car's mirror and checked her hair—the waves were sleek and shiny from her efforts early this morning, and her coral lipstick was immaculate.

She parked on the cobblestone driveway and walked to the house along a pathway bordered by flower beds. Even at this time of year the beds were bright with yellow blossoms, and she recognized flowering honeysuckle planted beyond. In summer she guessed they would be a riot of color.

The front door opened before she reached it.

"Afternoon, Cassie. Good to meet you. I'm Ryan."

The man who greeted her was a head taller than her, fit-looking and surprisingly young, with tousled, sandy-brown hair and piercing blue eyes. He was smiling, looking genuinely happy to see her, and he was wearing a faded Eminem T-shirt and a worn pair of jeans. She noticed a dishcloth was hooked into their waistband.

"Hi, Ryan."

She took his outstretched hand. His grip was warm and firm.

"You caught me in the middle of cleaning the kitchen, preparing for your arrival. The kettle's boiled—are you a tea drinker? It's such an English habit, I know, but there's also coffee if you'd prefer."

"I'd love some tea," Cassie said, reassured by his down to earth welcome.

As he closed the front door and led the way to the kitchen, she thought to herself that Ryan Ellis was very different from what she'd expected. He was friendlier than she'd thought he'd be, and she loved that he was prepared to clean the kitchen.

Cassie remembered her arrival at her last au pairing assignment. As soon as she'd walked into the French chateau, she'd sensed the charged, ugly atmosphere of conflict. In this house, she didn't pick that up at all.

Walking over polished wooden floorboards, she was impressed by how tidy it looked. There were even fresh flowers on the hall table.

"We spruced the place up for you," Ryan said, as if reading her mind. "It hasn't looked this good for months."

To her right, Cassie saw a family room with huge sliding doors leading onto a verandah. With comfortable-looking leather furniture and paintings of ships on the walls, the room appeared welcoming and tasteful. She couldn't help but compare it with the ostentatious showroom décor of the chateau where she'd previously worked. It felt like a real family lived in this home.

The kitchen was neat and clean, and Cassie noticed the quality of the appliances. The kettle, toaster, and food processor were a top brand. She recognized their bright designer patterns from an article she'd read in the in-flight magazine, and she remembered having been astonished by their price.

"Have you eaten lunch?" Ryan asked after pouring the tea.

"No, but it's fine—"

Ignoring her protests, he opened the fridge and took out a plate piled high with fruit, muffins, and sandwiches.

"On the weekend I like to have a stash of snacks available. I wish I could say this was especially for you, but it's standard fare for the children. Dylan is twelve and starting to eat like a teenager, Madison is nine and plays a lot of sports, and I'd rather they gorged on this than junk food or sweets."

"Where are the children?" Cassie asked, feeling another stab of nerves at the thought of meeting them. With such a fun, genuine dad they would probably be just as Jess had described them, but she needed to be sure.

"They cycled down the road after lunch to visit a friend. I told them to make the most of the afternoon before the weather turned. They should be back any minute—if not, I might have to take the Land Rover to pick them up."

Ryan glanced out the window at the darkening sky.

"Anyway, as I explained to you, I'm stuck for help over the next while. I'm a single parent now, the kids need as much distraction as they can get, and my work deadline is unbreakable."

"What do you do?" Cassie asked.

"I own a fleet of fishing and leisure boats which operates from the port in town. This time of year is when the boats get maintained, and I have a repair crew on site at the moment. They are hellishly busy, and the first storms of the season are almost here. That's why time's so tight, and my present circumstances aren't helping."

"It must be terrible to have gone through a divorce, especially now."

"It's been a very difficult time."

As Ryan turned away from the window, in the changing light, Cassie realized he wasn't just attractive, but exceptionally good-looking. His face was strong and chiseled, and from the defined muscles in his arms, she thought he looked to be extremely fit.

Cassie chastised herself for ogling this poor man's appearance when he was going through emotional hell. All the same, she had to admit he was compellingly handsome, so much so that she had to stop herself from staring.

"Ryan, the only problem is that I don't have a valid work visa at this point. I have one for France, and I've been fully cleared by the au pair agency, but I didn't realize it works differently here."

"You were referred to me by a friend," Ryan said, smiling. "That means you can stay with us as a guest. I will pay you cash, completely off the books, so you will receive it tax-free, if that works for you."

Cassie felt a surge of relief. Ryan understood her situation and was willing to accommodate it without any issues. This was a huge weight off her shoulders. She realized it might even be the deciding factor, and had to stop herself from accepting the job on the spot. She reminded herself to be careful, and to wait until she'd met the children before committing.

"How long would you need me for?"

"A maximum of three weeks. That will give me time to get this project done, and we'll be heading for the school holidays by then so we'll have a chance to bond as a family. Rebond, I should say, as a new family. They say divorce is the most stressful life experience, and I think the children and I can confirm that."

Cassie nodded in sympathy. She was sure his children would have suffered. She wondered how much Ryan and his wife had fought. Inevitably there would have been fights. It just depended whether they'd ended in shouting and recriminations, or in tense, smoldering silence.

Having experienced both as a child, she wasn't sure which was worse.

While Cassie's mother was alive she'd managed to keep the lid on the worst of her father's temper. Cassie remembered the tense silences from when she was younger, and it had allowed her to develop a finely tuned sense for conflict. She could walk into a room and pick up instantly if the people had been fighting. The silences were toxic and they wore you out emotionally because there was never an end to them.

If there was one thing you could say in favor of loud fighting, it was that eventually it ended, even if it was with glass being broken or emergency services being called. But that caused other trauma and lasting scars. It also brought a sense of fear, because shouting and physical violence showed that you could lose self-control and therefore could not be trusted.

That, in summary, had been her father after her mother had died.

Cassie looked around the cheerful, tidy kitchen and tried to imagine what might have happened there between Ryan and his wife. The worst fights, in her experience, took place in the kitchen and the bedroom.

"I'm so sorry you had to go through this," she said softly.

Ryan was looking at her closely and she returned his gaze, staring into pale, piercing blue eyes.

"Cassie, you seem to understand," he said.

She thought he was going to ask her something else, but at that moment the front door opened.

"The children are home, just in time." He sounded relieved.

Cassie glanced out the window. Raindrops were spattering the glass, and as the door slammed, a cold winter shower started pouring down.

"Hey, Dad!"

Footsteps thudded along the wooden floor and a slim young girl wearing cycle shorts and a green tracksuit top came sprinting into the kitchen. She stopped when she saw Cassie, looked her up and down, and then marched over and shook her hand.

"Hello. Are you the lady who'll be looking after us?"

"My name's Cassie. Are you Madison?" Cassie asked.

Madison nodded, and Ryan ruffled his daughter's shiny brown hair.

"Cassie is still deciding whether she wants to work for us. What do you think? Will you promise to be on your best behavior?"

Madison shrugged.

"You always tell us not to make promises we can't keep. But I'll try."

Ryan laughed and Cassie found herself smiling at the cheeky honesty of Madison's response.

"Where's Dylan?" Ryan asked.

"He's in the garage, oiling his bicycle. It was squeaking on the way up the hill and then the chain fell off." Madison took a deep breath and walked to the kitchen door.

"Dylan!" she yelled. "Come here!"

Cassie heard a distant shout. "Coming!"

"He'll take forever," Madison said. "Once he starts fussing with the bikes he doesn't stop."

Noticing the plate of snacks, she made a bee-line for them, her eyes lighting up. Then, looking down at the contents, she gave an exasperated sigh.

"Dad, you made egg sandwiches."

"Is that a problem?" Ryan asked, his eyebrows raised.

"You know my views on egg. It's like having sick in a sandwich."

She carefully selected a muffin from the opposite side of the plate.

"Sick in a sandwich?" Ryan's voice combined outrage and amusement. "Maddie, you shouldn't say that kind of thing in front of a visitor."

"Watch out, Cassie, that egg stuff sticks to everything," Madison warned, making an unrepentant face at her father.

Cassie suddenly felt a weird sense of belonging. This banter was exactly what she'd hoped for. So far, this seemed to be a normal, happy family, teasing each other, looking out for each other, even though she was sure each of them had their own quirks and difficulties. She realized how tense she'd been, anticipating that something would go wrong.

She hadn't yet taken any food because she had felt self-conscious about eating in front of Ryan. Now, she realized how hungry she was, and decided she'd better have something before her stomach embarrassed her by growling audibly.

"I'll be brave and try a sandwich," she volunteered.

"Thank you. I'm relieved somebody appreciates my culinary excellence," Ryan said.

"Egg-cellence," Madison added, making Cassie laugh.

Turning to Cassie she said, "Dad does all the cooking. He just hates to clean."

"That I do," Ryan said.

Madison took another deep breath and faced the kitchen door.

"Dylan," she yelled.

Then she added, in a normal voice, "Oh, there you are."

A tall, lanky boy strolled in. He had the same brown, shiny hair as his sister and Cassie wondered if he'd just had a growth spurt, because he looked to be all limbs and sinew.

"Hi, pleased to meet you," he said to Cassie, somewhat absently.

In his boyish features, she could see a similarity to Ryan. They shared the same strong jaw and well-defined cheekbones. In Madison's pretty, oval face she saw less of Ryan and wondered what the children's mother looked like. Were there family photos anywhere in the house? Or had the divorce been so acrimonious that these had been removed?

"You must shake hands," Ryan reminded his son, but Dylan turned his hands outward and Cassie saw the palms were black with oil.

"Uh-oh. Come over here."

Ryan hurried over to the sink, turned on the tap, and poured a generous amount of dishwashing liquid into his son's hands.

While Ryan was distracted, Cassie took another sandwich.

"What was wrong with the bike?" Ryan asked.

"The chain was skipping when I changed up the gears," Dylan explained.

"Did you fix it?" Ryan was monitoring the progress of the handwashing with some concern.

"Yes," Dylan said.

Cassie expected him to elaborate further but he didn't. Ryan passed him a towel and he dried his hands, grasped Cassie's hand briefly in a formal hello, and then turned his attention to the snacks.

Dylan didn't say much while he ate but Cassie was impressed by how much food he managed to put away in a few minutes. The plate was nearly empty by the time Ryan returned it to the fridge.

"You're not going to have an appetite for dinner if you keep eating, and I'm about to make spaghetti Bolognese," he said.

"I'll eat all the spag bol too," Dylan promised.

Ryan closed the fridge.

"Right, kids, I need you to go and change out of your cycling clothes now, or you'll catch a chill."

When they had gone, he turned back to Cassie and she noticed that he sounded anxious.

"What do you think? Are the children what you expected? They're good kids, although they can have their moments."

Cassie had liked the children immediately. Madison, in particular, seemed like an easy child and she couldn't imagine there being any shortage of conversation around the talkative young girl. Dylan seemed more complex, a quieter, more introverted person. But it could also be that he was older, heading into his teens. It made sense that he wouldn't have very much to say to a twenty-three-year-old au pair.

Ryan was right, they seemed like easy children, and more importantly, he came across as a supportive father who would help with any problems if they occurred.

Decision made, then. She would take this job.

"They seem lovely. I'll be happy to work for you for the next three weeks."

Ryan's face lit up.

"Oh, that's great. You know, Cassie, from the time I saw you—no, from the time I first spoke to you, I was hoping you'd agree. There's something about your energy that intrigues me. I would love to know what you've been through, what has shaped you, because you seem—I don't know how to describe it. Wise. Mature. At any rate, I feel my children will be in excellent hands."

Cassie didn't know what to say. Ryan's praise was making her feel awkward.

Ryan added, "The kids are going to be thrilled; I can see they like you already. Let's get you settled in and I'll give you a quick tour of the house. Do you have your bags with you?"

"Yes, I do."

Taking advantage of a lull in the rain, Ryan walked with her to the car and picked up her heavy bags with ease, carrying them into the hallway.

"We only have one garage, which is the Land Rover's domain, but parking on the street is totally safe. The house is simple. We have the living room on the right, the kitchen ahead, and on the left is a dining room we hardly ever use, so it's turned into a jigsaw puzzle, reading, and games room. As you can see."

Peering in, he sighed.

"Who's the puzzle enthusiast?"

"Madison. She loves working with her hands, crafts, anything she can get busy and do."

"And she's sporty?" Cassie asked. "She's multi-talented."

"I'm afraid with Maddie, schoolwork is the weak point. She needs help academically, especially in math. So any assistance you're able to offer, or even just moral support, will be great."

"What about Dylan?"

"He's a passionate cyclist, but can't be bothered with any other sport. He's very mechanically minded, and a straight A student. He's not sociable, though, and it's a fine balance with him because he can be a moody boy if he feels pressured."

Cassie nodded, grateful for the input on her new charges.

"Here's your room. Let's put these bags down."

The small room had a beautiful sea view. It was decorated in turquoise and white, and looked neat and welcoming. Ryan placed her larger bag by the foot of the bed, and the smaller one on the striped armchair.

"The guest bathroom is down the passage. We have Madison's room on the right, Dylan's room on the left, and finally mine. Then there's one other place I must show you."

He accompanied her back down the hall and they headed into the family room. Beyond it, through the glass doors, Cassie saw a covered balcony with wrought-iron furniture.

"Wow," she breathed. The sea view from this vantage point was exquisite. There was a dramatic drop to the ocean below, and she could hear the waves crashing against the rocks.

"This is my peaceful place. I sit here every evening after dinner to unwind, usually with a glass of wine. You're very welcome to join me any evening you choose—wine's optional, but warm, windproof clothing is compulsory. The balcony is solidly roofed, but not glassed in. I considered doing it but found I couldn't. Out there, with the sound of the sea and even an occasional gust of spray on stormy nights, you feel so connected to the ocean. Take a look."

He opened the sliding door.

Cassie walked out onto the balcony and headed to the edge, grasping the steel railing.

As she did so, dizziness flooded her, and suddenly, she wasn't looking down onto a Devon beach.

She was leaning over a stone parapet, staring in horror at the crumpled body far below, flooded with panic and confusion.

She could feel the stone, cold against her fingers.

She remembered the hint of perfume that had still lingered in the opulent bedroom, and the way that nausea had boiled inside her and her legs had gone so weak that she'd thought she would collapse. How she'd been unable to remember how the events of the previous night had played out. Her nightmares, always bad, had become far worse and more vivid after that shocking sight, so she'd been unable to tell where dreams ended and memories began.

Cassie thought she'd left that terrified person behind, but now, as the darkness rushed up to swallow her, she understood that the memories, and the fear, had become a part of her.

"No," she tried to scream, but her own voice seemed to come from a distant, faraway place and all that came out was a ragged, inaudible whisper.

CHAPTER FOUR

"There, take it easy. Just breathe. In, out, in, out."

Cassie opened her eyes and found herself looking at the deck's solid wooden floorboards.

She was seated on the soft cushion of one of the wrought-iron chairs, with her head on her knees. Firm hands were grasping her shoulders, supporting her.

It was Ryan, her new employer. His hands, his voice.

What had she done? She'd panicked and made a complete fool of herself. Hastily she struggled upright.

"Easy, take it slow."

Cassie gasped. Her head was whirling and she felt as if she was having an out-of-body experience.

"You had a serious attack of vertigo there. For a minute I thought you were going to fall over the railing," Ryan said. "I managed to grab you before you blacked out. How are you feeling?"

How was she feeling?

Icy cold, lightheaded, and mortified by what had happened. She'd been desperate to make a good impression and to live up to Ryan's praise of her. Instead, she'd screwed up badly and should explain why.

How could she, though? If he knew the horrors she'd been through, and that her ex-employer was facing trial for murder at this very moment, he might change his mind about her and feel that she was too unstable to care for his children at a time when they needed stability. Even a panic attack might be cause for concern.

It would be better to go along with what he'd assumed—that she'd suffered a bout of vertigo.

"I'm feeling much better," she answered him. "I'm so sorry. I should have remembered that I get severe vertigo if I haven't been around heights for a while. It does improve. In a day or two I'll be fine out here."

"That's good to know, but you must be careful in the meantime. Are you OK to stand up now? Keep holding my arm."

Cassie got up, leaning on Ryan until she was sure her legs would support her, and then he slowly walked her back into the family room.

"I'm good now."

"You sure?" He held her arm a moment longer before letting go.

"Take some time now to unpack, rest up, settle in, and I'll have supper ready by six-thirty."

Cassie took her time unpacking, making sure her belongings were neatly packed in the quaint white wardrobe, and that her meds were stashed at the back of the desk drawer. She didn't think this family would go through her stuff when she wasn't there, but she didn't want to field any embarrassing questions about the anxiety medications she took, especially after the panic attack she'd had earlier.

At least she'd recovered from the episode quickly, and that must be a sign that her anxiety was under control. She made a mental note to take her nighttime tablets before joining the family for dinner, just in case.

The delicious aroma of cooking garlic and browning meat wafted through the house long before six-thirty. Cassie waited until a quarter past six and then put on one of her prettiest tops, with beadwork around the neck, lip gloss, and a touch of mascara. She wanted Ryan to see her at her best. She told herself it was important to give a good impression because of the earlier panic attack, but when she thought back to those moments on the porch, she found what she remembered most clearly was the feel of Ryan's toned, muscular arms as he'd held her.

She felt lightheaded all over again when she remembered how strong, yet gentle with her he'd been.

Leaving her room, Cassie nearly bumped into Madison, who was heading eagerly for the kitchen.

"This food smells so good," Madison told Cassie.

"Is it your favorite dinner?"

"Well, I love spag bol the way Dad makes it, but not when we eat out in restaurants. They don't do it the same. So I'd say this is my favorite home food, and my second favorite is roast chicken, and my third favorite is toad in the hole. Then when we go out, I love fish and chips, which you get all over the place here, and I love pizza, and I hate hamburgers, which happen to be Dylan's favorite, but I think restaurant burgers are yuck."

"What's toad in the hole?" Cassie asked curiously, guessing it must be a traditional English dish.

"Have you never eaten it? It's sausages baked in a sort of pie, made with eggs and flour and milk. You have to have it with lots of gravy. I mean, lots. And peas and carrots."

The conversation had taken them all the way into the kitchen. The wooden table was laid for four, and Dylan was already sitting in his place, pouring a glass of orange juice.

"Burgers are not yuck. They're the food of the gods," he countered.

"My teacher at school said they're mostly cereal and bits of the animals you wouldn't eat otherwise, ground up finely."

"Your teacher is wrong."

"How can she be wrong? You're stupid to say that."

Cassie was about to intervene, thinking Madison's insult too personal, but Dylan got his comeback in first.

"Hey, Maddie." Dylan pointed a warning finger at her. "You're either with me or you're against me."

Cassie couldn't work out what he meant by that, but Madison rolled her eyes and stuck out her tongue at him before sitting down.

"Can I help you, Ryan?"

Cassie walked over to the stove, where Ryan was lifting a boiling pot of pasta off the heat.

He glanced at her and smiled.

"Everything's under control, I hope. Dinner time is T minus thirty seconds. Come on, kids. Grab your plates and let's dish up."

"I like your top, Cassie," Madison said.

"Thank you. I bought it in New York City."

"New York City. Wow. I'd love to go there," Madison said, wide-eyed.

"The sixth form economics students went in June on a school trip," Dylan said. "Study economics, and you might go, too."

"Does that involve math?" Madison asked.

Dylan nodded.

"I hate math. It's boring and difficult."

"Well then, you won't go."

Dylan turned his attention to his plate, piling it high with food, while Ryan rinsed the cooking utensils at the sink.

Seeing Madison was looking mutinous, Cassie changed the subject.

"Your dad told me you love sports. What's your favorite?"

"Running and gymnastics. I quite like tennis, we started it this summer."

"And you're a cyclist?" Cassie asked Dylan.

He nodded, piling grated cheese onto his food.

"Dylan wants to be a professional and win the Tour de France one day," Madison said.

Ryan sat down at the table.

"You're more than likely going to discover some obscure mathematical formula and get a full scholarship to Cambridge University," he said, gazing affectionately at his son.

Dylan shook his head.

"Tour de France all the way, Dad," he insisted.

"University first," Ryan retorted, his voice firm, and Dylan scowled in response. Madison interjected, asking for more juice, and Cassie poured it for her while the brief moment of discord passed.

Letting their conversation wash over her, Cassie ate her food, which was delicious. She'd never known anyone quite like Ryan, she decided. He was so capable and so caring. She wondered if the children knew how lucky they were, having a father who cooked for his family.

After dinner, she volunteered to do the cleaning up, which mainly involved loading the large, state-of-the-art dishwasher. Ryan explained that the children were allowed an hour of TV after dinner if their homework was finished, and that he turned off the Wi-Fi at bedtime.

"It's harmful for these screenagers to text on their phones all night," he said. "And they will, if the opportunity is there. Bedtime is sleep time."

When eight-thirty arrived, the two children went to bed obediently.

Dylan gave her a brief "Good night" and told her he'd be up very early in the morning to cycle around the village with his friends.

"Do you want me to wake you?" Cassie asked.

He shook his head.

"I'm good, thanks," he said, before closing his bedroom door.

Madison was chattier, and Cassie spent some time sitting on her bed, listening to her ideas of what they might do tomorrow and what the weather would be like.

"There's a sweet shop in the village and they sell the most beautiful striped candy bars that are like small walking sticks and taste of peppermint. Dad doesn't often let us go there, but maybe he'll let us go tomorrow."

"I'll ask," Cassie promised, before making sure the young girl was settled for the night, bringing her a glass of water, and turning out her light.

As she closed Madison's door gently, she remembered her first night at the previous job. How she'd fallen into an exhausted sleep, and had been late to respond when the youngest child had experienced a nightmare. She could still feel the pain and shock of the stinging slap she'd earned as a result. She should have walked out right then, but she hadn't.

Cassie was confident that Ryan would never do such a thing to her. She couldn't imagine him even giving a verbal admonishment.

Thinking of Ryan, she remembered about the glass of wine on the outside verandah, and she hesitated. She was tempted to spend more time with him but not sure if she should.

Had he meant it when he said she would be welcome to join him? Or had he offered out of politeness?

With indecision still churning in her mind, she found herself pulling on her thickest jacket. She could test the waters, see how he responded. If he didn't seem to want company, she could stay for a quick drink and then go to bed.

She headed down the hallway, still agonizing over her decision. As an employee, it wasn't right to have a glass of wine with her employer after working hours—or was it? If she wanted to be totally professional, she should go to bed. However, with Ryan being so accommodating about her lack of a visa, and promising to pay her cash, the lines of professionalism were already blurred.

She was a family friend, that's what Ryan had said. And sharing a glass of wine after dinner was exactly what a friend would do.

Ryan seemed delighted to see her. Relief and excitement uncoiled inside her as she saw his warm, genuine smile.

He stood up and took her arm and walked her across the verandah, making sure she was safely settled in a chair.

She saw with a skip of her heart that he'd set an extra wineglass out on the tray.

"Do you like Chardonnay?"

Cassie nodded. "I love it."

"Truth be told, I don't have a good palate for wine and my favorite is an ordinary rough red, but this excellent case was gifted to me by a grateful client after a successful fishing trip. I've been enjoying working my way through it. Cheers."

He leaned over and touched his glass to hers.

"Tell me more about your business," Cassie said.

"I started South Winds Sailing twelve years ago, just after Dylan was born. Having him come into the world made me rethink my purpose, and what I could offer my children. I spent three years in the Royal Navy after school, eventually becoming a merchant navy deck officer. The sea's in my blood and I've never imagined living or working inland."

Cassie nodded as he continued.

"When Dylan was born, tourism in this area was starting to boom, so I handed in my notice—at that stage I was the site manager at a shipyard in Cornwall—and bought my first boat. The second followed soon, and today I own a fleet of sixteen boats of various shapes and sizes. Motorboats, sailboats, paddleboards—and the jewel in my crown is a new charter yacht which is popular with corporate clients."

"That's amazing," Cassie said.

"It's been a fantastic journey. The business has given me so much. A comfortable income, a wonderful life, and a beautiful home, which I designed according to a dream I'd always had—although thankfully the architect toned down the wilder elements, or the house would probably have fallen over the cliff by now."

Cassie laughed.

"Your business must take a lot of hard work," she observed.

"Oh, yes." Putting his glass down, Ryan stared out at the sea. "As a business owner, you make constant sacrifices. You work extremely long hours. I seldom have a weekend off; today I asked my manager to stand in for me because I was meeting you. I think that's why—"

He turned toward her and met her gaze, his face serious.

"I think that's why my marriage eventually failed."

Cassie felt a tingle of anticipation that he was opening up to her about it. She nodded in sympathy, hoping he would keep on talking, and after a while, he did.

"When the children were younger, it was easier for Trish, my wife, to understand that I had to put work first. But as they grew older and became more independent, she started wanting me to—well, to replace their presence in her life, I guess. She demanded emotional support, time, and attention from me at an excessive level. I found it draining, and it started causing conflict. She was a strong woman. That was what first drew me to her, but people can change, and I think she did."

"That sounds very sad," Cassie said.

Her glass was almost empty, and Ryan refilled it before topping off his own.

"It was devastating. I can't explain what a tumultuous time it's been. When you love someone, you don't let go easily, and when love goes, you search nonstop for it. Hoping, praying, that you can get back what you valued so highly. I tried, Cassie. I tried with everything I had, and when it became clear it wasn't working, it felt like a defeat."

Cassie found herself leaning toward him.

"How scary that can happen."

"You picked the right word. It's terrifying. It left me feeling inadequate, and very much adrift. I don't take commitment lightly. To me, it means forever. When Trish left, I had to redefine my own impression of who I was."

Cassie blinked hard. She could hear the anguish in his voice. The pain he was going through sounded fresh and raw. It must take immense courage, she thought, to hide it under a joking and lighthearted exterior.

She was about to tell Ryan how much she admired him for the strength he was showing in adversity, but stopped herself just in time, realizing that this comment was far too forward. She barely knew Ryan, and had no right to make such personal observations to an employer after only a couple of hours in his company.

What was she thinking—if she was thinking at all?

She decided that the wine was going to her head and that she must choose her words carefully. Just because Ryan was so good-looking, intelligent, and kind was no reason to behave like a star-struck teenager around him. It had to stop, because she would only end up embarrassing herself dreadfully, or worse.

"I guess I'd better let you go to bed now," Ryan said, putting his empty glass down. "You must be exhausted after the drive, and meeting my two hooligans. Thank you for joining me out here. It means a lot to be able to speak to you like this."

"It's been an enjoyable end to the day, and such a lovely way to relax," Cassie agreed.

She didn't feel relaxed at all. She felt amped up by the intimacy of their conversation. As they stood up and headed inside, she couldn't stop thinking about what he had shared with her.

Back in her room, she took a quick look at her messages, feeling grateful that this house was connected to the Internet. At her last workplace, there had been no cell signal, and it had led to her becoming completely isolated. Until it happened, she hadn't realized how scary it was not to be able to communicate with the outside world when she needed to.

On her phone, Cassie saw there were a couple of hellos, and one or two memes from friends back in the US.

Then she saw one other message had been sent earlier in the evening. This one was from an unfamiliar UK cell phone number, which raised alarm bells when she saw it, and as she opened it, she felt cold fear clench her stomach.

"Be careful," the short message read.

Chapter Five

Cassie had expected to sleep well in her cozy room with the only sound the wash of surf outside. She was sure she would have, if it hadn't been for that disconcerting message, sent from an unknown number while she had been sitting out on the verandah with Ryan.

Her first panicked thought was that it concerned her ex-employer's murder trial; that somehow she'd been implicated and people were hunting for her. She tried to check the latest news, but found to her frustration that Ryan had turned the Wi-Fi off already.

She tossed and turned, worrying about what it could mean and who had sent it, trying to reassure herself that it was probably a wrong number and had been meant for somebody else.

After a restless night, she managed to drift into an uneasy sleep, and was woken by the sound of her alarm. She grabbed her phone and found to her relief that the signal was back.

Before she got out of bed, she searched for news on the trial.

Cassie learned that a postponement had been requested and it was due to resume in two weeks. Researching more carefully, she discovered this was because the defense team needed more time to contact additional witnesses.

That made her feel sick with fear.

She looked again at the strange message, "Be careful," wondering if she should reply to it and ask what it meant, but sometime during the night the sender must have blocked her because she found she couldn't send a message back.

In desperation, she tried to call the number.

It cut off immediately. Her calls had clearly been blocked, too.

Cassie sighed in frustration. Cutting off communication felt more like harassment than a genuine warning. She was going to go with it being a wrong number, which the sender had realized too late and blocked her as a result.

Feeling marginally comforted, she got out of bed and went to wake the children.

Dylan was already up—Cassie guessed he must have gone cycling. Hoping he wouldn't think it an intrusion, she went in, straightened up his duvet and pillows, and collected his discarded clothes.

His shelves were crammed with a huge variety of books, including quite a few on cycling. Two goldfish swam in a tank on top of the bookcase, and on a big table near the window was a rabbit hutch. A gray rabbit was eating a breakfast of lettuce and Cassie watched it happily for a minute.

Leaving his room, she tapped on Madison's door.

"Give me ten minutes," the young girl replied sleepily, so Cassie headed for the kitchen to get a start on breakfast.

There, she saw that Ryan had left a wad of money under the salt shaker with a handwritten note, "I've gone to work. Take the kids out and have fun! I'll be back this evening."

Cassie put a round of bread in the pretty floral toaster and filled the kettle. As she was busy making coffee, Madison walked in, wrapped in a pink robe and yawning.

"Good morning," Cassie greeted her.

"Morning. I'm glad you're here. Everyone else in this house gets up so early," she complained.

"Can I get you coffee? Tea? Juice?"

"Tea, please."

"Toast?"

Madison shook her head. "I'm not hungry yet, thanks."

"What would you like to do today? Your dad told us to go out somewhere," Cassie said, pouring tea as Madison requested it, with a splash of milk and no sugar.

"Let's go into town," Madison said. It's fun on the weekend. There's lots to do."

"Good idea. Do you know when Dylan will be back?"

"He usually goes for an hour." Madison cupped her hands around her mug and blew onto the steamy liquid.

Cassie was impressed by how independent the children seemed to be. Clearly, they were not used to being overprotected. She guessed the village was small and safe enough for them to treat it as an extension of their home.

Dylan arrived back soon afterward, and by nine they were dressed and ready to depart on their outing. Cassie assumed they'd take the car, but Dylan warned her against it.

"It's difficult to find parking on the weekend. We usually walk down—it's only a mile and a half—and take the bus back. It runs every two hours so you just have to time it right."

The walk down to the village could not have been more scenic. Cassie was charmed by the shifting views of the sea and the picturesque houses along the way. From somewhere in the distance she could hear church bells. The air was fresh and cool, and breathing in the smell of the sea was pure pleasure.

Madison skipped ahead, pointing out the houses of people she knew, which seemed to be almost everybody.

A few of the people driving past waved at them, and one woman stopped her Range Rover to offer them a ride.

"No thanks, Mrs. O'Donoghue, we're happy walking," Madison called. "We might need you on the way back though!"

"I'll look out for you!" the woman promised with a smile before pulling away. Madison explained that the woman and her husband lived further inland and ran a small organic farm.

"There's a shop selling their produce in town, and they sometimes have homemade fudge, too," Madison said.

"We'll definitely go there," Cassie promised.

"Her kids are lucky. They go to boarding school in Cornwall. I wish I could do that," Madison said.

Cassie frowned, wondering why Madison would want to spend any time away from such a perfect life. Unless, perhaps, the divorce had left her feeling insecure and she wanted a bigger community around her.

"Are you happy at your current school?" she asked, just in case.

"Oh, yes, it's great apart from that I have to study," Madison said.

Cassie was relieved that there didn't seem to be a hidden problem, such as bullying.

The shops were as quaint as she'd hoped. There were a few stores selling fishing tackle, warm clothing, and sports gear. Remembering her hands had been cold while drinking with Ryan the previous night, Cassie tried on a beautiful pair of gloves, but decided in view of her finances and her lack of available money, it would be better to wait and buy a cheaper pair.

The smell of baking bread drew them across the road to a cake shop. After some discussion with the children, she bought a sourdough loaf and a pecan pie to take home.

The only disappointment of the morning was the sweet shop.

When Madison marched expectantly up to the door she stopped, looking crestfallen.

The store was closed, with a handwritten note taped to the glass which read, "Dear Customers—we're out of town this weekend for a family birthday! We'll be back to serve you your favorite delicacies on Tuesday."

Madison sighed sadly.

"Their daughter usually runs the shop when they're away. I guess everyone went to this stupid party."

"I guess so. Never mind. We can come back next week."

"That's so far away." Head lowered, Madison turned away and Cassie bit her lip anxiously. She was desperate for this outing to be a success. She had been imagining how Ryan's face would light up as they spoke about their happy day, and how he might look at her with gratitude, or even give her a compliment.

"We'll come in next week," she repeated, knowing that this was little consolation to a nine-year-old who'd believed peppermint candy sticks were in her immediate future.

"And we might find sweets in other shops," she added.

"Come on, Maddie," Dylan said impatiently, and took her hand, marching her away from the shop. Ahead, Cassie noticed the store that Madison had told her about, owned by the woman who'd offered them a ride.

"One last stop there, and then we decide where to have lunch," she said.

Thinking of healthy suppers and snacks ahead, Cassie chose a few bags of chopped vegetables, a bag of pears, and some dried fruit.

"Can we buy chestnuts?" Madison asked. "They're delicious roasted on the fire. We did that last winter, with my mum."

It was the first time either of them had made mention of their mother and Cassie waited anxiously, watching Madison to see if the memory would cause her to become upset, or if this was a sign she wanted to talk about the divorce. To her relief, the young girl seemed calm.

"Of course we can. That's a lovely idea." Cassie added a bag to her basket.

"Look, there's the fudge!"

Madison pointed excitedly and Cassie guessed the moment was over. But having mentioned her mother once, she had broken the ice and might want to talk more about it later. Cassie reminded herself to be responsive to any signals. She didn't want to miss out on the opportunity to help either of the children through this difficult time.

The bags were displayed on a counter near the till, together with other sweet treats. There were toffee apples, fudge, mint humbugs, small bags of Turkish delight, and even miniature candy sticks.

"What would you like, Dylan and Madison?" she asked.

"A toffee apple, please. And fudge, and one of those candy sticks," Madison said.

"A toffee apple, two candy sticks, fudge, and Turkish delight," Dylan added.

"I think maybe just two sweets each for you will be enough or it'll spoil your lunch," Cassie said, remembering that excessive sugary treats were discouraged in this family. She took two toffee apples and two packets of fudge from the display.

"Do you think your father would like anything?" She felt a rush of warmth inside her as she spoke about Ryan.

"He likes nuts," Madison said, and pointed to a display of roasted cashews. "Those are his favorite."

Cassie added a bag to her basket and headed for the till.

"Afternoon," she greeted the shop assistant, a plump, blonde young lady with a name tag that read "Tina," who smiled at her and greeted Madison by name.

"Hello, Madison. How's your dad? Is he out of hospital yet?"

Cassie glanced in concern at Madison. Was this something she hadn't been told about? But Madison was frowning, confused.

"He hasn't been in hospital."

"Oh, I'm sorry, I must have misunderstood. When he was last here, he said—" Tina began.

Madison interrupted her, staring at the cashier curiously as she rang up the purchases.

"You've got fat."

Horrified by the tactlessness of this comment, Cassie felt her face going as crimson as Tina's was doing.

"I'm so sorry," she mumbled in apology.

"That's all right,"

Cassie saw Tina looked crestfallen at the comment. What had gotten into Madison? Had she never been taught not to say such things? Was she too young to realize how hurtful those words were?

Perceiving that no more apologies would redeem the situation, she grabbed her change and hustled the young girl out of the shop before she could think of anything else tactless and personal to announce.

"It's not polite to say things like that," she explained, when they were out of earshot.

"Why?" Madison asked. "It's the truth. She's much fatter than when I saw her in the August holidays."

"It's always better not to say anything if you notice something like that, especially if other people are listening. She might have a—a glandular problem or be taking medication that makes her fat, like corti-sone. Or she could be expecting a baby and not want anyone to know yet."

She glanced at Dylan on her left, to see if he was listening, but he was rummaging in his pockets and seemed preoccupied.

Madison frowned as she thought this over.

"OK," she said. "I'll remember for next time."

Cassie let out a deep breath of relief that her logic had been understood.

"Would you like a toffee apple?"

Cassie passed Madison her toffee apple, which she put into her pocket, and handed the other to Dylan. But when she gave it to him, he waved it away.

Looking at him in disbelief, Cassie saw he was unwrapping one of the candy sticks from the store they'd just visited.

"Dylan—" she began.

"Ah, no, I wanted one of those," Madison complained.

"I got you one." Dylan reached into the deep pocket of his coat and to Cassie's horror, pulled out several more.

"Here," he said, and passed her one.

"Dylan!" Cassie felt suddenly short of breath and her voice sounded high and stressed. Her mind was racing as she struggled to take in what had just happened. Had she misread the situation?

No. There was no way Dylan could have bought the candy. After Madison's embarrassing comment, she'd hustled them straight out of the store. There hadn't been time for Dylan to have paid, especially since the assistant hadn't been very adept at working the old-fashioned till.

"Yeah?" he asked, looking at her inquiringly, and Cassie felt chilled by the fact that there was no trace of emotion in his pale blue eyes.

"I think—I think you might have forgotten to pay for that."

"I didn't pay," he said casually.

Cassie stared at him, shocked beyond words.

Dylan had just coolly admitted to having shoplifted goods.

She'd never imagined that Ryan's son would do such a thing. This was beyond the scope of her experience and she was at a loss to know how she should react. She felt shaken that her impression of a perfect family, which she'd believed in, was far from reality. How could she have been so wrong?

Ryan's son had just committed a criminal act. Worse still, he was showing no remorse, no shame, nor even any sign that he understood the enormity of his action. He stared back at her calmly, seeming unconcerned by what he had done.

CHAPTER SIX

While Cassie stood, frozen in shock and clueless as to how she should handle Dylan's theft, she realized that Madison had already made up her mind.

"I'm not eating stolen goods," the young girl announced. "You can have it back."

She held out the candy stick to Dylan.

"Why are you giving it back? I took it for you because you wanted a candy stick, and the first shop didn't have them, and then Cassie was being stingy and wouldn't buy you one."

Dylan spoke in aggrieved tones, as if he'd expected thanks for saving the day.

"Yes, but I don't want a stolen one."

Shoving it into his hand, Madison folded her arms.

"If you don't take it, I won't offer it again."

"I said no."

Chin jutted, Madison marched away.

"You're with me or you're against me. You know what Mum always says," Dylan shouted after her. With worry surging inside her at another mention of their mother, Cassie detected more than a hint of menace in his tone.

"OK, enough now."

In a few fast steps, Cassie grabbed Madison's arm and turned her around, bringing her back so that they all stood facing each other on the cobbled sidewalk. She felt cold with dread. The situation was spiraling out of control, the children were starting to fight, and she hadn't even addressed the issue of the theft. No matter how traumatized they were, or what emotions they were suppressing, this was a criminal act.

She was all the more appalled that this store belonged to someone who was friendly with the family. The owner had even offered them a ride to town! You shouldn't steal from a person who'd offered you a ride. Well, you shouldn't steal from anybody, but particularly not from a woman who had generously tried to help that very morning.

"Let's go and sit down."

There was a tearoom on her left which looked full, but, spotting a couple getting up from a booth, she hustled the children to the door.

A minute later they were seated in the warm interior that smelled deliciously of coffee and crisp, buttery pastry.

Cassie stared down at the menu, feeling helpless, because every second that passed was proving to the children that she had no idea how to handle this.

Ideally, she supposed Dylan should be made to go back in and pay for what he'd taken, but what if he refused? She also wasn't clear what the penalties were for shoplifting here in the UK. He might end up in trouble if the store policy dictated that the clerk had to report it to the police.

Then Cassie thought back to the timeline of events and realized there might be a different perspective.

She remembered that Madison had mentioned roasting chestnuts with their mother just before Dylan had stolen the sweets. Perhaps this quiet boy had heard his sister's words and been reminded of the trauma the family had been through.

He might have been acting out his repressed emotions over the divorce by deliberately doing something forbidden. The more Cassie thought about it, the more the explanation made sense.

In which case, it would be better to handle this in a more sensitive way.

She glanced at Dylan, who was paging through his menu, looking completely unconcerned.

Madison also seemed to have gotten over her flare-up of temper. Having refused the stolen sweet and given Dylan a piece of her mind, the matter seemed to have been handled to her satisfaction. She was now engrossed in reading the descriptions of the various milkshakes.

"All right," Cassie said. "Dylan, please give me all the sweets you took. Clean out your pockets."

Dylan rummaged in his jacket and took out four candy sticks and a packet of Turkish delight.

Cassie stared down at the small pile.

He hadn't taken a lot. This wasn't theft on a grand scale. It was the fact he'd taken them at all that was the problem—and that he didn't think it was wrong.

"I'm going to confiscate those sweets because it's not right to take something without paying. That shop assistant could get into trouble if the money in the till doesn't match up with the stock. And you could have landed in bigger trouble. All these stores have cameras."

"OK," he said, looking bored.

"I'm going to have to tell your father, and we'll see what he decides to do. Please don't do this again, no matter how much you're trying to help, or how unfair you think the world is being to you, or how upset you are feeling about family issues. It could lead to serious consequences. Understand?"

She took the sweets and stashed them in her purse.

Watching the children, she saw that Madison, who didn't need the warning, was looking far more worried than Dylan was. He was staring at her with what she could only interpret as puzzlement. He gave a small nod, and she guessed that was all she was going to get.

She'd done what she could. All she could do now was pass the information on to Ryan and let him take it further.

"Are you thinking of a milkshake, Madison?" she asked.

"You can't go wrong with chocolate," Dylan advised, and just like that, the tension was broken and they were back to normal again.

Cassie was relieved beyond measure that she'd been able to manage the situation. She realized her hands were shaking and she put them under the table so the children wouldn't see.

She'd always avoided fights because it brought back memories of the times when she'd been an unwilling, helpless participant. She recalled fragmented scenes of bellowing voices and screams of pure rage. Smashing of dishes—hiding under the dining room table, she'd felt the shards sting her hands and face.

Given the choice, in any fight, she usually ended up doing the equivalent of hiding away.

Now, she was glad that she'd managed to assert her authority calmly but firmly, and that the day hadn't turned into a disaster as a result.

The tearoom manager hurried over to take their orders and Cassie started to realize how small this town was, because she also knew the family.

"Hello, Dylan and Madison. How are your parents?"

Cassie cringed, realizing the manager obviously didn't know the latest news, and she hadn't discussed with Ryan what she should say. As she was fumbling for the correct words, Dylan spoke.

"They're fine, thank you, Martha."

Cassie was grateful for Dylan's brief response, although she was surprised by how normal he'd sounded. She had thought he and Madison would be upset by the mention of their parents. Perhaps Ryan had told them not to discuss it if people didn't know. That was probably the reason, she decided, especially since the woman seemed to be in a rush and the question had only been a polite formality.

"Hello, Martha. I'm Cassie Vale," she said.

"You sound like you're from America. Are you working for the Ellises?"

Again, Cassie winced at their collective mention.

"Just helping out," she said, remembering that despite her informal agreement with Ryan, she needed to be careful.

"So difficult to find good help. We're very short-staffed at this time. One of our waitresses was deported yesterday, due to not having the correct paperwork."

She glanced at Cassie, who looked down hurriedly. What did the woman mean by this? Did she suspect from Cassie's accent that she didn't have a working visa?

Was this a hint that authorities in the neighborhood were clamping down?

Quickly, she and the children placed their orders and to Cassie's relief, the manager hurried away.

A short while later, a stressed-looking waitress, who was obviously a local, brought them their pies and chips.

Cassie didn't want to linger over her food and risk another round of chitchat, as the restaurant was starting to empty out. As soon as they'd finished, she went up to the front desk and paid.

Leaving the tearoom, they walked back the way they had come. They stopped off at a pet supplies store where she bought more food for Dylan's fish, which he told her were named Orange and Lemon, and a bag of bedding for his rabbit, Benjamin Bunny.

As they were heading toward the bus stop, Cassie heard music and noticed a crowd of people had gathered in the cobblestone town square.

"What do you think they're doing?" Madison noticed the activity at the same moment Cassie's head turned.

"Can we have a look, Cassie?" Dylan asked.

They headed across the road to find that there was a pop-up entertainment show in progress.

In the north corner of the square, a three-piece live band was playing. In the opposite corner, an artist was creating balloon animals. Already a line of parents with young children had formed.

In the center, a magician, formally dressed in a smart suit with a top hat, was performing tricks.

"Oh, wow. I absolutely love magic tricks," Madison breathed.

"Me, too," Dylan agreed. "I would like to study it. I want to know how it works."

Madison rolled her eyes.

"Easy. It's magic!"

Just as they arrived, the magician completed his trick, to gasps and applause, and then as the crowd dispersed, he turned to face them.

"Welcome, good people. Thank you for being here on this lovely afternoon. What a fine day it is. But tell me, little lady, are you not a bit cold?"

He beckoned Madison forward.

"Cold? Me? No." She stepped forward, half smiling in wary amusement.

He held out his empty hands and then moved forward and clapped them close to Madison's head.

She gasped. As he lowered his cupped hands, in them was a small toy snowman.

"How did you do that?" she asked.

He handed her the toy.

"It was on your shoulder all along, traveling with you," he explained, and Madison laughed in amazed disbelief.

"So now, let's see how quick your eyes are. This is how it works. You bet me—any amount you like, as I move four cards around. If you can guess where the queen lands, you double your money. If you can't, you leave empty-handed. So, would you like to place your bet?"

"I'll bet! Can I have some money?" Dylan asked.

"Sure. How much do you want to lose?" Cassie rummaged in her jacket pocket.

"I want to lose five pounds, please. Or win ten, of course."

Aware that a new crowd was gathering behind her, Cassie handed Dylan the money and he paid it over.

"This should be easy for you, young gentleman, I can see you have a quick eye, but remember, the queen is a wily lady and she has won many battles.

"Watch carefully as I deal four cards. See, I am placing them face up, for total disclosure. This is almost too easy. It's like giving the money away. The queen of hearts, the ace of spades, the nine of clubs, and the jack of diamonds. After all, as they say about marriage, it starts off with hearts and diamonds, but by the end all you need is a club and a spade."

There were roars of laughter from the audience.

The magician's allusion to marriage going bad had Cassie glancing nervously at the children, but Madison didn't seem to have understood the joke, and Dylan's attention was fixed on the cards.

"Now, I turn them over."

One by one he deliberately flipped the cards face down.

"And now, I move them."

Swiftly, but not too fast, he shuffled the four cards. It was a challenge to follow but by the time he stopped, Cassie was fairly sure that the queen was on the extreme right.

"Where is our lady queen?" the magician asked.

Dylan paused, then pointed to the card on the right.

"Are you sure, young sir?"

"I'm sure." Dylan nodded.

"You have one chance to change your mind."

"No, I'll stick with that one. She's got to be there."

"She's got to be there. Well, let us see if the queen agrees, or if one of her consorts has managed to spirit her away into hiding."

He flipped the card over and Dylan let out an audible groan.

It was the jack of diamonds.

"Dammit," he said.

"The jack. Always ready to cover for his queen. Loyal to the end. But our queen of hearts, the emblem of love, still eludes us."

"So where's the queen?"

"Where indeed?"

Cassie had noticed, while he shuffled the cards around, that there was one he hadn't touched at all—the one on the far left. That had been the ace of spades.

"I think she's there," she guessed, pointing to the card.

"Ah, so here we have a clever lady, pointing to the one card she knows it couldn't possibly be. But you know what? Miracles happen."

With a flourish, he uncovered the card—and there was the queen.

Laughter and applause rang through the square and Cassie felt a surge of delight as Dylan and Madison high-fived her.

"What a pity you didn't put money on it, my lady. You would have been richer now, but that's the way it goes. Who needs money, when love has chosen you?"

Cassie felt her cheeks redden. If only, she hoped.

"As a memento, you may have the card itself."

He dropped it into a paper bag and sealed it with a sticker before handing it to Cassie, who put it in the side pocket of her purse.

"I wonder what would have happened if I'd chosen that card," Dylan remarked as they walked away.

"I'm sure it would have been the jack of diamonds," Cassie said. "That's how he makes his money, by switching the cards when people bet."

"His hands were so fast," Dylan said, shaking his head.

"They must be naturally good and then train for years on top," Cassie guessed.

"I suppose they would have to," Dylan agreed, as they reached the bus stop.

"It's also misdirection, but I'm not sure how that applies when there are four cards so close together. But it must work somehow."

"OK, let's practice. Try and misdirect me, Cassie," Madison asked.

"I will, but the bus is coming. Let's get on it first."

Madison turned to look and while her attention was distracted, Cassie snatched the toffee apple out of her jacket pocket.

"Hey! What did you do? I felt something. And there's no bus." Madison turned back, saw Dylan burst out laughing, paused for a moment as she replayed what had happened, and started giggling herself.

"You got me!"

"It's not always that easy. I was just lucky."

"The bus is coming, Madison," Dylan said.

"I'm not looking. You can't trick me twice." Still snorting with laughter she folded her arms.

"Then you'll get left behind," Dylan told her as the sleek single-decker country bus pulled up at the stop.

During the short ride home they all did their best to misdirect each other. By the time they reached their stop, Cassie's stomach felt sore from laughing and she was warm with happiness that the day had been a success.

As they unlocked the front door, her cell phone buzzed. It was a message from Ryan, telling her he'd be bringing pizzas home, and were there any toppings she didn't like?

She typed back, "I'm easy, thanks," and then realized the connotations as she was about to press Send.

Her face felt hot as she erased the words and replaced them with, "Any toppings are good. Thank you."

A minute later her phone buzzed again and she grabbed it, eager for Ryan's next message.

This text wasn't from him. It was from Renee, one of her old school friends from back home.

"Hey, Cassie, someone was looking for you this morning. A woman, calling from France. She was trying to find you but she wouldn't say more. Can I give her your number?"

Cassie reread the message and suddenly the village didn't feel remote or safe anymore.

With her ex-employer's trial upcoming in Paris, and the defense team searching for more witnesses, she was terrified that the net was closing.

CHAPTER SEVEN

A s she helped the children with their evening routine of bath time and pajamas, Cassie couldn't get the disturbing message out of her mind. She tried to convince herself that Pierre Dubois's legal team could have called her directly, without needing to track down an old school friend, but the fact remained that someone was looking for her.

She urgently needed to find out who that person was.

After she'd tidied the bathroom, she messaged Renee back.

"Do you have a number for the lady? Did she give you her name?"

Leaving her phone behind, she headed through to the kitchen and helped Madison set the table with all the extras that accompanied pizza—salt and pepper, crushed garlic, Tabasco sauce, and mayonnaise.

"Dylan likes the mayo," she explained. "I think it's yuck."

"I do, too," Cassie confessed, and her heart leaped as she heard the front door open.

Madison rushed out of the kitchen, with Cassie close behind.

"Pizza delivery!" Ryan called, handing Madison the pile of boxes. "It's good to be indoors. It was getting icy out there, and dark, too."

He saw Cassie and just as she'd hoped, his face broke into that wickedly attractive grin.

"Hello, Cassie! You're looking beautiful. I see you have some color in your cheeks after all our seaside air. I can't wait to hear about your day."

Cassie smiled back at him, grateful that he'd assumed her flushed face was caused by the fresh air, and not by the fact that she'd started feeling excited and strangely self-conscious as soon as he'd walked in.

As she took the boxes from him, she told herself it would be a good thing when this crush on her boss calmed down.

A few minutes later, Ryan joined them in the kitchen, and Cassie saw he was holding a brown paper bag.

"I bought gifts for everyone," he announced.

"What did you get me?" Madison asked.

"Patience, sweetheart. Let's all sit down first."

When the children were seated at the table, he opened the bag.

"Maddie, I bought you this."

It was a black, fitted top with a pink glittery slogan that was written upside down.

"This is my Handstand Shirt," the slogan read.

"Oh, that's so pretty. I can't wait to wear it to gym," Madison said, beaming in delight as she turned the shirt, watching the light catch the sparkles.

"For you, Dylan, this."

His gift was a neon yellow, long-sleeved cycling top.

"Cool, Dad. Thanks."

"I hope it keeps you safe, now that the mornings are getting so dark. And for you, Cassie, I bought these."

To Cassie's amazement, Ryan took a pair of elegant, warm gloves from the bag. Her eyes widened as she realized they were almost identical to the ones she'd tried on in town.

"Oh, they're absolutely beautiful, and they will be so useful."

To her consternation, Cassie realized she was in the throes of her crush once again and was imagining herself wearing them while sitting outside and sipping wine with him.

"I hope they're the right size. I tried my best to picture your hands while I was buying them," Ryan said.

For a moment Cassie couldn't breathe as she wondered if he was thinking the same way she was.

"So, did you enjoy yourselves today?" Ryan asked.

"We had such fun. There was a magician in town. He gave me a snowman, and he tricked Dylan and took five pounds off him, but then Cassie guessed where the card was and won the card, although no money."

"What card did she win?" Ryan asked his daughter.

"The queen of hearts, so the magician said love is coming her way."

Cassie took a drink of orange juice because she didn't know where to look and was shy about meeting Ryan's gaze.

"Well, I think Cassie deserves that card and all it brings," Ryan said, and she nearly spilled her juice as she put the glass down.

"What did you do after that?" he asked.

"We started talking all about misdirection on the way to the bus, and Cassie misdirected me and stole my toffee apple!"

The words burst out of Madison, and although Dylan was too busy eating pizza to say much, he nodded enthusiastically.

"We bought you something as well," Cassie said, and shyly handed over the cashew nuts.

"My favorite! I have a busy day tomorrow and I'm going to take these with me and have them for lunch. What a treat. Thank you for such a thoughtful gift."

As he said the last words, he looked directly at Cassie and his blue gaze held hers for several moments.

After the pizzas had been devoured—Cassie hadn't had much of an appetite but the others had made up for it and finished every slice—she took the children through to the family room for their allotted TV time, and after watching a talent show they all enjoyed, she put them to bed.

Madison was still excited by the day's adventures and by the talent show, which had featured two groups of school gymnasts.

"I think I want to be a gymnast one day," she said.

"It takes hard work, but if it's your dream, you must follow it," Cassie advised.

"I feel like I can't sleep."

"Do you want to talk some more? Or should I read you a story?"

Cassie tried not to feel impatient at the thought of Ryan, sitting outside with his wine, waiting for her. Or perhaps he wouldn't wait, but would have an early night instead. In which case, she'd miss the opportunity to tell him about Dylan's shoplifting.

The memory jolted her. In her happiness over the thoughtful gift, and the chatter at the dinner table, she'd forgotten about that unpleasant incident. It was her duty to tell Ryan, even if it ended up spoiling what had been a wonderful day.

"I'd like to read for a while."

Madison scrambled out from between the sheets, headed for the shelf, and selected a book she had obviously read many times, because its spine was creased and its pages dog-eared.

"This is the story of an ordinary girl who becomes a ballet dancer. I really enjoy it, it's exciting. Every time I read it, it's exciting. Don't you think that's strange?"

"No, not at all. The best stories always make you feel that way," Cassie said.

"Cassie, do you think they teach gymnastics at boarding school?"

That mention of boarding again. Cassie paused.

"Yes, especially since boarding schools are usually bigger schools. They'll have lots of sports facilities there I should think."

Madison seemed satisfied with that answer, but then she had another thought.

"Do boarding schools let you stay there during the holidays?"

"No, you have to come home for the holidays. Why would you want to stay at school?"

Cassie hoped Madison would answer, but she pulled the duvet up to her chin and opened her book.

"I just wondered. Good night. I'll turn my light out later."

"I'll check on you," Cassie promised, before closing the door.

She sprinted to her room, grabbed her coat and pulled on the beautiful new gloves, and rushed to the balcony.

To her relief, Ryan was still there. In fact, she saw with a thrill of happiness that he'd waited for her before pouring the wine. As soon as he saw her he got to his feet, moved her chair closer to his, and plumped up the cushion before she sat down.

"Cheers. Thank you so much for today. It's the best feeling in the world to see the kids so happy."

"Cheers."

As she touched her wineglass to his, she remembered that it hadn't been a perfect day. There had been a serious incident. How was she going to tell him? What if he criticized her and said she should have handled it differently?

It would be better to ease into it, she decided, and to bring the topic up in a conversational way. She hoped Ryan might mention his divorce again, because that would provide the perfect opening for her to say, "You know, I think this divorce might have been troubling Dylan more than we've been realizing, because just after Madison mentioned her mother, he stole some sweets from the store."

They spoke for a while about the weather—tomorrow was supposed to be a fine day—and the children's schedule. Ryan explained that the school bus would pick them up at seven-thirty in the morning, by which time he would already be gone, and that the children would tell her what time school ended, and if they needed to be taken to any activities.

"There's a timetable on the inside of my cupboard door, if you want to check," he said. "I update it whenever there's a change in timing."

"Thank you so much. I'll check it if I need to," Cassie said.

"You know," Ryan said, and Cassie tensed, draining the last of her wine, because the tone of his voice had changed, becoming more serious. She was sure he was going to mention his divorce, and that meant it would be time for her to bring up the difficult topic of Dylan's shoplifting.

He refilled their glasses before continuing.

"You know, you were very much on my mind today. As soon as I saw those gloves I thought of you and I realized how much I enjoyed our chat outside yesterday The gloves were really a way of saying that I would love you to spend every evening out here with me."

For a moment Cassie didn't know what to say. She couldn't believe what Ryan had just said. Then, as his words sank in, she felt happiness fill her.

"I'll be glad to. I loved the time we spent together last night."

She wanted to add more, but stopped herself. She must be careful of spilling out the emotions that were rising inside her, because Ryan's comment might just have been politeness.

"Do they fit well?" He took her left hand in his cupped palm and ran his thumb gently over her fingers.

"Yes, they are a perfect fit. And I can't feel the cold in them at all."

Her heart was beating so fast she wondered if he'd be able to feel her pulse pounding as he gently stroked his fingers over her wrist, before releasing his grasp.

"I admire you so much, taking such a big step to travel overseas. Did you decide to do this all on your own? Or with a friend?"

"All on my own," Cassie said, glad that he appreciated what it took.

"That's incredible. What do your family think?"

Cassie didn't want to lie, so she did her best to skirt the issue.

"Everyone was supportive. Friends, family, and my previous employers. I did have a few friends tell me I would be homesick and would come back soon, but that hasn't happened."

"And did you leave anyone special behind? A boyfriend, perhaps?"

Cassie could hardly breathe as she realized what this question might imply. Was Ryan hinting at something? Or was it just a conversational question, finding out more about her? She needed to be cautious because she was so star-struck by him that she could easily babble out something inappropriate.

"I don't have a boyfriend. I dated a guy earlier this year, back in the States, but we broke up a while before I left."

That wasn't true. She'd broken up with her abusive ex only a couple of weeks before leaving, and one of her main reasons for traveling overseas had been to get so far away that he couldn't follow and she couldn't change her mind.

Cassie couldn't give Ryan the correct version. Right here and now, watching the white crests of the distant waves roll to shore, she wanted him to think that her last relationship was far in her past. That she was serene and unscarred and ready for a new one.

"I'm glad you shared that with me. It would be wrong of me not to make sure," Ryan said softly. "And I assume you must have ended things, because I can't see it being the other way round."

Cassie stared at him, hypnotized by his pale blue eyes, feeling as if she were in a dream.

"Yes, I did. It wasn't working out and I had to make a hard decision."

He nodded.

"That's what I sensed about you from the first time we spoke. Your inner strength. That ability to know what you want, and to strive for it, and yet you have this amazing empathy and gentleness and wisdom."

"Well, I don't know about wise. I don't feel very wise most of the time."

Ryan laughed. "That's because you're too busy living life to be overly introspective. Another great quality."

"Hey, I feel that while I'm here, I might learn from an expert in that regard," she countered.

"Isn't life the most fun when you spend it with somebody who makes it worth living?"

His words were teasing, but his face was serious, and she found she couldn't look away.

"Yes, definitely," she whispered.

This didn't feel like a normal conversation. It meant something more. It must.

Ryan put his glass down and took her hand, helping her out of the deep cushion. His arm slid round her waist, casually, for a few moments as she turned to go back inside.

"I hope you sleep well," he said, when they reached her bedroom door.

His hand brushed the small of her back as he leaned toward her and for a moment her amazed eyes took in the shape of his mouth, sensual and firm, framed by a soft outline of stubble.

Then his lips touched hers for just a moment before he drew away and said, softly, "Good night."

Cassie watched until he'd closed his bedroom door and then, feeling as if she were floating on air, she checked that Madison's light was out and returned to her room.

With a jolt, she realized she'd forgotten to tell Ryan about the shoplifting.

There hadn't been the opportunity. The evening had not turned out that way. It had gone in a completely different direction, an unexpected one that had left her feeling amazed and hopeful and expectant. With that kiss, she felt as if a door had opened, and beyond it she'd glimpsed something that might change her entire world.

Had he meant it in a friendly way? Or had he meant something more by it? She wasn't sure, but thought it had. The uncertainty made her feel nervous and excited, but in a good way.

Back in her room, she checked her messages again and found Renee had texted her back.

"The woman said she was calling from a pay phone. So no number. If she calls again I'll ask her name."

As she read the message, Cassie had a sudden idea.

This mystery woman had called from a pay phone, fearful to leave her details, and had contacted a school friend who was one of Cassie's only friends who still lived in her old hometown.

Cassie's father had moved away from where they'd grown up. He'd moved several times, changing jobs, changing girlfriends, and losing his phone just about every time he went on a drunken rampage. She hadn't been in touch with him for ages and never wanted to see him again. He was aging, his health was broken, and he'd created the life he deserved for himself. However, this meant he was no longer contactable by family looking to get in touch. Even she wouldn't know how to get hold of her dad now.

There was a chance—a chance that seemed stronger the more she thought about it—that this caller was her sister, Jacqui, doing her best to trace Cassie again. An old school friend would be the only connection if you weren't on social media, and Jacqui wasn't. Cassie looked for her often, searching whenever she had the time, hopeful that her detective work might uncover a clue to her sister's whereabouts.

Goosebumps prickled Cassie's spine as she considered the possibility that it had been Jacqui who'd called.

It didn't mean Jacqui was in a good situation, but then, she'd never thought she was. If Jacqui had been settled down, with a stable job and an apartment, she would have been in touch long ago.

When Cassie thought of Jacqui she always imagined uncertainty, precariousness. She visualized a life teetering on a fragile balance— between money and poverty, drugs and rehab, boyfriends and abusers, who knew the details? The more uncertain Jacqui's life was, the harder it would be for her to make contact with family she'd left long ago. Perhaps her circumstances didn't allow it, or she was ashamed of the situation she was in. She might be spending weeks and months on the road or off the grid, high out of her mind, or begging for food, or who knew what?

Cassie decided she was going to have faith, and take the chance this was Jacqui reaching out.

Quickly, knowing that Ryan might turn off the Wi-Fi at any moment, she messaged Renee back.

"It could be my sister. If she calls again, please give her my number."

Hoping that her hunch was right, Cassie closed her eyes, feeling she'd done what she could to reestablish contact with the only family she still cared about.

CHAPTER EIGHT

The next morning was organized chaos, as Cassie tried to help the children dress for school. School uniform items were missing, shoes were muddy, socks were mismatched. She found herself running back and forth between the kitchen and the bedrooms, juggling breakfast with everything else.

The children wolfed down tea, toast, and jam before resuming the search for school items that seemed to have migrated to an alternate universe over the weekend.

"I've lost my badge!" Madison announced, pulling on her blazer.

"What does it look like?" Cassie asked, her heart sinking. She'd thought that they were finally done.

"It's round in shape and bright green. I can't go to school without it, I was last week's class captain and someone else has to get the button today."

In a flat panic, Cassie got on her hands and knees and searched the whole room, eventually finding the badge on the closet floor.

After this crisis had been averted, Dylan shouted that his pencil case had vanished. It was only after the children had left that Cassie found it behind the rabbit's cage, and rushed down the road to the bus stop where they were waiting.

When they'd safely boarded the bus, she took a deep breath, and the happy thoughts from the previous night bubbled up inside her again.

As she tidied the house, she replayed the interaction between her and Ryan in her head.

He'd been flirting, she was certain of it.

The way he'd touched her, taken her hand, asked her if she had a boyfriend. That on its own was an innocent enough question, but it was what else he'd said.

"It's wrong of me not to make sure."

That indicated he was asking for a reason. Making sure.

And that kiss. She closed her eyes as she thought of it, feeling warmth bloom inside her. It had been so unexpected, so perfect.

It had felt friendly, but as if he might have meant more by it. It was impossible to say. She felt filled with uncertainty, but in a positive way.

The morning flew by and since Ryan had said he would be arriving home late, she decided to get a start on supper. She had a very limited repertoire of dishes, but there was a kitchen shelf full of recipe books.

Cassie chose the one on family dinners. She'd assumed it was Ryan's book but was surprised to find a handwritten message on the first page—Happy Birthday Trish.

So this was Trish's book. It must have been gifted to her by a friend; perhaps a friend who didn't realize Ryan did most of the cooking. At any rate, she hadn't taken it with her.

Cassie's thoughts were interrupted by a loud knocking on the front door.

She hurried to answer it.

A man in black leathers was standing outside. A large motorbike was parked on the sidewalk behind him.

As soon as Cassie opened the door, he stepped forward so he was halfway in, and very much in her space. He was tall, broad-shouldered, with dark spiky hair and a mustache. She sensed a low level of aggression in the way he pushed inside and his expression as he looked down at her.

She stepped back, flustered by his invading presence. She wished she had put the inside chain on the door before opening it, but she hadn't thought it necessary in this small, quiet village.

"This the Ellis residence?" the man asked.

"Yes, it is," Cassie said, wondering what this was all about.

"Mr. Ryan Ellis in today?"

"No, he's at work. Can I help you?"

Cassie was panicking inwardly. For her own safety, she should have said Ryan had gone next door for a minute. She didn't know who this man was. He was pushy and entitled, and this was not how a delivery person would interact with a customer.

"And you are?" The man smiled slightly, leaning a hand on the doorframe.

"I'm the au pair," Cassie said defensively, remembering too late she should have said she was a family friend.

"Ah, so he's hired you? He's paying you, eh? Where you from? The States?"

Cassie felt breathless. She hadn't expected this at all, and thought immediately of the deported waitress that the tearoom manager had spoken about yesterday.

She didn't answer him. Instead, she repeated, "How can I help you?"

She hoped he couldn't sense how frightened he was.

"I've got a special delivery for Mr. Ryan Ellis."

The man handed her a large manila envelope with Ryan's name and address handwritten on it.

She placed it on the hall table and he passed her a clipboard.

"Sign here. Your full name, time of delivery, and your phone number."

So it was just a delivery after all. Cassie felt relieved, but she wasn't going to relax until this creepy guy was out of the door.

"And your passport, please."

"My what?"

She stared at him in horror.

"I have to photograph it. If you don't mind."

His tone of voice told her that he didn't care if she minded. He leaned against the wall and checked his watch.

Cassie felt thoroughly flustered. What was this all about? She dreaded it was some sort of illegal worker clampdown.

She couldn't tell him to get out, although she wanted to. Was photographing this document even legal, or an infringement of her rights? It felt like an attempt at intimidation, but she couldn't think of a way out without landing herself in even bigger trouble.

"Would you wait outside while I fetch it?" she asked.

He took his time moving onto the porch. Arms folded and that half smile on his round, pale face, he stood and watched.

She closed the front door, wishing she didn't have to open it again, and rushed to her bedroom to get her passport, with its incriminating visitor's visa.

Then she went back, opened the door, and handed it to him.

In the meantime he'd lit a cigarette. Placing it between his lips, he took his phone out and flipped through the document's pages.

She heard the repetitive click of the phone camera. It looked like he was photographing more than one page.

Then he handed it back and took the cigarette out of his mouth.

"Righto. That's it. Tell Mr. Ellis I'll be back soon if the notice is not attended to."

He flicked his smoldering cigarette butt onto the paving, turned away, and strode back to his bike. A minute later, the engine roared and he was gone.

On her hands and knees, Cassie scrabbled to pick up the burning cigarette. She stubbed it out on the damp grass and took the butt to the kitchen, where she threw it away. Her hands were shaking. What had that been about?

She stared at the envelope, held it up to the light, and even turned it over to see if there was any hint as to the sender's identity, but she could see nothing.

She would have to wait until Ryan got home and tell him about it.

Cassie began to fear that through her presence here, and Ryan's accommodating kindness, she'd landed him in serious trouble.

CHAPTER NINE

When it was time to fetch the children from school, Cassie did her best to put her worries aside. With the recent divorce, she knew the children had their own stress to deal with, and she didn't want them to sense her anxiety on top of it all.

Both were waiting at the school gate, and Madison in particular seemed pleased to see her. On the scenic drive home, the young girl talked nonstop about the day's lessons, which were boring, and math was getting too difficult, and the sport—they'd gone for a cross-country fun run which she'd enjoyed. Cassie found herself smiling, momentarily distracted by the girl's cheery comments.

The children made short work of the sandwiches she'd made, devouring them in a few minutes before heading purposefully out of the kitchen.

Cassie tidied away lunch and spent a while longer in the kitchen, trying to focus on the food preparation and not worry about what was inside the envelope on the hall table, or what Ryan's reaction might be when he came home.

It suddenly occurred to her that the house was very quiet.

"Dylan?" she called. "Madison?"

There was no answer.

Anxiety clenched her stomach, like an unwelcome guest who'd been temporarily banished but was waiting to return.

Cassie left the kitchen and checked their rooms. They weren't there, so she headed out to the backyard, noticing that the chilly wind had dropped.

Dylan, dressed in blue jeans and a red parka, was on the far side of the grassy slope, standing on the bluff that overlooked the ocean. He had his back to the sea and was messaging on his phone. It looked as if he was on the very edge, and there was no rail, only a sheer drop down sandstone cliffs to the gray waters below.

"Dylan, do you mind moving away from there?" she called.

He looked up curiously.

"If you're texting, don't go too near the edge," she explained. "You're distracted. You could fall over, and sandstone crumbles."

"Oh. OK."

He moved a step further in.

"Where's Madison?"

He shrugged.

"I dunno. I've just come out here. I've been messaging my mate."

Dylan lowered his head and turned his full attention back to his phone.

But Cassie had spotted something nearby. She headed to the bluff to see what it was.

A pink sneaker lay on the grass near the cliff's edge. Where was the other one? And where was Madison?

Cassie felt panic rising inside her, so sharp and sudden it seemed to choke her.

She hurried to the edge of the cliff.

Once there, she forced herself to take a moment to collect her thoughts and make sure she was on steady footing. If the steep drop triggered another flashback to the horrors she'd seen while in France, there would be nobody to help her.

Carefully, she peered over.

Far below, on the rocks, she saw a flash of pink.

Looking more closely, she confirmed, to her horror, that it was the other shoe.

"Madison!" she screamed, so loud that Dylan's head jerked up from his messaging in alarm.

"Madison, where are you?"

She felt a rush of panic and staggered back from the dizzying drop.

"Dylan, she's down there. I can see her shoe. She must have fallen."

Cassie clapped her hands over her mouth to smother her sobs. Self-recrimination crushed her. She'd been so preoccupied that she hadn't thought to check on the children. She'd been neglectful and irresponsible, focusing on less important matters instead of properly caring for the children, and in one terrible moment a catastrophe had occurred.

Had Madison fallen? Had the two of them fought and Dylan pushed her? Had she been trying to do gymnastics, or acrobatics, too close to the edge?

She felt sick with guilt as she wondered whether she could have prevented the accident if she'd bothered to check on them earlier.

"How do we get down there?"

Cassie shouted the question in a high, shrill voice, frantically considering what emergency action she should take and what the likelihood would be of surviving such a fall. The rocks looked lethally sharp, and Madison must have been washed out to sea, because there was no sign of her apart from the terrible sight of that one lonely shoe.

In a flash, Cassie realized that the fragile sense of security she'd achieved with this family was only a flimsy veneer covering the deep wounds that festered inside her. Now that veneer had been ripped away and exposed her for what she really was.

How could she ever have thought she was suitable to look after children? She was incompetent, unreliable, and the baggage she carried with her was going to prevent her from ever making a success of her life.

"Dylan, quick. Pass me your phone. What's the emergency services number?"

As Cassie spoke, Dylan started to laugh.

For a moment she stared at him, shocked beyond words at his reaction.

Then she followed his gaze to see Madison emerging from the garage side door, holding wads of crumpled up newspaper in her hands.

She walked a few steps away from the door and then stared down at the grass, frowning.

"Where have my shoes gone?" she asked.

For a moment, Cassie couldn't speak. A storm of emotion was raging in her head.

Then she managed to get the words out.

"Dylan, what happened here?" Her voice was still hoarse with tension, but she hoped it was loud enough to be authoritative.

"I moved your shoes. One of them fell off the edge," Dylan said to Madison.

"What? Over the cliff? Dylan, those are my favorite trainers! Go fetch it, now."

"He can't—" Cassie began, but Dylan interrupted.

"It's on the rocks. The tide's on the way out. I'll walk there in half an hour." He looked at Cassie. "There's a path that goes down."

"Why did you do that?" Madison still sounded angry. "I washed them because they were muddy after the run. I brought the newspaper to put inside so they would dry, like Dad taught us to do. And now you moved them and the one will be all dirty again."

"I thought it would be a game. I didn't mean for it to fall over."

Cassie cleared her throat.

"Madison could have fallen while fetching the shoe. You could even have slipped off the edge while putting it there. Dylan, that was a nasty thing to do."

He stared at her calmly.

"Neither of us have vertigo," he said.

The word hit Cassie like a slap in the face. It dragged her straight back to the moment when she'd looked over the balcony with Ryan.

Dylan knew what had happened. The way he'd said it told her so. He must have been passing by the family room at the time and seen them outside. Now he was using the word intentionally to show her that he knew, and this put a different spin on his behavior.

Cassie suspected that this was some sort of revenge move.

Dylan was getting Madison, or herself, or both of them, back for something, and she was sure it was because of what had taken place in town. They had criticized him, accused him of theft. He hadn't shown much emotion at the time but their words must have stung, and now he was retaliating.

Fury surged inside her and she knew was about to lose it. She was going to scream at him, let rip with the most vicious, hurtful things she could think of, to try and break through his nonchalant shell and force him to feel the same pain she was feeling now.

She almost did it, she almost couldn't stop herself, and she saw from his wary expression that he was expecting it.

At the very last moment, she paused.

Was she screaming because she felt angry at him? Or was she angry at herself, for having been so wrapped up in what she was doing that she hadn't checked on the children?

It would be unfair to make Dylan the target when she was the one to blame.

Dylan's behavior was troubling, and a little scary, but it hadn't been malicious. It had been a mean joke, that was all; his way of showing her how clever he was, and how sensitive, too.

She remembered his words, defensive and ever so slightly threatening.

"You're with me or you're against me."

Instead of shouting, she kept her voice calm as she spoke.

"It's no problem, Dylan. I'll walk down the path with you as soon as the tide's far enough out, and we will rescue Madison's shoe. Deal?"

Dylan looked surprised, as if he hadn't expected this response from her at all and hadn't thought about how to handle it.

"Deal," he said hesitantly, and Cassie knew with a surge of relief that she'd made the right call.

The path down to the sea was a few hundred yards away, in a place where the cliff face was less sheer. Cassie had worried that it might be danger-ous, but although it was steep and stony, the winding trail was not risky to negotiate.

Once she and Dylan were at the bottom, they walked single file along the exposed section of narrow, stony beach.

"When the tide's in, this is completely covered," Dylan called to her. "The sea breaks onto the cliffs, basically."

It was freezing cold down here and the spray from the waves was shocking but exhilarating. Cassie guessed that on a windy day, you'd be drenched just walking alongside the sea.

"There you are."

The pink trainer was lying on a rock and Dylan picked his way between the sharp boulders to collect it. He handed it to Cassie and they hurried back, scrunching over the pebbled beach and scrambling up the path again.

Cassie realized the good weather was passing by, and she was glad they'd managed to get the shoe when they had. The afternoon was clouding over and the wind was starting up again, icy and strong and blowing from the north.

When she checked on Madison, she found she was in her bedroom, doing a puzzle on a tray. Dylan headed into the dining room with a book and sprawled down onto the bean bag in the corner.

Cassie stuffed both the shoes with newspaper and set them near the radiator in the laundry to dry.

Only then did she allow herself to return to the kitchen, and she made sure to keep her thoughts on a tight rein. When she wasn't focusing on the food, she listened out for any sounds that meant Dylan or Madison might need her.

When she heard the click of the front door opening, her heart leaped, despite the stern talking-to she'd given herself. It was only two thirty in the afternoon. She hoped everything was all right, and that Ryan hadn't had a crisis at his work. She rushed out of the kitchen to say hello.

As she reached the hallway, Cassie stopped, staring in astonishment.

A young woman with pale pink hair had come in and was locking the door behind her.

She turned, saw Cassie, did a double take, and regarded her with the same surprise.

"Who're you?" she asked.

CHAPTER TEN

Cassie stared at the pink-haired woman with suspicion.

"I'm helping out here," she said, this time remembering to be careful about how she worded her role. "I arrived on the weekend. But who are you?"

The woman had just let herself in. She obviously had a key. Surely Ryan would have mentioned that to her?

She looked to be a couple of years younger than Cassie, and was very pretty, wearing faded, low-rise jeans that showed off her hourglass figure. With her fair skin and local accent she was clearly from the area.

"My name's Harriet. I work for Maids of Devon, and I clean here two afternoons a week. Usually Mondays and Fridays, unless the Monday is a bank holiday."

"Oh," Cassie said.

She was still distrustful, wondering if she should call Ryan to make sure, when Dylan shouted from the dining room, "Hi, Harriet!"

"Hey, Dylan," Harriet called back.

She removed her lilac jacket, hung it on the coat stand, and took a smock out of her backpack.

"Anything special needs doing today?" she asked.

Her tone wasn't friendly.

"What do you usually do?" Cassie felt at a loss.

With a shake of her candy floss hair, Harriet replied. "Usually put on a load of washing, get it in the dryer, fold it. Change the bedding weekly in all rooms—today's bedding day. Clean the bathrooms and the kitchen weekly, usually on Friday. Vacuum the house, dust, tidy, and then do any other jobs that need doing, but not ironing. If you don't have anything else today, I generally start in the rooms."

She headed purposefully for Ryan's room.

Cassie still felt totally confused. She wanted to follow Harriet into the bedroom and question her further but thought it would be rude. She had to accept that Ryan had just forgotten to tell her. After all, he'd left so early this morning he'd been gone before she was out of bed.

Even so, when she'd arrived on Saturday, Ryan had told her he'd cleaned especially for her. He hadn't mentioned that a housekeeper had been in the day before and done it all.

Feeling flustered by the alternative version of events that now existed, Cassie returned to the kitchen and finished preparing supper. She'd seasoned and spiced the pumpkin she'd bought yesterday, which was now ready to roast. She had cooked and mashed some potatoes, and made onion gravy to accompany the chicken pies she'd found in the freezer.

Harriet sashayed into the kitchen carrying a laundry basket piled high with bedding and towels.

She headed through the back door to the laundry room and in a minute, the washing machine started up.

Then she returned to the kitchen.

"I see you've been busy," she said, looking at the results of Cassie's efforts.

"I thought I'd help out today," Cassie said.

"You were hired as a cook, or to help with the kids?"

"I'm mostly helping with the kids."

Rattled, Cassie wondered whether Ryan had omitted to tell her about other staff, and a cook might make an appearance at the front door tomorrow.

Harriet left the kitchen again, returning with the empty wine bottle and the glasses that they'd left out on the balcony the previous night. She stared at the two glasses for a moment before packing them in the dishwasher and then glanced back at Cassie.

"So you're from the States, right?"

"Yes."

"You been here long?"

"In the country, about three weeks. I started this job on the weekend."

"How'd you hear about it? This isn't where most people go. Usually it's London."

"My friend au paired for Ryan last year during the school holidays and she told me he was looking again," she said.

"So you came all the way down here?"

"I have a car so I drove down. It's parked outside."

"Ah, yeah, I saw it. The little white Vauxhall?"

"That's the one."

"Where're you sleeping?" Harriet put on a pair of rubber gloves and wrung a cleaning cloth out at the sink.

"Sleeping? In—in the spare bedroom, of course."

Her nonstop questions were disconcerting for Cassie.

"Oh, I didn't mean where in the house, I just wondered if you're sleep-in or sleep-out."

"Sleep-in," Cassie confirmed, but she doubted whether that was what Harriet had meant by the question.

Seeing Harriet was hard at work cleaning, and since Cassie had had enough of the unsettling conversation, she left the room and went to check on the children.

Lounging on the bean bag and engrossed in his book, Dylan reassured her he didn't need anything and had no homework. Madison, on the other hand, had completed her puzzle and was frowning over a math worksheet.

"These sums are confusing," she complained.

Perching on the bed, Cassie leaned across the desk and did her best to help her by explaining, rather than solving the problems for her. She thought she had made some headway when the front door opened again and this time it was Ryan.

"Hello, all," he called, and Madison shouted back an excited, "Hi, Dad!"

Cassie leaped up from the bed and rushed to the front door. She was looking forward to seeing Ryan after his day at work, but felt anxious when she remembered about the delivery of the envelope.

She was fast, but Harriet was faster, and Cassie found her already at the door.

"Hel-lo, Mr. E," she greeted him, smoothing back her pretty pink hair.

"Afternoon, Harriet." Ryan gave her a friendly nod before turning to Cassie.

"I'm so sorry, I was in a rush this morning and completely forgot to tell you we have a cleaner come in twice a week."

"That's no problem. We've introduced ourselves."

With Harriet practically treading on her toes, Cassie decided it would be better to wait before telling Ryan about the unpleasant delivery man.

"Good, good." Ryan turned toward the bedroom but Harriet stepped in front of him.

"Did you notice?" she asked, shaking her head back.

Ryan stared at her and then glanced at Cassie, perplexed.

"Notice?"

Harriet sighed.

"My hair."

"Oh." Frowning, Ryan looked.

"It's pink." Harriet smiled, twirling a lock around her finger.

"Ah, so it is. Did Madison see yet? You know how much she loves pink, right?"

Ryan sounded at a loss, as if he wasn't getting what she was trying to say. And Cassie thought that Harriet was becoming frustrated. She wondered if Harriet had wanted to prove that she was more valued by her employer than Cassie was.

To Cassie's surprise, Harriet then said, "I made you your tea already, Mr. E. Where would you like it?"

"That's very kind, but I had tea at work. Perhaps the children want some?"

She didn't miss the flash of anger that darkened Harriet's face.

"I'll ask them," Cassie said, and headed down the hall, wondering why Harriet was so upset.

After she'd put dinner into the oven, she and Madison ended up sharing the tea in the family room while Harriet mopped the kitchen floor. Harriet seemed to be putting a lot of energy into her efforts. The bucket clattered across the tiles.

As soon as she was finished, Cassie returned to the kitchen, anxious to move ahead with her cooking. As she opened the oven, the delicious aroma of spicy pumpkin and cooking pastry wafted out. Ryan, who was passing, stopped in his tracks.

"Did you make food? Cassie, you're an angel. It smells wonderful."

From the broom cupboard, Cassie heard a loud bang as Harriet shoved the mop inside.

"Thanks. I hope it tastes as good as it looks. It will be ready in about half an hour," she said, putting the bowl of mash in to warm up and the pot of gravy onto the burner.

The cupboard door slammed.

Harriet marched out of the kitchen, pushing past Cassie.

As she passed her, she muttered something, and a moment later, the front door slammed and she was gone.

Perplexed, Cassie turned back to the stove.

She didn't like Harriet, and wondered if she might be bipolar. She'd seemed very moody and the cryptic words she'd snapped in an undertone as she departed hadn't made sense.

Cassie thought she had said, "Don't get too close."

CHAPTER ELEVEN

As soon as Harriet had left, Cassie hurried to find Ryan, picking up the manila envelope on the way.

He was in the family room, paging through a brochure advertising boats.

"Ryan, someone delivered this earlier today." Cassie handed him the envelope. "The delivery person took a photo of my passport. I don't know why, and I'm worried that it might somehow get you or me into trouble."

She felt bad saying the words, as if she'd brought the trouble here herself.

Ryan frowned as he turned the envelope over.

"You mustn't worry. This is probably something I need to sign for the divorce. I had papers delivered last week that looked similar. I was home at the time so took them myself."

As he made to open it, his phone rang. Cassie realized it would be rude to listen in. She forced herself to walk out of the room, even though she longed to hover nervously nearby so that he could open it, and she could be sure.

She guessed that if a legal document was delivered, proof of identity of the recipient would be required. That must be why the unfriendly man had photographed her passport.

Even so, she remembered how he'd threatened that he'd be back soon if the notice was not attended to. The repairs at Ryan's business seemed to be reaching a crucial stage, and with so much to think about, she hoped that the document would not slip his mind. If there was anything to sign, she needed him to sign it, because she felt uneasy at the thought of the dark-haired man coming back.

❧   ❧   ❧

On Tuesday morning, Madison reminded Ryan that she would be having extra math lessons on Monday and Wednesday the next week, and would need to be picked up an hour later from school.

Cassie could see Ryan was completely distracted. He'd already taken two phone calls that morning, speaking in angry tones to the repair company. She guessed from the conversation that he was a different person at work and that he must have a hard, uncompromising side that was hidden at home.

"You won't forget, Dad?" Madison asked anxiously.

"I'll write it on the timetable," Cassie promised, as Ryan strode out of the room with his phone ringing yet again.

As soon as the children had left, she went into Ryan's room to adjust it.

She hadn't been in his bedroom for longer than it took to dart in, pick up an empty cup, and head out again. She was trying to stay away because the room felt so much like his personal space. It smelled of the deodorant he wore, and there were books on the bedside table that he was reading, a beautiful sea view painting on the wall opposite the bed that she was sure he would have chosen, and even a notepad with a few words scribbled in his forward-tilted, precise hand.

Cassie couldn't help it. She stood in the middle of the room, on the shiny floorboards, and closed her eyes and breathed in the smell. She imagined him in this room, whistling softly to himself as he pulled off his shirt and walked over to the white-curtained window, staring out for a moment at the restless sea. Then she imagined herself there, too.

At that point she opened her eyes, abandoning the vivid images that were becoming way too personal.

A quick glance around the room confirmed there were no family photos. No wedding portraits, not even pictures of the kids. She wondered if there had been photos in the room before the divorce, or whether Ryan kept everything online.

He'd said the timetable was on the inside of a cupboard. Which one?

She opened one at random and blinked in surprise, because inside, neatly arranged on hangers, were several sets of women's clothes.

Smart business suits, high-heeled shoes, a variety of blouses in neutral colors.

It looked tidy and untouched, but the presence of the clothes bothered Cassie. It meant that there hadn't been closure. Either Trish was coming back for them, or else she hadn't wanted them, and if she hadn't wanted them, surely a plan should be made? They could be given away to a second-hand store or charity shop. They looked like top-quality garments that were relatively new. They could be used again, rather than moldering in here.

Frowning, she closed the door and moved to the next cupboard.

This was Ryan's space. A couple of leather jackets and dress shirts, many more T-shirts and casual tops, piles of jeans, and a few tracksuits. On the inside of the door, as he had promised, was the children's timetable.

Cassie made a note on the relevant days.

She wondered if she should ask Ryan about it, and that night, while they were having their glass of wine, she plucked up the courage to do it.

"I noticed that there are still some of Trish's clothes in the cupboard," she said.

Ryan nodded, grimacing.

"She took what she could fit into the boxes she'd brought, and she promised she'd be back to get the rest. She hasn't been, and I don't mind. It means she's not here and not in my space and I don't have to think about it, if you see where I'm going with this."

Cassie nodded.

"If you want to give them away, let me know. I can do it for you."

"That's a very kind offer, and I think I might just take you up on it, for most of the clothes, anyway. There are a few that I know she will still want, so as soon as I have a chance, I'll go through them. Once that's done, I can parcel up what she needs."

"That sounds like a good idea," Cassie agreed.

"You know, you're an absolute life saver. I'm so grateful that you're here." He smiled.

Cassie had been working hard on keeping the lid on her crush, and she was pleased that she was able to smile in a professional way, without blushing or stammering or showing him that his words were making her melt inside.

Telling him how she felt could only lead down the dangerous road to disappointment. After all, Ryan was a wealthy business owner with film star good looks, while she was just a penniless traveler, even if his kindness and praise made her feel like somebody more special.

The next day, as Ryan had another long day at work, she cooked again. This time, she tried her hand at shrimp pasta with lemon and garlic. She was worried that it might not be to the children's taste, although she'd asked them if they were willing to try it, and was delighted when they both declared it delicious.

"You're a cookery genius," Ryan said after taking the first bite.

"I'm not. I don't know much at all about it and all I've been doing is following the recipes in the cookbooks,"

Ryan shook his head.

"Cooking is more than that. Even with a recipe, there's still feel and instinct involved. People either have a flair for it or they don't, and you do."

Madison nodded.

"You're a great cook, Cassie. You haven't made one yuck thing the whole time you've been here. I love your food. Could you dish me some more, please?"

Ryan smiled fondly at his daughter.

"I'm pleased you are enjoying shrimp. Remember the last time you tried it, when we went on holiday to Madrid last year, and you hated the paella so much that the waiter had to bring you a hamburger instead?"

"That wasn't me, though," Madison corrected him. "It was Cousin Tess. She wouldn't eat the paella and so she got a burger but she didn't like the burger either so she just had chips. I ate the paella but I picked the shrimp out."

"Your cousin wasn't with us at that meal, though," Ryan said.

"She was. Tess and her mum came along with us."

"No, I remember it clearly, Madison," Ryan said in a decisive tone. "It was you who refused the paella, because I remember thinking to myself how strange it was that my own daughter wouldn't eat a bite of the very best food we had on that whole holiday."

Madison looked appealingly at Dylan, but he just shrugged. Cassie expected her to keep arguing back, because she was usually as tenacious about her opinions as a bulldog with a bone. But to her surprise, Madison just lowered her head and devoured her second helping. She didn't look happy, but she didn't speak about the incident again, and after a short silence, Cassie filled the uncomfortable gap in the conversation by asking what the program was for school tomorrow.

"We're both in the school play and there's a dress rehearsal at the town hall after school," Madison said.

"Where must I fetch you from?" Cassie asked.

"We can catch the bus back," Madison said. "It runs right past the town hall."

Intrigued by the mention of a performance, Cassie asked, "What's the play about? What are your roles?"

"Dylan is backstage crew, but they appear on stage, they wear these shirts saying "Crew" and run on and change the scenes."

"It's a very important role," Dylan added. "We have to be fast, but at the same time we also have to look like factory workers while making the audience laugh, so we're actors too. There are five of us, and they only picked people who were tall and strong."

"I can see you're crucial to the action," Cassie agreed. "What about you, Maddie?"

"I am Veruca Salt." Madison looked proud.

"That's one of the main characters, isn't it?" Cassie said, trying to remember the book, which she'd read as a child.

"Yes, it is. I'm the spoiled brat whose father gives her everything!"

Ryan laughed, shaking his head.

"And I'm the youngest person to have a speaking part," she continued.

"That's incredible. When's the play itself?"

"It's on Saturday afternoon."

Madison scraped her fork across the empty plate to get the last of the sauce, licked it, and put it neatly down.

"I have tickets," Ryan said.

"And don't forget, we have a cast sleepover that night," Madison reminded him.

"What's that?" Cassie asked.

"They're performing the play the following morning as part of an inter-school arts festival in Canterbury. So the cast are traveling to a hotel after the Saturday show, and staying overnight. Then they'll be dropped back at school later on Sunday," Ryan explained.

"I'll put it on the timetable and be there to pick you up when you get back," Cassie said.

In the morning she awoke to find the first winter storm had arrived.

A massive cold front had blown in, bringing with it howling winds and driving rain. Cassie was woken by the gusts of rain drumming against her window, and realized as soon as she got out of bed that the temperature had dropped sharply. Suddenly the low setting of the central heating seemed uncomfortable, and she rushed to get dressed, putting on thick socks and several layers of clothing.

Concerned about the children standing outside in this icy, blowing rain, she drove them to the bus stop and waited until the bus arrived. Then they made a run for it, sprinting through the rain and leaping over puddles before reaching the bus doors.

Arriving home cold and wet after the short run from the car to the house, Cassie headed to the kitchen to warm up by the fire. Here, she was surprised to see Ryan making a pot of tea.

"Good morning, lovely," he greeted her and she felt herself flush with the pleasure of the compliment, and the prospect of being able to spend some unexpected time with him.

"Is everything all right?" she asked. "I thought I heard you leave earlier."

"I only stayed at work long enough to make a call on the weather. There's no repair work going to be done today with this storm. I've postponed the new crew. It's supposed to clear for a while this afternoon, but we can't get any work started till tomorrow."

"Oh dear. That must be playing havoc with your timing."

"I always factor in a few non-operational days this time of year, so it's not a catastrophe. The main problem was the previous repair crew's schedule. Thankfully we have some extra time now, with a new team on board."

"What are you going to do today?" Cassie asked, pouring the tea.

"I've got some paperwork to catch up on, but it won't take long. So if I can give you a hand doing anything, let me know."

"I will," Cassie replied, delighted to have Ryan to herself for the day.

The paperwork seemed to take him no time at all, and he helped her with the chores she'd become used to doing—tidying the rooms, emptying the dishwasher, putting on a load of laundry.

"You know, this really does feel like domestic bliss," he commented jokingly. "I'm sure chores become mundane and annoying when you do them every day, but once in a while, and especially with such pleasant company, I'm finding this fun."

"You think you'd be a good house-husband?" Cassie joked, then blushed crimson as she realized how forward the comment must have sounded. But Ryan winked at her before replying in a serious tone.

"I think I'd be a brilliant one."

By lunchtime, all the chores were done and the house was tidy.

"I have to admit, as an outdoor person, this weather gives me cabin fever," Ryan said. "Do you want to head down the pub for lunch? We'll get absolutely soaked on the walk, but they have a roaring fire there so we can eat, dry out, and have a pint or two—and then do the same thing all over again on the way back if it's still raining. I know it will be fun, and I'd love to do it with you."

"That sounds wonderful," Cassie said, thrilled to be going on an outing with him, and thanking her lucky stars that the children were catching the bus back home and that she wouldn't have to drive anywhere.

As she headed to her room to put on another, waterproof, layer, she remembered one final chore she needed to do—clean the rabbit's cage in Dylan's room and put some fresh sawdust down.

She headed into the room, grabbing the bag of shavings from the bookcase.

"Come, little twitchy-nose, I need to clean your cage quick-quick," she said, bending down.

She froze, staring in horror.

Benjamin Bunny's lettuce leaves were untouched. He was lying very still at the back of his cage and when she reached in hesitantly to feel his gray fur, his body was cold and stiff.

Benjamin Bunny was dead.

Chapter Twelve

"Ryan!" Cassie shouted. "Come quickly."

She couldn't take her eyes off the shocking sight of the prone rabbit and she felt tears welling up.

Ryan's footsteps thudded on the wooden floor and a moment later he was at Dylan's door, his face filled with concern.

"What is it?"

"Benjamin Bunny. He's dead, Ryan."

She pointed to the cage, noticing her hands were shaking.

"Dead? Are you sure?"

Ryan hurried into the room.

He reached into the cage and gently took the rabbit out.

Its head lolled sideways in his grasp.

"Oh, no, this is terrible. He's ice cold and you can see his limbs are starting to stiffen. Poor little thing."

"What do you think could have happened to him?"

Cassie sniffed, rubbing her eyes hard.

"I don't know. I've no idea about rabbits. Dylan's only had him three weeks but I know he was an older pet; he got him from someone who was moving and didn't want to take him with them. So it could be that his time was up."

"A heart attack?" Cassie hazarded.

"Perhaps. He doesn't look to have suffered," Ryan said.

"Could it have been the cold snap?"

"No, Dylan researched his care. Rabbits are cold weather animals and prefer cooler temperatures. And I can see nothing changed in his diet, his water's fresh. He must have just had a heart attack or a stroke or something. Dylan's going to be gutted. He adored Benjamin."

Cassie felt sobs rising inside her again and fought to control them. She didn't want to break down and weep in front of Ryan.

"I'll go out and bury him now in the back garden near the compost heap. And I'll think of the best way to break it to Dylan."

With the furry body held carefully in his hands, he walked out of the room.

Cassie took a deep, trembling breath.

"I'm sorry, little bunny," she said, blinking hard.

She checked on Orange and Lemon, but the two fish looked healthy and well, swimming around their mini aquarium.

Then she sat on Dylan's bed for a while with her head in her hands, unable to stop the tears from flowing when she thought about the loss of the small gray rabbit, and the devastation it would cause Dylan when he found out.

After a while she felt Ryan's hands gently rubbing her shoulders.

"I've buried the little guy," he said. "Come on. You need to take your mind off this so I say we go out, have a drink, toast bunny's life, and cheer up. It won't do Dylan any good if we're in pieces about it."

Two hours in the warmth and chatter of the local pub took Cassie's mind off the shock and she was glad that they had a chance to talk it through.

"Losing a pet is such a wrench, no matter how it happens," Ryan said.

"Have the children had other pets?" Cassie asked, feeling that this home would be made even friendlier by the presence of a cat or dog.

"I grew up with cats in our home, but after I was married, that wasn't possible, due to allergy problems," Ryan explained.

From the way he worded it, Cassie wasn't sure whether one of the children was allergic, or if it had been his ex-wife.

"What about you?" he asked.

"When my mom was alive, we had a dog. He was a good companion and so much fun to have around. We used to walk him, feed him, train him. Or try to. He was quite old, and not very trainable."

"Did your mom pass away when you were younger?" Ryan asked sympathetically.

"Yes. She died in an accident. After that, my sister and I were raised by my dad, together with—various girlfriends along the way. It wasn't a happy home life. My dad was an angry person and he became worse after she died. My sister, Jacqui, ran away from home when I was twelve. She'd protected me for so long but it reached a stage where she just couldn't anymore. After that it became even worse. I left home as soon as I could, too."

"Oh, Cassie. You've had such a rough time. No wonder you're so mature and wise. I told you I sensed that in you, and now I see why it's there."

Ryan's voice was filled with sympathy as he leaned closer to her. She felt grateful for his compassion. Trusting him with these details felt like an important step—for her, and also for the two of them.

"Where is Jacqui now?"

"I don't know," Cassie said, confessing the awful truth that had filled so many of her thoughts and nightmares over the years.

"You don't know?"

"She never contacted me again. For years I hoped she would. Every time the phone rang at home, I thought it might be her. Then I moved away, and my dad moved house, and every time there was another degree of separation, I would think of Jacqui and how it would be more and more difficult for her to find me again."

"There's social media," Ryan said.

"My account's super-private, and I don't think she has an online presence at all. I've looked for her often but never seen a trace of her."

"Where do you think she went?"

"I think she went to Europe, and I don't know what happened to her after that. I thought for a while she was dead, but recently I've changed my mind. I think she's alive, and I believe I will see her again one day."

Cassie thought of Renee's message about the mystery woman who'd refused to give her name.

It might be Jacqui. Scared, damaged, and surely feeling guilty about all the years of silence. It might take a while for her to get the courage to call again.

"I hope that happens, Cassie. Living with that uncertainty for so long is a burden you don't deserve to be carrying."

Ryan checked his watch.

"We'd better be getting back. We have our boy to think about now."

She glanced at him sharply, wondering if he realized what he'd said and how he'd used the word "our," but he didn't seem to notice, or regret, the words that he had used.

The rain was easing off as they headed home, although the wind was still strong. After two beers, Cassie was glad of the brisk, sobering walk. She hadn't realized until she had gotten up how much the alcohol had affected her and she was worried she would become over-emotional when Ryan broke the news to his son.

When Dylan and Madison arrived back, they burst into the house, with Madison shrieking and laughing from the short run to the front door.

"Hello, Dad, hello, Cassie. Dress rehearsal went really well. My costume is awesome! I get to wear this really sparkly, pretty dress because I'm rich and I'm spoiled."

"Glad to hear it, lovely. Come into the kitchen now. Do you two want a cup of tea?"

"No, thanks."

Looking curious, Madison came into the kitchen, with Dylan close behind.

Cassie took a deep breath as she saw Ryan's serious face. She hoped she wouldn't start crying.

"Dylan, I'm afraid I have some bad news about Benjamin Bunny."

Cassie heard the sharp intake of Madison's breath. Glancing at the children, she saw Madison looked stricken. Dylan, however, was expressionless.

"What happened, Dad?" he asked.

"When Cassie cleaned the cage, she noticed that the little guy wasn't looking well."

Now Cassie's head jerked around and she stared at Ryan, wide-eyed. This wasn't what had happened. Where was he going with this?

"We immediately rushed him to the vet, and they confirmed that he was an older animal who had started to experience heart failure. They said that if this continued Benjamin would undoubtedly suffer, and feel progressively worse for the remainder of his life, and that the condition was irreversible and terminal."

Cassie couldn't breathe as she listened.

"They advised putting Benjy to sleep to prevent any further suffering. Cassie and I held him and he didn't know a thing about it; he was calm and comfortable, and with the painkillers they gave him, he was even feeling well enough to take a small bite of carrot before he went to sleep."

Madison burst into tears, and Dylan nodded somberly. His face was still empty of emotion. Needing comfort herself, Cassie hugged Madison, rubbing her shoulders, and dug in her pocket for the wad of Kleenex she'd put there in preparation.

She felt completely thrown by this alternative version. She had no idea why Ryan had said what he did. He hadn't discussed this with her first, or even hinted he would say anything other than the truth.

Surely he should have asked Dylan if he'd noticed anything wrong, or if there had been any change in the rabbit's food, or if he'd been accidentally injured, or any of the myriad other things that could have happened?

Well, it was too late now, and she couldn't step in. She was about to stammer out some comforting words herself, to scrape something coherent together, when Ryan took her voice away all over again.

"Here are his ashes," he said, and produced a glass jar filled with ash.

It could only have come from the fireplace. Cassie had noticed he'd cleaned it out after they had arrived back from the pub. He'd buried Benjamin—well, she guessed that much was true. He certainly hadn't burned the rabbit and a house fire wasn't hot enough to cremate a bunny in any case; it would just have roasted him.

Nausea flooded her at that thought, and she swallowed hard.

"I thought we could all have a cup of tea now and talk about Benjamin, remember him for the amazing bunny he was. And then when the rain has stopped, we can go and scatter his ashes into the sea."

Madison was still shuddering with sobs. "That's so sad. But it sounds good, Dad."

Dylan's face was like stone.

Cassie suddenly felt a stab of horror. What if the rabbit's death had affected her own memory and she was the one who had misremembered everything? Gaps in her memory had occurred before, admittedly when she'd been under stress, but that didn't mean they couldn't recur at other times. Those gaps had been terrifying. Days later, she'd recalled incidents that her mind had completely blanked out at the time—and her overactive subconscious had presented alternative versions in the form of nightmares, so that after a while, she hadn't known what was true and what not.

It was horrific to think that Ryan might have said, "Let's take the little guy to the vet—he could just be in a deep coma," and she had heard, "I'll bury him in the garden."

Cassie resolved that she would ask Ryan that night, while they were having their customary glass of wine that had turned into a nightly ritual.

She wanted to know for sure if she was remembering this right, or if the nightmares and false memories were starting up again.

CHAPTER THIRTEEN

As soon as the rain cleared, Cassie headed out to the bluff with the family.

Dylan led the way carrying the jar of ashes, Ryan followed close behind him, and Cassie walked at the back, holding Madison's gloved hand tightly in her own. She was feeling tearful again, and knew it would take all her self-control not to break down.

"You were a good bunny, Benjamin," Dylan said solemnly.

Cassie pressed her lips together to prevent sobs erupting. This was Dylan's chance to grieve; it was not for her to grab attention away from him. Hopefully she could blame the cold wind for the tears in her eyes.

"You were the best," Ryan added.

"An amazing bunny. I'll miss you," Madison agreed.

Madison had been tearful earlier but was calmer now, and Cassie thought that perhaps Ryan's instincts had been right, because although unusual, the ceremony was allowing them all to have closure for the death of their pet.

"I thought you were lovely, Benjamin. Rest well," Cassie said.

She hiccupped out a sob before holding her breath to try and prevent an onslaught of tears.

She had expected that Dylan would open the jar and scatter the fire-place ashes to the wind, but he didn't. He weighed it briefly in his hand and then tossed it out over the bluff.

The setting sun glinted on the glass as it tumbled and fell out of sight. The sea was raging so hard that she didn't hear it hit the rocks, far below.

That did it for Cassie.

Letting go of Madison's hand, she dropped to her knees, doubling over on the soaking, muddy grass with her head buried in her arms. Sobs burst out of her, rough and unstoppable.

"I'm so sorry," she gasped. "It's all my fault, I'm to blame. I should have done more. If I had done something earlier it might all have been OK."

Grief overcame her and her sobs turned into cries.

"Oh, Cassie, don't be sad."

Madison wrapped her arms tightly around her, just about climbing on top of her as she tried to comfort her.

"It's not your fault. Not at all."

Ryan crouched down beside her, stroking her hair, pushing the locks away from her tear-drenched face.

"Don't be sad, lovely," he murmured to her. "Or I'm going to start to cry, too."

Gradually, Cassie regained control and climbed to her feet. Her jeans and top were sodden.

"I'm sorry for that," she muttered.

"I understand. Sometimes you need to let out what's inside you, and that can only happen when you feel safe enough," Ryan said.

She felt grateful that he understood.

"Now we'd better get you into some dry clothes. Let's all have a glass of sherry and roast those chestnuts over the fire, so we can warm up before supper."

Ryan and Madison helped her to her feet and they walked into the house. In her bedroom, Cassie spent a few minutes breathing deeply, until she was sure there would be no more outbursts of tears. Then she changed into a dry top and fresh pair of jeans and dabbed a cold cotton-wool pad over her swollen eyes. Finally, she felt ready to rejoin the family.

As she left her bedroom, she almost bumped into Dylan, who was standing outside. She felt a wave of guilt about being complicit in the alternative story he'd been told. Did he suspect it wasn't the truth?

To her astonishment, he gave her a quick, clumsy hug.

"Feel better?" he asked in a low voice.

"Yes, I do. What about you?"

He shrugged.

"I'm OK."

She waited for him to move aside, but he didn't. Instead, he asked her, "You never told my dad that I took those sweets from the shop, did you?"

Cassie took a deep, shaky breath.

"I never found the right moment and in the end I decided not to. If you do it again, I'll have to, though."

He considered this in silence for a few moments and she looked at his expressionless face and wondered what exactly this highly intelligent, but strangely dissociated boy was thinking.

"I like you, Cassie," he said.

"Thank you." She felt taken aback by the compliment, which she'd never expected to receive.

"We can talk more another time. And I'll tell you other stuff you need to know."

Now she felt a twinge of misgiving; where was this conversation headed?

But Dylan seemed to have had his say. He turned around and headed for the kitchen, with Cassie following close behind.

In the kitchen, Ryan poured sherry for the whole family—Madison received a tiny sip, just a thimbleful, and Dylan received a child's glass. They all toasted the bunny and drank their sherry, and then the children showed her the best way to roast the chestnuts, while Ryan cooked fish fingers and chips.

Cassie felt grateful for the close support of this family, and realized how much she felt a part of it already. She knew she would always remember this evening; the smell of the chestnuts roasting, the children's faces flushed in the warmth after the cold outdoors, and Ryan preparing comfort food which everyone would enjoy.

Even so, she felt unsettled by what had happened that afternoon. When she and Ryan joined each other for their nightly glass of wine, she promised herself she would ask him why he'd done what he did.

❧   ❧   ❧

For the first time ever, Ryan wasn't sitting out on the balcony but was in the family room, on the settee overlooking the ocean.

"It's not just the cold, it's the wind," he explained when she arrived. "It would blow the glasses right out of our hands."

He patted the cushion beside him and she sat down, being careful to keep some space between them and not to involuntarily brush against him, or do anything that might hint to him how head-over-heels she was.

"I wanted to discuss the way you explained Benjamin Bunny to Dylan," she said hesitantly.

She was nervous about bringing the subject up—so nervous that she felt it would be better to get it over and done with.

"Yes. It wasn't what happened, was it?"

"No. That's what I'd like to talk about."

She felt a pang of relief that she hadn't misremembered and wasn't going mad. There had been an alternative version.

"I'll gladly explain. I was very troubled, and thought hard about what to do, and I only reached a decision after we were back from the pub. You see, Dylan's an extremely sensitive child. His IQ is off the charts. Super intelligent. I think, at times, it can put him at a disadvantage. He reacts differently from other children."

Cassie understood what he meant. Dylan didn't behave normally, and he acted out his anger in strange ways.

Ryan continued. "I thought that it would be more comforting for him to know that Benjamin had a proper diagnosis and was cared for as he passed away. Otherwise he might have gotten upset, or even blamed us. There's the school play coming up, it's his chance to shine in public, which is very new to him, and I don't want anything to spoil that."

Cassie nodded reluctantly. She accepted the explanation—sort of. She took a sip of wine and put her glass down on the table.

"There's another reason," Ryan said softly.

"What's that?" Cassie turned to him, anxious to know.

"Oh, Cassie, can't you tell?" Ryan moved closer to her and she felt a jolt of pure electricity as his blue gaze met hers.

"It's because you're here. I'm desperate for you to love us as a family, and not to want to leave. Look, we are as we are. I'm not hiding anything from you. But I want you to see us at our best, without any unnecessary drama. You make me want to be my best."

He leaned toward her, so close she could see the tiny gold flecks in his pale blue irises. She had enough time to feel a jolt of excitement and panic at what was going to happen. Then they were kissing, and as the kiss deepened her head started spinning with delight and the sheer physical desire that this intimate contact was awakening.

Ryan pulled away. He was breathing hard.

"I'm sorry," he whispered. "Please forgive me, that was way out of line and I apologize for it."

Cassie's heart was pounding so hard she was sure he could feel it. But she had to seize the moment. This was her chance to tell him, and show him, how she felt. She pulled him close, locking her arms round him.

"Don't apologize. I've been longing to do this—well, ever since I met you."

"Oh, Cassie. From the moment we met, I hoped this would happen," Ryan murmured. "I know you've only been here a short time, but it doesn't seem that way. You've become a part of us, and I can't imagine life without you. It's as if you were always meant to be here."

Then they were kissing again, more passionately, and she felt his hands slip under her shirt, warm against her skin, and although a tiny voice inside her was protesting that this was not the time or place to go so far, she didn't have the power to silence it.

But Ryan eventually drew away.

"We can't go on like this, Cassie, it's not right."

Hearing this, reality hit her with a slap. Of course he was right. It was not appropriate and could not continue, and from now on she'd better try to have some damned control over herself.

Then she took in his next words.

"I haven't even taken you on a date yet. And I want to do that first, and to do this properly, because you deserve the very best."

He drew her toward him again, and that roguish smile warmed his face and eyes.

"Are you free tomorrow night?" he whispered.

Chapter Fourteen

When Cassie woke up the next morning, she found an envelope pushed under her bedroom door.

In Ryan's forward-tilted hand it read:

Treat yourself to a new outfit! It's Date Night tonight! See you later—R

The envelope was filled with cash—Cassie was overwhelmed by Ryan's generosity. This would cover everything from shoes, to dress, to coat—and, most importantly, underwear. She was amazed by his thoughtfulness.

Cassie read his note over and over again and in between reading it, she immersed herself in the memories of what had happened last night. The passion of their kiss, and the way he had touched her. The way he had looked at her, as if she was everything in the world to him, and the words he had spoken. He'd told her that she was needed and valued, a part of the family, and that he couldn't imagine life without her. That meant more to her than he would ever know.

Without a doubt, Cassie knew Ryan was the man she'd always dreamed of.

She hugged herself, feeling a sense of unreality that she had landed in a fairytale come true. It could easily have turned out differently. Imagine if she'd ignored Jess's advice to call Ryan, and missed out on everything that had followed.

Cassie could see herself living in this house forever. She could make a life for herself in this beautiful village, a life filled with happiness and love.

Both the children remarked on her good mood as she cracked jokes about the rainy weather and tested them on their lines for the school play the next day.

As it was a wet day, she drove them to the bus stop again and waited until they were safely on board. Then, instead of going back home, she headed into town to buy her date night outfit.

Two hours later, she'd chosen the most beautiful dress she could find. Ryan's generous allowance covered every item of clothing she needed, as well as makeup, and there was still money left over so she bought Ryan a travel pack of shampoo and shower gel—choosing what the saleslady assured her was the hottest men's brand on the market. It was a useful gift, and also a hint that one day, they could travel together.

She found it bizarre to think that a week ago, she'd been deliberating about going back to the States and in fact had almost done so.

Now, the States felt like a distant dream, and the desire to go back seemed foolish and shortsighted. Her adventure, her future, her reality was here.

She spent the rest of the morning tidying up and preparing a simple supper for the children. It felt weird, but exciting, that she wouldn't be there to share it with them.

At two o'clock she heard the front door open and realized with a twinge of annoyance that the unpleasant cleaner, Harriet, had arrived. She'd forgotten that Friday was her other day. Trying to channel her inner goodness, Cassie resolved to be polite to her and to assume that she'd been in a bad mood on Monday.

Today, Harriet did in fact seem in a better frame of mind. Her hair color had washed out, and was now the barest hint of pink, but her fingernails looked freshly painted in silver glitter. Cassie couldn't help noticing once again how pretty she was, as she responded politely to Cassie's greeting.

The mood in the house darkened when Harriet came out of Cassie's bedroom.

"You been shopping?" she asked, carrying the plastic bin liner that contained some used Kleenex, and the packaging and labels that Cassie had cut off all the clothes she'd bought.

Cassie looked up, alarmed. Was it an accepted thing to root through people's dustbins when you emptied them?

"That's the evening gown shop in town," Harriet commented, reading the label. "Pricey."

"The school play's coming up. I wanted something nice to wear tomorrow," Cassie said.

She knew it was a lie, but sensed that the truth would send Harriet's mood over the edge. Cassie still didn't know if she had an actual crush on Ryan, or was simply a jealous type who didn't like anyone having something she didn't.

There wasn't much to do in the house. When she left to fetch the children, she was confident that Harriet would be gone by the time she returned.

Harriet wasn't. She'd been tidying the already tidy kitchen, and had taken out all the coffee cups and glasses and put them through the dishwasher. Now she was putting them away.

Suspicion filled Cassie as she wondered whether Harriet was deliberately killing time so that she would be home when Ryan arrived.

"Are we all done here?" she asked, trying to sound cheerful. "Come into the kitchen, Maddie, I'll make you some tea."

"I've still got to tidy the lounge and sweep the porch," Harriet said.

Cassie felt like asking her in an outraged tone, "Sweep the porch?" It was still drizzling and anyone could see there was absolutely no point in sweeping or tidying anywhere outside with more wind and rain expected.

She forced herself to smile sweetly, not wanting to end up in an argument with the cleaner. At least Harriet was going to be out of the kitchen, which meant Cassie could make tea, lay the table, and get the children's supper into the oven.

Eventually Harriet returned to the kitchen. Glancing at the clock, Cassie saw that it was now after six o'clock. Long past her finishing time, and still she was here.

"I found this on the couch," she said, holding up a vanilla chapstick. "Belong to anyone?"

"That's mine. Thanks so much. It must have fallen out of my pocket last night."

Cassie took the chapstick, glad to have it back. She'd looked for it at lunchtime and when she hadn't found it, had assumed she'd dropped it in town while she was trying on clothes.

"That was when you were kissing my dad," Madison said, looking up from the word game book she was busy with at the kitchen table.

Cassie gaped at her, shocked beyond words, as she heard Harriet's sharp intake of breath.

Madison continued, relaying the information in a factual tone as if she wasn't bothered by it and was simply passing it on.

"I went to get some water last night and saw you kissing each other. Maybe that's when it fell out," she told Cassie helpfully.

Looking at Harriet, Cassie could see the raw hatred in her face. Harriet was glaring at her as if she were a poisonous snake she was about to kill.

"Is that so?" the cleaner taunted. "That's why you're here? To get a little piece of Dad, eh? That didn't take you long. You're quite the mover."

Cassie stood up so suddenly she jolted the table, causing the salt and pepper shakers to fall over with a bang.

"Madison, come with me," she ordered.

She wasn't going to let the young girl sit here while hateful insinuations about herself and her father were flung around. She knew how deeply words could scar.

"Did he pay you for that? Perk of the job? Or was it an extra freebie?" Harriet spat the words out.

Cassie grabbed Madison's hand and headed for the door, hustling her toward the bedrooms and out of earshot.

Dylan, reclining on the bean bag in the dining room and engrossed in a book, glanced up as they passed.

"What's happening?" Madison asked.

Breathlessly, Cassie explained as she marched Madison into her room.

"Harriet's lost her temper and is saying hurtful things. You shouldn't have to hear things that are ugly and untrue. It will be better for us to stay in our rooms until she's gone."

It didn't sound as if that would take too long. Madison's announcement had clearly put an end to the delaying tactics. As she went to her own room, Cassie heard the brief hiss of the kitchen tap, a cupboard slamming, and then the stomp of angry feet as Harriet headed for the front door.

Then her heart leaped into her mouth as she heard it unlock, and Ryan's voice calling out.

"Knock knock! Hello, everyone. Oh, hello, Harriet, you still here?"

"Screw you, you bastard," Harriet spat the words out.

The front door slammed with a crash that reverberated through the house.

CHAPTER FIFTEEN

Cassie burst out of her bedroom and ran to the hallway where Ryan was standing, frozen, staring at the front door.

She felt consumed by anxiety about Harriet's behavior and had started to fear the worst. What if Harriet and Ryan had already had a relationship? What if Ryan had slept with her? He might have done so in a moment of passion, as a fling, but even so, it was troubling that he hadn't told her about it. She needed to know what was going on. She couldn't bear to think of anything destroying their potential happiness.

When Ryan turned and saw her, his face softened.

"Good afternoon, lovely," he said, and put his arms around her.

She hugged him back, reassured by how strong and tightly he held her.

"Did you have some kind of a fall-out with Harriet?" he asked softly, smoothing his hand over her hair.

"Madison told Harriet we'd kissed. She must have seen us last night."

Cassie felt sick inside as she described in a low voice what had played out.

"Harriet completely lost it. It was as if she'd been looking for things to do so she could be here when you came home, but when Madison said that, she stormed out."

"That makes sense." Ryan's hands cupped her waist. "I think she's been building a fantasy world for herself. She told me a while ago that she and her boyfriend broke up. It sounded like he broke her heart. Since then the poor girl's been looking for attention. I guess she thought I might be interested."

"Really? Is that all?" Cassie asked, frowning.

"Last Friday she hugged me hello when I came home, and goodbye, when she left a little while later, and she gave me a big kiss on my cheek. She's never done that before. Then she asked me if I'd like to come down to the pub with her for a drink, as it was her birthday the next day. I was rather taken aback by the offer, coming out of the blue as it did, so I told her unfortunately not."

Ryan smiled down at her ruefully.

"That makes sense," Cassie said, wondering how she herself would have behaved if a boss she'd built a fantasy around had turned out to be seeing someone else.

"Perhaps I should have been firmer with her and said that I wasn't interested, but there seemed no need. Obviously I was wrong, and I should have been more direct. I don't think she's a mean or nasty person; she's just going through a difficult time."

He raised his voice.

"Come on, kids. Come say hello to your poor hardworking dad!"

The family gathered in the kitchen.

"You two have got a special evening tonight," he said. "We're off to try out a new restaurant, so Lisa from down the road is looking after you, and I've said you can watch a movie as a treat. I've given her a list of films that you can choose from—but the list is a surprise. You can only decide when she gets here at half past six."

"Yay," Madison cheered.

"Let's dish your dinner up, and we're going to get ready."

Cassie hurried to her room, showered quickly—she'd already washed and dried her hair earlier that day in preparation—and got changed into her beautiful new dress. She did her makeup, realizing her hand was shaking with excitement. She wasn't used to seeing herself so made up. She looked like a different person.

She left her room with her heart in her mouth, guessing that she'd say goodbye to the children and meet Lisa before they headed out.

But Ryan was waiting for her in the hallway.

"You look beautiful. What a stunning dress, it suits you perfectly."

"Thank you." Cassie felt as if she was walking on air as she joined him.

"Lisa's already here, and the kids have started watching the film. Let's sneak away and leave them to their treat," he whispered. "The cab's just arrived."

A minute later they were seated in the spacious back seat of the silver Mercedes that Ryan had booked.

"Where are we going?"

"It's a fine dining restaurant that opened recently, an hour's drive away from here. I've wanted to go ever since I heard about it. I think we're going to have an amazing experience."

"I've never been to anything like that."

"You'll love it. There's a dance floor in the basement, I believe, so we can celebrate the night in style."

The conversation kept flowing as they drove, and by the time they reached the restaurant, Cassie had learned that Ryan loved to eat out, and his father, who had died at the age of sixty while deep-sea diving, had been a restaurant aficionado who enjoyed new tastes and experiences.

She also found out that despite their twelve-year age difference their tastes in music were very similar, and that two of her dream travel destinations—Thailand and Morocco—were at the top of his list too.

The restaurant was glamorous and clearly very expensive. It wasn't the kind of place Cassie had ever dreamed of going on a first date, and she was glad she'd had the chance to buy the perfect outfit. They were welcomed with a glass of champagne, before making their choice from the mouthwatering dishes on the menu.

"Isn't this fun?" Ryan said when they'd finished their delicious starters.

He reached across the table and took her hand, caressing her palm. Then he added, anxiously, "Are you enjoying yourself, too?"

"This is the experience of a lifetime," Cassie told him. "I'm going to remember this night forever."

She wondered if Ryan knew she wouldn't remember it for the fine food or the exquisite surroundings, but because of his presence opposite her, and the touch of his hand on hers.

After dessert, chocolates, and coffee, they headed downstairs to the dance floor. Cassie felt dizzy from all the wine she'd had, and was glad of the chance to be able to blow off some steam. Dancing with Ryan was incredible. She couldn't remember how long it had been since she'd had so much fun on the dance floor, and he confessed that he felt the same. They finished the night locked in each other's arms as the last song played.

And then they were heading home. In the cab, she gave him the gift she'd bought, and he was every bit as touched and grateful as she'd hoped.

"You're incredible, Cassie. Every time I use these, I will think of this night with you."

They started kissing, and by the time the cab arrived home, she knew there wasn't any question of going to her own room.

Because it was raining heavily, Ryan asked her to wait in the cab while he went inside, paid Lisa, and fetched an umbrella for her.

Then, in the shelter of the umbrella, they walked arm in arm through the rain and into the quiet house, past the children's bedroom doors, and into his room.

As he closed the door behind them and took her into his arms, Cassie thought she had never felt so happy in her life.

Much later, Cassie was woken by a slow, persistent scratching at the window.

It was icy, colder than she had expected it to be; she must have kicked the covers off.

She was alone in bed. She had no idea where Ryan had gone. It was pitch-black and the only dim light came from beyond the glass. She couldn't hear the rhythmic breaking of the waves. Only that odd scratching.

Perhaps it was a tree branch, scraping the glass. If so, it must be windy, but if it was, the waves should be roaring over the rocks and foaming back again, and she would hear them.

She sat up in bed, shivering, her skin prickled into gooseflesh. What was the noise? She should find out, and then she should check where

Ryan had gone. There was no reason for him to have left the room unless, perhaps, he'd gone to find out why the heating wasn't working.

"Ryan?" she called softly, but there was no answer. Only another scrape; this one harder. It was an unpleasant sound, as if something was cutting into the glass.

Her worry was escalating to frantic anxiety. She climbed out of bed and padded over the chilly floorboards to the window.

Peering through the darkened glass, she saw there was a claw-like branch scraping back and forth over the window.

Only it wasn't a branch.

As she looked more closely, Cassie saw to her horror that it was a hand. A pale, bony hand with ragged fingernails. The nail beds were etched with something dark, and she thought immediately about dried blood.

Where was Ryan? She was filled with fear at his unexplained disappearance—had he gone, or been taken?

She drew in a deep, terrified breath, ready to scream for help, but before she could, the scrabbling hand smashed through the glass and grabbed her wrist.

Icy cold, impossibly strong fingers clasped her tight.

Then the face came into view—sheet-white skin, framed by tendrils of dripping hair. It looked skeletally thin, as if she'd been underwater for eons before grasping onto life again.

"Jacqui," Cassie whispered. "You're alive."

It was Jacqui but yet it was not. She recognized her sister's features although they were haggard, dripping with icy water. She had seen those hazel eyes before. But the expression in them was new. A blank, hungry gaze, as if another entity had possessed her and was on the hunt.

The apparition's lips parted in a grin, showing teeth that were jagged and missing, like the mouth of a shark.

"Yes," Jacqui hissed. "And coming to find you."

Then she lunged at Cassie, who recoiled, screaming in terror, struggling to wrench herself away from the death grip on her hand and the glistening, ragged teeth and the freezing air that was rushing in to surround her.

But she couldn't escape. She was tugged out of the room, over the sill. Broken glass scraped over her skin, tearing it open so that she felt the blood stream out, causing a red glow of excitement to flare in Jacqui's hungry gaze.

Then she was falling—they were both falling, and Jacqui's limbs were wrapping around her with hideous strength, binding her as tight as wire as they reached the water and plunged into the dark, bottomless sea.

Cassie's own screams pulled her out of the nightmare and she sat up, breathing rapidly.

She could hear the sea again, and Ryan was beside her. Everything was all right. She'd had one of her crazy nightmares again, and should be grateful that the earth-shattering cries of her dream had been nothing more than whimpers in reality, because Ryan hadn't woken and was sleeping peacefully on his side.

Cassie felt weak with relief as the last tendrils of her nightmare released their hold.

She hadn't taken her meds. There had been no chance to do so. She'd been immersed in the fairytale ending to her wonderful evening, and she hugged herself as she remembered exactly how Ryan had touched her while they had made love, and the words he'd whispered.

She wanted to lie down, press herself against him, and go back to sleep.

But she needed to take her meds now. She couldn't wait till morning and risk having another nightmare.

Cassie climbed out of bed and tiptoed across the room, taking Ryan's robe off the hook on the back of the door, because she couldn't walk back through the house naked.

She switched on the light in the corridor and headed down the hall, past the children's closed bedroom doors, and quietly into her own room. She took the pills in her cupped hand, went to the kitchen, and poured a glass of water to drink them down.

Then she returned to Ryan's room, glancing left and right at the children's doors as she passed.

On the way back, she saw Dylan's door was no longer closed.

It was wide open, and she could see him inside.

He was sitting up in bed, his face turned to the open doorway, silently watching as she passed.

"Hey, Dylan, is everything OK?" she whispered, but he didn't respond, just kept staring at her.

Looking at his unreadable, expressionless face and the stillness of his posture, Cassie felt a chill of fear.

CHAPTER SIXTEEN

It was pitch-dark when Cassie woke again, and as she opened her eyes there was a crash of thunder.

Hail drummed the window as she fumbled for the light switch and snapped it on.

Ryan was gone. Cassie glanced at the rumpled bedcovers and let out a happy sigh.

She forgot all about the stormy weather as she remembered the feel of his skin on hers, and how she'd been filled with a sense of safety and love as she'd fallen asleep beside him.

He'd left a cup of coffee on her bedside table which was still warm, and her jeans and a warm top were folded at the foot of the bed. She was touched by his thoughtfulness. It meant a lot that she could walk out of the room properly dressed instead of sneaking down the hallway in his borrowed dressing gown. She guessed that, with the onset of bad weather, he had probably rushed off to make sure all was well at the harbor—but he'd still found the time to show her that he cared.

As she pulled on her clothes and hurried with her coffee to her own room, she thought how surreal it was that she'd only arrived a week ago. She had never dreamed that she'd end up falling for him and that he would feel the same way about her.

She hoped that the children would adjust to the fact that she was now sleeping in his bed. Well, some of the time, at least. She didn't know how this would play out or what Ryan would want her to do. With his divorce so recent, she guessed they would need to be discreet for now.

They hadn't been discreet enough, though. Cassie frowned as she remembered walking back down the hall last night, and how Dylan had been sitting up in bed and staring directly at her.

His silence, his watchful stance, had creeped her out, especially since it was obvious that she was heading toward his dad's room, wrapped in his distinctive burgundy robe.

Cassie wondered if she should take Dylan aside and speak to him about it in private, but the thought of doing that made her nervous.

She drank her lukewarm coffee, nearly dropping the cup as another massive thunderclap seemed to come from directly above the house.

The light flickered and then went out.

"Oh, hell," she said.

She put her cup down carefully and pulled back the curtains. There was just enough light in the grim, deep gray sky for her to navigate around the bed and leave the room.

"Dad?"

On hearing Madison's anxious voice, Cassie opened the door.

"Hey, Maddie. I think the lightning's caused a power outage."

She ran back to Ryan's room and grabbed her phone out of her purse. She hadn't charged it last night, but there was enough battery for her to use the flashlight for a few minutes.

With its help, she set out some clothes for Madison.

"What time's your play?"

"It starts at eleven but we need to be there at ten to get ready."

"It's quarter to eight now, so we still have lots of time," she reassured her.

She knocked on Dylan's door and found that he was already up and warmly dressed, reading a book by the light of his phone's flashlight.

He didn't mention that he'd seen her last night, or make any reference to why he'd opened his door to watch her passing by.

"Breakfast will be ready in ten minutes," she said, and headed to the kitchen to see what plan she could make.

Cassie checked the electricity box in the laundry room, but couldn't find a blown fuse, so she guessed the power in the whole area was down.

She found candles in the broom cupboard and set a few out on the table. Then she did her best to pull together a makeshift breakfast, assembling a pot of tea from the still-warm water in the kettle, and raiding the fridge for sandwich ingredients.

Then she, Dylan, and Madison sat down in the semi-dark kitchen. "Isn't this fun?" Cassie said. "It's just like—"

At that moment she felt something run over her foot.

Cassie let out a piercing shriek.

"What's happening?" Madison sounded just as startled, and Cassie saw she'd spilled her tea all over the table.

"An animal ran right across my foot," Cassie explained. "I felt it scampering on my skin."

Cassie's heart was pounding and she held her feet up above the floor, spooked by the scrabble of legs she'd felt. What had it been, and where was it now?

"I think I heard it," Dylan said.

"Whereabouts?" Cassie wished she'd put her shoes on, but she'd been so busy after the power outage that she hadn't had the chance.

What had it been? A rat? A giant spider?"

Dylan shone his phone's light onto the baseboards, and leaning down, she saw the gleam of eyes.

"It's a mouse!"

She clapped her hands at it and the mouse darted away, disappearing under the kitchen counter.

"That must have been so scary," Madison said.

"It was."

Now that the mouse had gone, Cassie dared to put her feet on the floor again. She headed to the sink and fetched a dishcloth to mop up the spilled tea.

A minute later, the front door opened and Ryan was back, slipping his drenched parka off his shoulders and kicking off his waterlogged shoes.

"It's vile out there. Oh, Cassie, you're a superstar. You got breakfast together."

"Is the power out everywhere?"

"Yes, the lightning hit a transformer."

"A mouse just ran over Cassie's foot and made her scream," Madison told him, with her mouth full of sandwich.

"What, now?"

"Yes, while we were all sitting here. It went under there." Cassie pointed.

Ryan grimaced. "They sometimes come in when it storms, I don't know why. The problem is they don't like going out again. Last year we ended up with an infestation. We need to buy a few traps immediately."

"I'll go," Cassie offered, seeing that Ryan had only just come in from the rain and hadn't had breakfast yet.

"You're an angel. The hardware store's in the opposite direction from the village. Drive about two miles west, then turn left at the first intersection and you'll see it."

Ryan handed her some cash, and Cassie put on her shoes and jacket and made a run for her car.

Ten minutes later, she walked into the hardware store. The small building was already packed with customers and Cassie guessed a lot of people must be doing emergency repairs and leak fixing after the storm.

It took her a while to find the correct aisle, and when she did, she couldn't see any traps.

A store employee was at the end of the row, stocking shelves.

"We're out of traps," he said. "Stock's coming in next week sometime."

"It's an emergency," Cassie explained. "What would you recommend for a mouse that's just moved in?"

"Rodenticide's your best bet. This is our most popular one, and it should sort your problem."

He handed her a box.

Cassie headed out of the shop, glad that the rain had reduced to a fine drizzle. She was preoccupied, wondering if there would be time for a final run-through of lines with the children before they had to leave for the play.

She climbed into her car and turned the ignition key.

There was a click. Nothing more.

Frowning, Cassie tried again.

The same result. The engine wasn't even catching.

Cassie tried yet again, twisting the key harder as if it might make a difference and give the car impetus to start. The little runabout had never given a moment's problem so far. She wondered if the storm had caused an electrical short.

Wishing she knew more about cars, Cassie fumbled under the dash and popped the hood, but when she pulled the lever, the hood didn't release.

With worry surging inside her she scrambled out.

To her consternation, she saw that the hood hadn't released because it was already open.

She hadn't locked the car. She hadn't even thought about it. In this safe, small village she had started being far too casual about security, and now, she had paid the price.

Suddenly this scenic town felt like an unfriendly place.

Who had done this? Had it been a bored kid, or was there a more sinister motive behind it? Looking around at the neat parking lot, Cassie could see no rowdy teens loitering around waiting to vandalize vehicles. The place was busy, but everyone seemed to be hurrying about their own business.

Cassie began to fear that someone might have targeted her.

She opened the hood, and her heart plummeted as she saw the sharp edges of severed wires that led to the battery. Someone had deliberately cut them and that fact made her feel vulnerable and afraid and very alone. She'd thought she was safe here, hidden away and protected in this small community. Now it was clear that nowhere was safe and that this must have been deliberately done.

Had her ex-employer in France managed to locate her? Cassie wondered whether this was the start of a twisted revenge game, or something worse. Disabling her car was a way of ensuring she couldn't disappear on short notice, which might mean he had other plans in store.

Cassie was suddenly desperate to speak to Ryan, to tell him what had happened and to hear his reassuring voice. She rooted in her purse for a minute before remembering she hadn't brought her phone with her. The battery had been about to die so she'd left it plugged into her charger, ready for when the power came back.

"Damn it," she shouted, slamming the hood in frustration. With no way of contacting him to explain her predicament, she was going to have to walk.

She yanked her keys out of the ignition and took her purse, and the hardware store bag, from the seat. Then she locked it, wishing bitterly she'd thought to do that before going into the store.

Cassie stomped out of the parking lot and headed toward the narrow lane which—two long miles later—would lead back to the house.

While walking, she found herself worrying about who could have wanted to sabotage her car this way.

There were only two options she could think of. Either it was random vandalism or else somebody had been following her and waiting for the opportunity.

Cassie hoped it had been random vandalism because the alternative, that she'd been targeted, was terrifying. She didn't want to think about how or why this might have happened.

She'd thought nobody could find her here. What if somebody had?

Wrapped in her disturbing thoughts, Cassie heard the loud rev of an engine behind her.

Her first thought was that this person could maybe offer her a ride home.

A heartbeat later her instincts started screaming.

Too fast, too close, too loud.

The roar of the engine was directly behind her.

Twisting round, she saw the grille, accelerating fast.

She dove sideways, crushing against the prickly bulk of the hedge.

The car shot past, so close that it brushed the leafy shoots growing from the hedge. So close that when Cassie looked down she saw the muddy tire track was only a few inches from where her foot had been.

One of the branches had scratched her hand and she stared down at the tattered line of blood welling from her skin. The hardware store bag had been torn. Looking down, she saw her jeans were spattered with mud and fragments of grass.

If she hadn't jumped into the hedge, she would have been hit.

Cassie realized she was shaking.

She stared down at the tire track and looked back. She could see the exact spot where the car had swerved off the tarmac and crushed the muddy grass by the hedge. The tracks followed a perfect curve. Off the tarmac, over the grass, and back to the road again.

She had been at the furthest point of the curve.

"What the hell?" she said aloud.

The letters FRZ, or had it been FZR? In her panic she couldn't remember their exact order. A white, low-slung car with a registration including the letters F, Z, and R had almost run her down.

If she hadn't dived out of the way, that car would have hit her. Smashed her legs, ridden over her, who knew?

If this was also deliberate, then she was in serious trouble now. In the space of an hour, someone had disabled her car and then tried to kill her as she walked home. If her ex-employer was behind this, she had no idea what she would do about it, or where she could hide.

Cassie continued walking, but every few steps she glanced behind her, terrified.

CHAPTER SEVENTEEN

B y the time Cassie reached home, stressed and scared and worried that she would make the family late for the play, she was on the point of tears.

As she reached the front door, Ryan opened it. He was wearing a dress shirt and chinos, ready to go, and Cassie realized how disheveled she must look.

"Hello, gorgeous. Glad to see you. I was starting to worry where you were."

He glanced outside at the empty road. "Where's your car?"

"It's at the hardware store. Ryan, it wouldn't start, and when I opened the hood, I found it was already open and I could see wires had been cut inside."

"What?" His voice was incredulous.

"Yes." Cassie's breathing was morphing into sobs.

"You think someone did it deliberately? The wires couldn't just have snapped?"

"They were cut. And the engine wouldn't even turn over. The only sound was the click of the key."

Ryan shook his head.

"That's unacceptable. Do you want to report it? We probably should."

That mention of police again. Cassie felt nervous.

"I doubt they could do anything and I have no proof."

Cassie didn't want to tell him that she feared her ex-employer might be behind this. It would complicate the situation and might cause Ryan to mistrust her. Even so, Ryan had to know everything that had happened.

"Then, when I was walking back, a driver behind me swerved into my path and almost hit me. I jumped aside just in time. The tire marks were on the grass. I scratched myself on the hedge."

"Cassie, this is terrible. I'm so sorry."

Ryan enfolded her in his arms, holding her close.

"I feel personally responsible. I feel like we—our community—should have done better for you."

"Don't worry, Ryan."

His words sounded so heartfelt that Cassie found herself laughing even though she was tearful.

"It definitely wasn't your fault!"

"All the same, I can help to make amends. I'm going to call our local mechanic, Dave Sidley, who runs Dave's Auto Repairs. He can tow your car to his workshop and get it fixed. I'll ask him to ensure it's in perfect working order. That, at least, we can do immediately. I'll get on the phone to him straight away. Give me your keys."

Cassie handed them to him.

"As regards the swerving incident, it is very common. Drivers unfamiliar with this area don't understand how narrow our roads are. A moment of distraction and you're in the hedge. I can't tell you how often it happens. So don't worry about that. I am sure that's what it was. You shouldn't have walked back. Why didn't you call me?"

"My phone was about to die, so I left it here."

Ryan sighed, gently releasing her from his arms.

"Of course. That damned storm. Power was restored half an hour ago so we're up and running again now."

He stared at her, his face serious.

"Cassie, please don't be scared. I can see how upset you are. I will look after you, I promise. I will not let anything like this happen to you again. Not while you are here, with my family, in my home and under my care."

Cassie was reassured by his words, and by his calm analysis of the situation, which made her feel less vulnerable. Perhaps the swerving had been accidental after all.

She remembered the reason for her outing and handed him the bag.

"They didn't have traps. They were only getting stock this week, so I bought poison."

"Oh, dear. It will be better to wait for new stock. I don't like using poison as it can affect the entire food chain. We can exchange it for traps during the week. Now, you'd better get yourself ready. We've got a play to attend."

Cassie rushed inside to get changed, and as soon as she was dressed, the family was ready to leave.

Ryan was uncharacteristically quiet on the drive to the theater, and Cassie wondered if he was nervous. Both the children had important roles, and it was the first time they were participating in something like this.

When they arrived, Ryan headed around to the back of the theater, where the backstage entrance was.

"If everyone gets out here, I'll go and park. Cassie, do you want to go in with the kids, in case they need help?"

Cassie noticed that Madison was looking pale, and had been much less talkative than usual on the drive. She suspected the young girl was having last-minute nerves about appearing on stage, and decided to go in with her.

"I'll catch up with you in the foyer," she said to Ryan.

When they arrived at the dressing room, she was greeted by a harassed-looking teacher.

"Our makeup artist is running behind. Would you be able to give us a hand?"

"Sure," Cassie agreed. "I don't have much experience in stage makeup, so tell me what you need."

"The brighter, the better. Go overboard," the teacher encouraged her.

Dylan sat down on the chair in front of the mirror, and she thought it was the first time she'd seen him look unsure.

"You'll be fine," Cassie reassured him. "Let's think about what a factory worker would look like and I'll do my best."

Madison stood quietly, offering no suggestions, which troubled Cassie even more. She'd been sure that Madison would have plenty to say.

"Dirty. Dusty," Dylan ventured.

"OK, so we'll make a big dirty mark on your cheek. And how about your hair? We can gel it to make it look wild."

"Hey, I also want a tattoo," Dylan said, and Cassie saw Madison give the tiniest smile before relapsing into seriousness.

"I'll draw a tattoo on your neck," she said.

After she'd accentuated his eyes and cheeks, and created a realistic-looking smudge, Cassie drew a tattoo with eyebrow pencil. Then she mixed gel with water and spiked up his hair.

"Hey, I look really cool," Dylan said delightedly. He seemed to have forgotten his nerves. "Thank you, Cassie."

"I'd hire you in my factory if I had one. Now you'd better hurry and get dressed. Maddie, it's your turn. What do you want to look like?"

Madison sat down but she shrugged, refusing to look at herself in the mirror.

"Freckles, maybe? Do you want curls?" Cassie suggested, feeling more and more anxious.

Madison shook her head.

"What's the matter?" Cassie asked gently, staring at Madison's reflection in the brightly lit glass.

"I don't want to be in the play," Madison said, and burst into tears.

"Madison!"

Horrified, Cassie grabbed a handful of Kleenex from the box in the makeup kit.

"Maddie, why not?"

Madison shook her head without answering, and Cassie guessed it could only be nerves. Hastily she tried to distract her from them and allay her fears.

"Remember how you enjoyed rehearsals, and how you couldn't stop talking about how much fun it was? You know all your lines perfectly and if you forget, your drama teacher is there to prompt you like you explained to me."

"It's not that," Madison sobbed.

"What is it?" Cassie hunkered down so that she was on a level with Madison rather than standing above her.

"I didn't get good enough marks to do the play."

Cassie frowned, taken aback by this argument.

"How do you mean? The play has nothing to do with marks. You got the part when you auditioned. You told me how you were chosen."

"I should never have done it. I should have told them that I couldn't, and that another girl should take my place. We still can, Cassie, let's go find a teacher and explain."

Cassie stared at her in confusion. This must be nerves. There was nothing else it could be.

"You're the best person for the part. This is as important as good marks in math."

"You think so?" Madison asked, her voice filled with doubt.

"Absolutely," Cassie said, hoping she wasn't contradicting anything Ryan might have said in the past.

"Math is useful, sure, but your phone has a calculator. And computers can do a lot of sums. There are computer programs that add things up and you just need to know how to work the program."

"OK." Madison was regarding her with the glimmerings of hope.

"But you know what is difficult and not everyone can do?"

"What's that?"

"Performing on stage. Not everyone has the talent or the ability for that. Now you have to prove yourself by going out there and wowing the audience."

"I won't get into trouble?"

Cassie squeezed her hand, wishing she could get inside the young girl's head and understand her fears better, because her words were very confusing.

"Absolutely not. Remember, if you feel unsure, look at your drama teacher, and she'll help you."

Cassie wiped Madison's eyes gently.

"Are you feeling better now?"

"I guess so."

"So how shall we make you up? Do you think a spoiled girl would have curls in her hair, and maybe we can draw some cute freckles on your face?"

"OK."

Using the hair gel with a blow dryer, Cassie managed to create some curls in Madison's thick brown hair, and drew large freckles on her cheeks and nose. She painted her lips bright pink and drew eyeliner around her eyes and brows for an exaggerated effect, hoping Madison wouldn't start crying again or her face would be a mess.

Dylan strolled back in, wearing the torn overalls that was his costume.

"You look one hundred percent the part," he complimented his sister, and Maddie gave a shaky smile.

It was time for her to leave. The teacher was hurrying over, holding the sparkly dress that would go perfectly with the makeup she'd just applied.

"Good luck to both of you," Cassie said.

But Dylan shook his head. "For plays, you're not supposed to say that. You're supposed to say 'Break a leg.'"

"Why's that?" Cassie asked, surprised.

"It's because it is the worst thing that could possibly happen to you. So actors wish it to each other and then because you have said it out loud, it won't happen."

"So it's a superstition. Well, break a leg, Dylan. Break a leg, Madison. And enjoy it."

Cassie made her way out of the makeup room, which was now crowded with actors and filled with the babble of excited voices.

Ryan was waiting outside the theater door, and they hurried to take their seats.

Seated in the front row of the auditorium, Cassie started growing even more anxious about Madison's behavior earlier.

"Ryan, did anyone tell Madison she wouldn't be able to do the play if her marks weren't good enough?" she whispered.

Ryan frowned. "I don't think so. Surely a teacher wouldn't do that? Her marks haven't been that bad."

"She didn't want to go on stage. I thought maybe it was nerves, but it sounds like there's a genuine reason."

Ryan shook his head.

"Perhaps she misunderstood the situation. I did tell her that doing the play was an extra activity and mustn't interfere with her schoolwork."

Cassie wasn't convinced, but then remembered that Madison was only nine, and might have misinterpreted what she'd been told.

"That might be it. I hope she'll be OK once the curtain goes up."

"I hope so, too," Ryan said.

In a few more minutes the hall was full, and it was time for the performance to start.

In the dark, Ryan's hand found hers.

The words "Break a leg" kept repeating themselves in her mind as the curtain rose. She hoped that the worst would not happen, and wished she'd been able to stay with Madison longer to ensure she was back to her normal self.

Her worry increased when Madison walked onto stage.

Cassie could see immediately, from the young girl's body language, that she was unhappy and didn't want to be there. Madison glanced at the audience, her eyes narrowed against the bright lights, and then looked down.

"No, Madison," Cassie whispered soundlessly. "Don't give up on it. You can do this."

Then it was her moment to speak, and in the play, her first lines couldn't be easier. All she had to do was introduce herself and say, "I'm Veruca Salt."

But Madison said nothing, and the silence stretched on and on, every moment filling Cassie with greater fear.

CHAPTER EIGHTEEN

Cassie could see Madison's drama teacher waving anxiously from below the stage, ready to help the young girl with her cue. Madison wasn't looking at her. Instead, she raised her head again and stared at the audience, as if taking in the entire hall.

Cassie could hear concerned murmurs from around her. People had realized this silence had gone on too long. She wished she knew what to do, but short of running onto stage and holding her hand, she felt utterly helpless.

"Go, Madison," she heard Ryan whisper.

Then it was as if Madison reached a decision that this was all OK. Cassie saw, with pride and relief filling her, how the young girl lifted her chin and summoned her confidence from deep inside herself.

"Well, Mr. Wonka. I'm ..." she began, and surveyed the crowd, aware of the tension her pause had created.

"Veruca Salt," she finished, spitting the words out in a haughty tone, with an arrogant shake of her curly head.

The audience erupted into delighted applause.

From that moment, Madison aced her performance. Word-perfect and on cue, she epitomized the spoiled brat she was playing. Especially after her nerve-racking crisis at the start, she was the star of the show whenever she spoke. Cassie's heart swelled with pride.

Dylan, running on stage during the scene changes, showed more of a sense of humor than Cassie had thought he possessed, and seemed to feed off the audience's energy to embrace his role. She could tell how delighted Ryan was, because every time the audience laughed, his hand tightened involuntarily in hers.

When the cast took their final bows and the curtain fell, Cassie was so emotional she was on the point of tears. She couldn't have been prouder of Madison's courage and the way she'd managed to defeat whatever demons had been tormenting her before the start.

"She was brilliant. Dylan, too. I'm so proud."

She felt like kissing Ryan, but with everyone filing out of their seats, there wasn't the chance.

"They were stars. We'd better go and congratulate them personally, and make sure their overnight bags get put onto the bus," Ryan said.

When Madison saw Cassie she ran up to her and hugged her tight.

"You were a hit," Cassie reassured her. "The superstar of the show. You can do it again, can't you? You'll be fine tomorrow?"

"I will," Madison whispered to her. "You know, Cassie, I stood on stage and I looked at every single person in the audience. Then I knew it would be OK. I remembered what you told me, and I decided to be brave."

"You were very brave," Cassie agreed.

After Dylan had received his congratulations and back-slaps, it was time for the children to get changed before they boarded the bus, where Ryan had already stowed their overnight bags.

The drama teacher remained behind.

"A quick question, please, Mr. Ellis. We're starting a drama club for the under-twelve students next year, and I'd like to invite Madison to be the club's first president. She's very talented and I think she'll be a great role model for the younger juniors as she's well liked. I wanted to ask your permission before we announce it. The club will probably meet twice a month and of course there'll be rehearsals when they do a show."

Cassie felt a surge of excitement. What an achievement for Madison. This was a feather in her cap.

She expected Ryan to agree instantly but to her surprise, he hesitated.

"Let me give it some thought," he said. "Can I confirm with you on Monday?"

The teacher also looked surprised and rather perturbed.

"Of course. We were hoping to announce it after tomorrow's performance, but we can wait a couple more days."

"Thank you," Ryan said.

As they walked to the car, Cassie wondered why Ryan hadn't said yes immediately. She was tempted to ask him, but it felt too much like questioning his authority, especially since their relationship was in the early days. There must be a good reason, perhaps something to do with Madison's sports commitments.

"You know what, Cassie?" he said as they climbed inside.

Cassie felt a surge of relief. He was going to share the reason with her.

"What?" she asked.

I have an idea. Let's go away for the night. The kids are out of town. That happens once in a blue moon. We'd be crazy not to make the most of it."

Cassie was blown away by his words. She couldn't have imagined a more perfect suggestion. Only yesterday, while buying his travel kit, she'd dreamed of going away with Ryan and had wondered if they ever would.

"It's a brilliant idea. Where shall we go?" she asked.

"There's a beautiful hotel on the coast to the north of here. I was invited to its opening event last year. This morning, I received an email to say that they have a room available due to a last-minute cancellation, so I booked it. I hope that's OK with you?"

"It's more than OK. It's wonderful," Cassie said. She was floating on her cloud of happiness again. A romantic overnight getaway was the next step in their relationship, and much sooner than she'd dared hope.

"It's the last word in luxury. Huge bathtubs, roaring log fires, sumptuous food. I can't wait to go there with you."

As they headed home, Cassie wondered when she should tell her friends about her incredible new relationship.

Even though she wasn't ready to announce anything on social media, there were a few close friends who deserved to know what a fairytale her life had become.

❧   ❧   ❧

When Cassie arrived home the next day, bubbling over with joy and excitement, she knew it was time to share the news.

The night at the five-star lodge had been the most incredible experience of her life. She needed to tell somebody about it, and share the fact that she and Ryan were an item now.

With a happy sigh, she collapsed onto her bed and took her phone out of her purse, smiling as she saw the thoughtful gift he'd given her on arrival at the hotel—a gorgeous silver and white leather wallet which she knew she would treasure forever.

She was home alone, because Ryan had rushed off to check the progress at work as soon as they'd arrived back. That meant she had plenty of time to compose an email and start telling her friends how her life had changed.

Cassie decided her first email should be to Jess. She owed Jess a huge debt of gratitude, because if they hadn't met for lunch on that exact day, and if Jess hadn't recommended Ryan and practically forced Cassie to give him a call, she would never have ended up here.

She still couldn't believe what a lucky coincidence it had been.

"Hey, Jess," she began, feeling warm inside as she chose the words. "I hope you enjoyed the rest of your trip to London, and I wanted to say thanks a million for putting me in touch with Ryan. This job has turned out to be more than I ever thought it would—and by 'more' I mean much more! Long story short, Ryan is divorced—that's why he was looking for help. He and the kids have had a tough time but they are coping well. The kids are great, just like you said they would be.

"Now for the happy ending to all of this. Ryan and I are dating! Jess, the minute I arrived I felt there was a spark between us. You didn't warn me he was so super cute! Anyway, it turned out that he feels the same way (lucky me) and we've just gotten back from an incredible overnight stay at a luxury hotel.

"I'm obviously taking it slow and not letting myself fall for him too much, too soon, but I have to admit I've fallen for him quite a lot. He is so generous, so caring, and such a genuine person. Who would have thought that I would find someone so special in this small seaside village where I was just hoping to get on my feet and earn a bit of extra cash!

"Anyway, I wanted you to know first.

"Write soon, I can't wait to hear your news!

"Love, Cassie."

She checked the message quickly and then pressed Send. She was sure Jess would be thrilled to hear about her good fortune, although Cassie reminded herself that she must be careful about what she shared, as her life had become so magical that some people might be jealous.

As Cassie started her next email, she heard the front door open.

"Hey," she called, getting up from off the bed. "That didn't take long."

She hurried down the corridor.

Cassie stopped in her tracks as she saw that a stranger had just walked in.

A tall, slender, well-dressed woman with shiny brown hair was wheeling a suitcase inside.

When she heard Cassie she spun around and stared at her, frowning.

"Who are you?" she asked.

"Wait a minute," Cassie said, feeling completely unsettled and on the back foot. "I should be asking you that. Are you sure you're in the right place?"

She wondered if Ryan had locked the door when he left. There was a guesthouse a block away and she wondered if that was where this rather rude mystery woman had meant to go.

"Oh, I'm very sure about that."

Folding her arms, the woman looked Cassie up and down in a way that made her feel awkward. It seemed as if this woman was entitled to be here. At any rate, she believed she was. Cassie wondered if Ryan might have a lawyer's appointment, or some other business arrangement. She'd have to phone him and tell him that the person he was meeting had arrived here.

"So, what are you doing here? Are you a cleaner?" the woman asked.

Intimidated by her stare, and not wanting to offend her if she was Ryan's friend or business associate, Cassie capitulated.

"I'm not a cleaner. My name is Cassandra Vale, and I'm staying here and helping with the children."

The woman frowned.

"Ryan never told me he was hiring anyone."

A dark suspicion was starting to form in Cassie's mind.

"I'm sorry, could I ask for your name?"

"Trish Ellis," the woman told her, sounding impatient. "I'm Ryan's wife."

As Cassie stared at her, frozen in shock, the woman brushed past her and headed toward the master bedroom, her suitcase wheels whirring over the wooden floorboards.

CHAPTER NINETEEN

Cassie stared after her, aghast at the bombshell the woman had dropped.

This was Ryan's ex-wife. Did Ryan know she was going to be here? Why had she just walked in and not called first? And why on earth was she disapproving about him hiring staff? It wasn't as if she was around to look after the kids.

Then another horrific thought struck Cassie.

Trish had headed straight for the master bedroom, and in the craziness of the previous morning, Cassie couldn't remember if she'd made the bed after sleeping there the other night. After the power had gone out, she probably hadn't even thought of it. If Trish had come to pack up the rest of her clothes, she would notice that both sides of the bed had been slept in, and that the covers were rumpled.

Cassie didn't want to have to explain that she had been sleeping there. It could get awkward or even acrimonious and it might put Ryan in a difficult situation.

She tiptoed along the hallway, treading as quietly as possible over the shiny wooden boards. From inside the master bedroom, she heard the bathroom door close. Quickly, Cassie opened the bedroom and peered inside to check.

To her relief, the bed had been made. Very neatly; Ryan must have done it yesterday.

Then a realization hit Cassie and she felt physically jolted as she saw it.

She and Ryan had slept under pale blue bedding. She remembered it vividly. Now, there was a cream duvet and beige pillowcases on the bed.

Ryan hadn't just made up the bed, he'd changed the sheets completely. Why? There was no reason to have done that, unless he'd known Trish would be arriving, and if so why hadn't he told her?

With another shock, she realized Trish had put her suitcase on the ottoman and opened it. It wasn't empty, as Cassie had expected. It was full of clothes. Packed full of shirts and folded blouses and a toiletry bag and a few pairs of shoes in clear plastic holders.

From inside the bathroom she heard the toilet flush and she turned hastily away from the door and hurried back to her own room, not wanting to be caught peeking.

She collapsed on her bed, her head spinning from confusion. What was happening? She felt as if someone had taken her familiar world and yanked it sideways so that nothing was as it seemed.

Then another thought hit her, this one the most shocking yet.

When she was introducing herself, Trish hadn't said she was Ryan's ex, or that they were separated.

She had said she was Ryan's wife.

Cassie's head shot up as she heard the heels click past her bedroom. Trish must be on her way to the kitchen. Much as Cassie didn't want to have to face her again, and was worried she'd made a complete fool of herself, she had to find out more.

Drawing a deep breath and summoning every fragment of courage she possessed, Cassie got up and followed Trish to the kitchen.

She was pouring herself a glass of water, and the kettle was on.

"Tea?" she asked in a not-very-friendly tone, seeing Cassie come in.

Cassie stared at her. She couldn't believe how long it had taken her to realize that this woman was Trish. Looking at her features, and her thick, perfectly bobbed hair, she could see the resemblance to both the children, particularly Madison.

"I was rude earlier," she said. "I haven't been here very long and for some reason I thought that Ryan stayed here alone. I thought I'd better check with you. Do you live here?"

Trish was regarding Cassie with puzzlement.

"I do live here, most of the time anyway. I travel often. I'm an international events organizer, so I'm frequently abroad."

Cassie felt breathless with shock, as if Trish had punched her in the face. Somehow she got herself down onto a chair.

"That must be a fun job," she said.

She was trying for a conversational tone, but she didn't actually have a clue how she was coming across—whether she sounded normal or if Trish thought she was a raving lunatic, because she couldn't get past the panicked confusion in her own head.

Trish shook her head.

"I wouldn't describe my career that way. It's extremely demanding. I'm a senior manager in a global communications company that specializes in large-scale events worldwide. I work with elite industry leaders across the board, who are top professionals in their field. Scientists, politicians, celebrities, you name it, they know my firm and they use us. I specialize in the hands-on running of these events, and have just coordinated an eight-day speaker tour across the USA. Five experts on the world economy, six cities, a total audience of thirty thousand. That was one of our smaller events."

She poured her tea and then glanced at the hardware bag on the counter.

"What's in there?"

In her shock, Cassie found herself babbling.

"It's rodenticide. I bought it because they were out of traps and there's a mouse in the house."

She was about to continue, and explain that Ryan had asked her to return it as poisons affected the food chain, but Trish interrupted.

"Well, are you going to put some out? It won't kill any mice standing on the counter. Now, if you'll excuse me, I'm exhausted. I was supposed to return yesterday morning, but we had to stay on to organize additional press conferences. I'll be resting now, until I have to fetch the children."

She walked out of the kitchen with her drinks.

Cassie watched her go, feeling sick with doubt.

She'd had a chance to look at Trish's neatly manicured hands while she was carrying the tea, and on the third finger of her left hand there was an elegant gold ring.

The evidence was indisputable.

There was a valid reason for Trish's extended absences. None of her actions since she'd arrived back had hinted that there was any conflict between herself and Ryan, never mind a divorce being in the cards.

Cassie was starting to suspect that she had been misled in the worst, most terrible way. How was any of this possible?

She'd slept with Ryan—slept with him—believing he was genuinely divorced when in fact he was married and had been spinning a sob story.

What would happen if Trish found out?

Cassie buried her face in her hands as the horror of her situation hit home.

Here she was, living as part of the family, under the delusion that the man of the house was divorced and available. She'd kissed him; she'd slept with him and spent the night in his room. She hadn't made a secret of it because she'd seen no need to.

Had Ryan been lying to her all along?

Cassie never wanted to open her eyes again.

Eventually, she managed to pull herself together enough to stand up. She stared numbly at the hardware store bag on the counter.

Trish had said she must use it, Ryan had said not to. Until she was told otherwise, she was going to go with what Ryan said. She put the bag in the broom cupboard.

Then she walked back to her room, with fresh waves of horror hitting her every step of the way as she thought about her situation, how trusting she had been, how recklessly she'd behaved as a result.

When she saw her phone lying on the bedside table, her heart nearly stopped as she remembered the cheerful email she'd sent to Jess. It was insane that an hour ago she'd believed herself to be in a completely different situation.

At some stage, Jess would open that mail and read its outdated, incriminating content. Her tell-all, when she thought she'd had nothing to hide.

No wonder the children had never shared with her about the divorce. It was because their family was still together, although their mother was away a lot. Which they were presumably used to, and why they hadn't mentioned her much.

Cassie stayed holed up in her room for the afternoon, hiding away from Trish in a state of utter shock. She'd never felt so miserable, or so alone, in her life. She thought of calling Ryan but didn't know what she should say, and what if Trish overheard her speaking to him?

When it was time for the children to be picked up, she heard Trish walk down the corridor and the click of the front door as she left. Cassie heard the sound of a car starting up, and she was gone.

The front door opened again ten minutes later and she heard Ryan call out, "Hello!"

At the sound of his voice, adrenaline surged inside her. She didn't feel as if she was welcoming her lover home, but rather as if she was preparing to do battle with an enemy.

She burst out of her room and marched down the hall to find Ryan taking off his coat.

"Afternoon, gorgeous," he greeted her.

Cassie was having none of it.

"Ryan, what the hell is going on? Your wife just arrived back from an overseas trip. Your wife. Not your ex. Your actual wife. She said she lives here. You didn't tell me about any of this. I had no idea you were still married, or that she was coming back here. Do you know how much of a fool I felt when she explained?"

Cassie could feel herself hyperventilating. She feared she would explode from the emotions boiling inside her.

"It's OK. It's OK. Calm down, Cassie," Ryan said.

"Calm down? You want me to calm down after she walked into your bedroom and put her bag in there, and told me she travels overseas a lot, and the rest of the time she lives here? What the hell am I supposed to be calm about?"

"She—" Ryan began, but Cassie was unstoppable.

"And there is a wedding ring on her finger. A wedding ring! I saw it, right there on the third finger of her left hand. Ryan, you need to tell me the truth now. I am not accepting any more lies."

Her voice was rising to a scream.

"Cassie, please. Don't be upset. Come here."

Ryan spoke gently.

"Please, come into the lounge. Sit down."

Cassie didn't feel like sitting. She was far too angry. But Ryan shepherded her into the family room and somehow she found herself on the couch, remembering that this was where they had first kissed, and where he'd first told her that he wanted her to be a part of his life.

"Cassie, listen to me. Please."

He sat next to her, his knee touching hers. Angrily, Cassie pulled her legs away. She didn't want to touch him, ever again. It was all she could do to look into his handsome, lying face.

"We are separated. The divorce is pending. The only step that has to be completed is that some of the documents need signing. You are right, and I must apologize because I didn't tell you how badly Trish was taking all of this."

Cassie glared at him, challenging him to make her believe his version.

"She has been acting very erratically since we started the process. Coming back on short notice like this is just one example. There have been a few others."

Cassie was going to demand that he name them, but Ryan continued.

"She suffers from depression. It's been a problem for a while. Remember I said how demanding, how needy, she was becoming?"

Reluctantly Cassie nodded.

"It was symptomatic of what she was suffering, because I do understand it's an illness. It meant I had to proceed very slowly with this. Even though our relationship isn't what it was, I still feel responsible for her. I couldn't even make a start on the process until her medication was right. That took months, and Cassie, they were not happy months."

She stared at Ryan and no matter how hard she looked, she could only see truth in his eyes.

Then she remembered that Trish hadn't looked like a depressed person. She knew herself what depression was like, how anxiety was the devil on your shoulder that never went away.

Although, perhaps Trish was able to hide it well, if her meds were finally in balance.

"She's the mother of my children," Ryan continued. "I would never forgive myself if my actions, my own selfishness, caused her to harm herself. So I have been patient. More patient, and more accommodating, than you'll ever know."

He sighed.

"This is just the latest hurdle but it's the final one. I didn't want her to come back here—but if she has had a hectic business trip and wants somewhere familiar to lay her head while this whole process wraps up, I can't say no. Would you say no?"

"Where's she been living?" Cassie challenged him.

"She has been renting an apartment close to Heathrow Airport. It makes sense for her to be there because she travels so much, but the problem is she has no friends or support structure nearby. I told her she should rent within the village until all this was finalized, but she refused. I guess she was worried that people might talk."

Cassie shook her head.

"You didn't even tell me. Do you have any idea how upset I felt when she walked in?"

Ryan leaned closer and she thought he wanted to take her hand, so she pulled it away and bunched her hands together in her lap.

"I didn't know she was arriving now. She told me she was stopping by work first, and would get here after supper. I intended to sit down with you before we collected the children, and explain what was going to happen. I see she's had a look at the timetable and has gone off to pick up the kids herself."

"Yes," Cassie said.

She suddenly felt like bursting into tears because she'd been longing to catch up with the children and to find out how their big performance in Canterbury had gone. It would have meant a lot to her to have been waiting when the bus arrived.

"Please, Cassie, help me get through this. It's not going to be easy, but it hopefully won't be for too long. If you want proof of my feelings toward you, I brought you a present. As a thank-you for being so special, and to remember the amazing experience we had while away."

To Cassie's astonishment, he produced a small velvet box from his pocket and handed it to her.

She opened it, realizing her hands were shaking.

Inside was a pair of gold earrings, with beautiful green jewels set in the shape of flowers.

"The stones are emeralds. When I saw them, I thought how beautiful that color would look on you. It's a gift from the heart, because you've brought so much joy into my life, but it's also a promise. We have a future together. We just have to get through the next few days. You are strong enough. I hope I'm strong enough."

Cassie stared down at the earrings.

Did they make a difference?

She decided they did. Ryan's calm, logical words had finally gotten through to her and they made sense. She accepted that this was just the final, difficult phase of a tricky divorce.

"Thank you," she said. "I'll try. But please, Ryan, this can't go on too long."

"It won't," he promised.

Trish arrived home with the children at five.

Cassie had hoped to hear all about their adventures, but when she came out of her room to greet them, she found herself facing two sullen children who barely acknowledged her. Madison headed straight for the bathroom, and Dylan folded himself down on his bean bag in the dining room.

Cassie hovered nervously at the dining room door.

"How was your trip?" she asked.

Dylan looked up from his book reluctantly.

"It was OK," he said, and then turned back to his reading.

The bathroom door slammed, and Cassie hurried off, hoping to catch up with Madison, but she marched into her bedroom and closed the door firmly.

Standing outside, Cassie frowned. She was sure Madison had seen her, but the closed door was a clear message she didn't want to talk.

Then, to her surprise, she smelled food cooking in the kitchen.

Ryan had told her that the family had fast food on Sundays, usually pizza. Trish either hadn't remembered about this, or maybe it only happened when she was away. Either way, she was cooking for the family and that unsettled Cassie, because what had happened to Ryan preparing all the meals? It felt as if Trish was entrenching herself.

Cassie went back to her own room, feeling like a dog with its tail between its legs. She didn't venture out again until she heard Trish calling out for everyone to come for supper.

The square kitchen table was made for four. Five was a squeeze. Trish had set a place for her next to Madison, but there wasn't enough space and Cassie had to shift sideways so that her legs were on either side of the table leg. It was awkward and uncomfortable, and gave her the feeling that she truly was a fifth wheel in the home.

The children ate in silence, and Trish updated Ryan on her trip and asked after people Cassie knew nothing about. From the context she realized some of them lived in the village.

"The Richardsons are opening a stationery store in town," Ryan said.

"Part of the post office? Or separate?"

"I believe it's opposite. On the other side of the road."

"I'm unconvinced about the viability of a stationery store in this small town," Trish said. "If it was part of the post office, it would be different. But separate, I'm not sure."

Cassie could contribute nothing toward this conversation. She ate her food, discovering that Trish was a substandard cook and the chicken pasta she had made was bland and under-seasoned. She wished she could be somewhere else. Sitting at this table made her remember all the other times she'd enjoyed meals here, and how during every dinner, she'd been looking forward to sharing wine with Ryan outside. That would be impossible now.

"There was a power outage yesterday morning," Madison said.

"Really?" Trish asked.

"There was a scary storm and then everything went dark."

"That must have been frightening," Trish said. "Are there flashlights in the bathroom and in your bedrooms? That's something you could see to tomorrow," she said, addressing Cassie for the first time.

"During storm season these outages are fairly frequent," she continued. "If there are flashlights in everyone's rooms, you won't have to find your way to the bathroom in the dark."

"I know my way around," Madison protested. "Sometimes I test myself by walking to the bathroom with my eyes closed."

"You must think of others. It's a long walk from the guest bedroom to your bathroom."

Madison frowned, puzzled.

"Cassie wasn't sleeping—"

Just in time, Cassie realized what the young girl was going to say.

With a mouth full of food, she had no way of stopping the innocent statement that was going to land both her and Ryan in an ocean of trouble.

CHAPTER TWENTY

C assie knocked her water over.

It was the only conversation-stopper she could think of.

She slammed the back of her hand into the glass, and it thumped down onto its side. Water sluiced all over Madison's plate, which was almost untouched, and into Madison's lap.

Madison uttered a dismayed shout.

"It's cold! Yuck!"

Cassie hastily swallowed her food.

"Sorry, Maddie. That was clumsy of me," she apologized.

Ryan jumped up and grabbed a dish towel from the hook above the sink.

Cassie's heart was pounding from delayed shock at the bombshell Madison had come so close to dropping. She helped Madison mop up the splashes on her lap and dried the table while Ryan dished another helping of food for her.

"Do you want some more water?" Trish asked Cassie, coolly polite, once everything was back to normal.

"No, thanks. I'm fine," Cassie said. She felt even more on edge than before, knowing that at any moment, innocent dinner table conversation could give the game away

She glanced at Madison anxiously, but she was not her talkative self, and had relapsed into silence again.

Once everyone had finished their food, Trish checked her watch.

"It's already after seven, and we are meeting the Robinsons at half past. Do you need to get changed?" she asked Ryan.

Cassie couldn't stop herself from gaping in astonishment at what was unfolding before her eyes.

"It's only drinks at the Seafarer's Arms. It'll be fairly casual," Ryan said.

"Well, we'd better get going." Trish turned to Cassie. "You'll ensure the children are put to bed by eight thirty? And could you tidy the kitchen?"

"Sure, I—sure. I'll do that."

Cassie had to bite back a stinging retort, realizing it would be completely out of place. After all, she had been hired to do this work. She just hadn't thought she would be taking instructions from Ryan's wife.

Ryan walked out of the kitchen, humming to himself, and a minute later, he and Trish were on their way out.

Cassie turned on the TV for the children and then headed back to the kitchen, agonizing over Ryan and Trish. She'd never been to the Seafarer's Arms but guessed it was among the pubs and restaurants down by the harbor. From the sounds of it they were meeting a married couple.

Another married couple, Cassie corrected herself.

This seemed like a normal life being lived; that was the most worrying part of this whole inexplicable situation. When had this drinks arrangement been made? Why had it even been made if there was so much uncertainty surrounding their relationship?

She wished she could drive down to the pub and peer through the windows and see how Ryan and Trish were interacting, whether they seemed friendly, or even loving. Was Trish going to try and use this outing to make Ryan change his mind and rethink the divorce?

Cassie stopped herself as she was putting the salt and pepper shakers into the dishwasher, realizing she was so distracted she was messing up horribly with the simple job of tidying.

Rechecking, she found a few idiotic errors. The cheese was in the cupboard and she'd folded a dirty dish towel and put it back with the clean ones. Quickly she corrected her mistakes, now frantic with worry that she would keep buckling under stress. Trish seemed to be a stickler for correctness and Cassie didn't think she looked like the forgiving type. Even a small slip-up might land her in trouble.

She went back into the family room to find that Dylan had already gone to bed, and Madison was dozing on the sofa. She'd been doing a puzzle, but the tray had tipped sideways and some of the pieces had fallen onto the floor.

"Come on. It's bedtime. You've had a busy day," Cassie said, carefully righting the tray to salvage as much of Madison's work as possible.

"What time is it?" Madison asked, confused.

Cassie glanced at the clock on the mantelpiece.

"It's a quarter to nine."

She'd run late without even realizing it.

On her hands and knees, Cassie picked up the puzzle pieces and peered under the couch to make sure none of the others had fallen out of sight.

She could see no puzzle pieces, but something else, pushed far under the low-slung couch, caught her eye.

Scrabbling her fingers along the carpet, Cassie grasped it and pulled it out, before staring at it in consternation.

It was the manila envelope that the unpleasant, dark-haired man had delivered a few days ago. She recognized the handwritten address on the front. Ryan had opened it, but the papers were still inside. So this was surely nothing to do with any divorce.

Suspicion crystallized inside her as she wondered why Ryan had hidden it away after opening it.

Now she had found it, and Cassie resolved that as soon as she was alone in her room, she was going to look inside.

She put the envelope in her jacket pocket and picked up Madison's tray.

Madison followed Cassie to her bedroom in sullen silence.

Cassie had no idea why she was so moody, but she was starting to suspect it had nothing to do with the so-called divorce. On the spur of the moment, she decided to ask Madison some careful questions. She was desperate to find out what she knew.

"Madison," she asked softly, "do you know if your mum and dad have been planning to live in different places? Did they talk to you about it at all?"

Madison frowned at her.

"How do you mean?" she asked.

"If your mum was moving out?"

She didn't want to put ideas into Madison's head, and felt as if she was walking a tightrope. Madison could so easily pass this information on to Trish. Cassie clenched her hands tightly, realizing her palms felt damp.

"No. She hasn't moved out. She spends a lot of time at work though."

"You haven't felt sad about that?"

Madison looked confused.

"No," she said.

Rage flared inside Cassie and she had to struggle not to show Madison, through words or gestures, how furious she was.

This was not what Ryan had told her, not at all. He'd said the children knew about the divorce, and it had affected them so badly they weren't willing to speak about it.

Not true. In fact, they knew nothing about it and that was why they had said nothing about it. All the nuances she thought she'd picked up in their behavior had simply been coincidence. Even Dylan's shoplifting had nothing to do with the mention of the children's mother.

God, what a fool she'd been. If she had asked them about this at the start, she could have gotten to the truth of the situation and not become embroiled the way she had. She hadn't asked them because Ryan had told her how traumatized they were.

He'd covered all his bases like a seasoned liar, and Cassie was starting to fear that was what he was.

"I'm very tired, Cassie," Madison said.

Cassie climbed hastily off her bed.

"Sleep well. I hope you will feel happy in the morning," she said.

She switched Madison's light off and closed her door.

Rage was still simmering inside her as she sat on her bed and took the manila envelope out of her pocket. She pulled out the papers, noticing that her hands were shaking, and then stared at them, appalled.

This was no divorce document. It was a final demand for payment from a loan agency.

Cassie read it carefully. It was for a substantial amount, and Ryan was months overdue with it. From the printed statement, it looked as if he'd defaulted on every single repayment. Either he hadn't had money, or he'd ignored the payment requests completely.

Now she realized why the delivery man had been so unpleasant to her—and she was the one who'd bear the brunt of his attentions if Ryan continued to default, and he came back again.

"He told me it was divorce papers. This has nothing to do with any divorce," she said aloud. "Is there even a divorce? I doubt there is!"

Anger was making her reckless. She was entitled to know the truth. If it wasn't being told to her, there were ways she could find it out.

Cassie left her room and walked quietly to the master bedroom, where she eased open the door.

Ryan had said that Trish was here to sign divorce papers. Those papers hadn't been in the manila envelope, so if Ryan was telling the truth, they must be elsewhere.

The logical place was in the wooden filing cabinet in the corner—it contained two large drawers, one neatly labeled "Work," and the other "Children/Personal."

If divorce papers needed signing, they must be filed away for safe-keeping. If they were there, Cassie was determined to find them.

CHAPTER TWENTY ONE

C assie felt sick with tension as she stepped into the tidy master bedroom. She felt so angry, so violated and outraged by the lies she'd been told, that she was tempted to upend the files and rip through them. She warned herself that would only cause repercussions. She must keep control, and be methodical.

She opened the first drawer, relieved that it wasn't locked.

Everything was in its place. Tax documents, the house plans, the papers for Ryan's business. Birth certificates. Marriage certificates.

Cassie paused when she saw that folder and anger filled her again.

Reading the document, she saw that Trish and Ryan had been married ten years ago, but both parents' names appeared on the children's birth certificates. So they had lived together as a family before being married.

Then Cassie checked the house purchase documents and saw, to her surprise, that Trish was the owner of the house, and had been for the past twelve years since she had bought it.

That didn't tie in with what Ryan had told her about the house being a reward from his business.

Aware that this was taking time, and that the Ellises might already be heading home, Cassie sped up her search.

She sifted through every folder without success. She didn't find anything. Not an attorney's letter, nor the papers Ryan had mentioned. Nothing.

She did find something else, though.

One of the folders in the Children/Personal drawer was labeled "Other." Inside, there was a copy of an invitation that had been sent earlier in the year.

Cassie read it and felt cold with shock as she stared down at the pretty, floral paper.

"Dear..." the invite read.

"On Spring Bank Holiday, Trish and Ryan request the pleasure of your company at a Luncheon Party and Family Celebration.

"Venue: The Conservatory Gardens, Lakeside Hotel

"Time: From 12 noon

"Dress: Elegant

"Occasion: Our 10 Year Wedding Anniversary and Vow Renewal."

Cassie stared down at the crisp, expensive paper and felt consumed by a murderous rage. For the first time she understood what the term "seeing red" meant, and if she'd been holding a weapon and Ryan had walked in at that moment, she knew she would have attacked him with it.

Their marriage hadn't been falling apart. Quite the contrary.

Six months earlier, they'd renewed their promises at a public ceremony to show they were more in love than ever.

Cassie wanted to tear up the invitation and scatter it like confetti around the room, letting the strewn fragments of paper show Ryan that she knew how he'd lied.

Putting it carefully away and closing the cabinet without a sound made her head want to explode with frustration.

Closing the door softly, Cassie headed back down the hall, but as she passed Dylan's room she drew in her breath sharply.

His door was open, and this time he was standing by his bed, facing her.

Cassie froze, shivers running down her spine as she wondered if Dylan was awake or asleep. Perhaps he was prone to sleepwalking and opened his door every time.

She realized he was awake when he whispered, "Pssst. Come here."

Reluctantly, because she felt spooked and had no idea what this was all about, she stepped into his room.

"What is it, Dylan?" she whispered.

"You were in my dad's room," he said.

He must have heard her in there, rooting around in his father's filing cabinets, even though she'd done her best to be quiet. How could she explain this? Knowing she'd been found out made Cassie feel suddenly ashamed.

No point in denying it.

Cassie nodded.

She thought Dylan would demand to know why, but he didn't.

Instead, he muttered, sympathetically, "Sometimes you have to check up on what the old man says. He doesn't always tell the right story."

Cassie didn't even dare to breathe as she considered Dylan's words. She was at a loss how to respond. Agreeing would feel disloyal and she couldn't talk badly to a son about his own father.

She settled for a nod.

"I tried to warn you," Dylan said. "The first night you were here, I got my mate to send you a message."

Cassie stared at him in consternation.

"'Be careful'?" she asked. "That message? You asked your friend to send it?"

Dylan sighed.

"Yes. I wanted my mate to say more, but he chickened out. It was something, but not enough, maybe."

"Why did you tell me that?" Cassie whispered.

"Because my dad gets—weird—when you accuse him of not being truthful. So you just have to go along with it."

Dylan continued softly.

"Like with Benjamin Bunny. That made me want to laugh. He went to a lot of effort there. What a story. He could have just said the bunny escaped. But then I suppose he knew Madison would spend the rest of her life searching for him."

Once again, Cassie felt uncertain how to respond.

"He only did it to try and comfort you," she said eventually. "So you wouldn't be too sad."

Dylan nodded.

"I know, I know. So I went along with it."

From outside, Cassie heard a car pass by, sluicing along the wet tarmac. The noise reminded her that it was getting late and Ryan and Trish might come home at any time.

"You should get into bed now," she told Dylan. "You don't want to be tired tomorrow."

"Yeah, OK," he agreed.

He climbed into bed. As he pulled the covers up, a thought suddenly occurred to Cassie. How had Dylan guessed that Ryan had been lying about Benjamin? The story about the bunny had seemed plausible. The ashes had been a bit far-fetched, but how had that clued Dylan that the whole episode with the vet had been an invention?

"How did you know it wasn't true?" she whispered.

He stared up at her, and in the soft light filtering through the curtains she could just make out his features, calm and strangely blank.

"Because I killed Benjamin that morning, before I left for school. I broke his neck."

CHAPTER TWENTY TWO

Cassie took in a horrified gulp of air.

Was Dylan joking?

She knew he wasn't. He sounded perfectly matter-of-fact, and that only made his words more chilling. In any case, his version was the more plausible. A healthy rabbit, suddenly dead.

Cassie remembered the way Benjamin's head had hung, limp and disjointed. At the time she had wondered about it and now it made sense.

Why had Dylan done that? Killing an innocent pet was a psychopathic act. No normal boy would do such a thing. What had his reasons been, or had he simply wanted to kill, to feel the bone break in his grasp, to snuff out a harmless little life?

What kind of a creature was he? She'd thought him to be a normal boy, if rather shy and introverted. Now she was finding out that behind his quiet exterior, a monster lurked.

His words had rendered her speechless, and she shuddered, as if a bucket of ice had been poured down her back. She had no idea what to say, what to do next. But Dylan seemed unconcerned.

"Good night," he said, and turned over in bed so that his back was facing her.

Blindsided by this sickening revelation, Cassie stumbled out of the room. Back in her bedroom, she huddled under her duvet, in a state of shock at what she had discovered that night.

Ryan was a liar. What she'd found, and what she hadn't found, tonight had proven it. He'd been feeding her falsehoods, stringing her along, making empty promises that were based on nothing but his own warped imagination.

His own son had confirmed he did this—and thinking back on the conversation with Dylan, Cassie buried her face in her pillow.

His words, and the casual way he'd spoken them, had terrified her. He'd talked about killing in cold blood as if it meant nothing to him. If he could do that to a rabbit, what else could he do? What might he do to her?

With fear and anger warring inside her, sleep was impossible for Cassie, and she was still awake when, much later, she heard the sound of Ryan and Trish returning home.

As they walked down the hallway, laughing softly and whispering in their efforts to be quiet, she checked her phone.

It was after eleven. They must have stayed at the pub till closing time. This hadn't just been a polite get-together, it had been a festive evening.

Listening to their giggles as they passed her door, she imagined they must be walking close together, perhaps even arm in arm. What would happen when they got into the room, and into that immaculately made bed?

Cassie shut her eyes as tight as she could, squeezing them painfully closed to try and block out her imaginings.

Then she got up and opened her window. Even though it would make the room freezing cold, she wanted to hear the scream of the wind and the roar of the sea as it foamed over those dark, glossy pebbles, and she wanted to drown herself in its rage.

She knew the alternative—hearing any whisper of lovemaking from the room down the hall—would push her over the edge.

"You bastard," she whispered viciously as she climbed back into bed. "I hate you for what you've done."

Cassie hadn't thought she wouldn't sleep at all, but she must have at some stage during that terrible night, because she woke abruptly to the sound of laughter from the kitchen.

She sat bolt upright, gritting her teeth as she heard Ryan's guffaw and Trish's piercing, bell-like laugh. She threw on clothes, and then although her hands were shaking with anger, she did her makeup carefully to conceal the paleness of her face and the dark shadows under her eyes. She was going to show Ryan that she wasn't in pieces about this and, in fact, didn't care at all.

She checked the time on her phone, and to her consternation, she saw that she had an email from Jess.

The happy letter she'd written just yesterday explaining that she and Ryan were an item felt like it came from a different lifetime. How stupid, how gullible she had been.

She was mortified by the confession she'd made, but at least she could now vent her anger to Jess in a caustically worded reply.

She opened the email and as she read it, she felt her heart sink.

"Hi, Cassie," Jess wrote.

"I think we might have a situation here! I am totally confused and feel I have done the wrong thing.

"You know I told you I worked for friends of friends. That's how I met Ryan and his family. Well, his friend, whom I know quite well, is named Olive and she lives in one of the nearby towns.

"Anyway I told her the good news and she emailed me back. She said that you were lying because they attended Ryan's birthday party two weeks ago and everything was perfect. Ryan and his wife were making plans for a family holiday over New Year.

"I don't know what to say or do! I feel terrible that I might have given the wrong info or misunderstood your email. Would these friends not know if they were divorced? I need to know what to say to her because she's demanding answers. Please can you help me!

"Love, Jess."

Cassie stared at the letter in panic.

Jess had innocently spilled the beans, and now there was every chance that the angry friend would tell the Ellises.

Crimson with shame, she reread the email she'd sent Jess. There wasn't much room for doubt in it. Cassie had said there was a spark, she'd mentioned the nonexistent divorce, she'd used the word "dating," and worst of all, she'd told Jess about the overnight stay at a hotel.

There was no way to back out of this; it was totally incriminating. She'd been truthful and now her own honesty had come back to bite her.

She could ask Jess to lie, but that would be unfair and Jess might refuse.

As Cassie frantically considered her options, she realized there might be another way out of this that wouldn't put such an unfair burden on her innocent friend, especially since she didn't know where Jess's loyalties lay.

That would mean telling Jess that she, Cassie, was a liar.

Cassie's hands shook as she composed a hasty reply.

"Jess, I feel so embarrassed. I ended up saying things that weren't true.

"I thought there was a spark between Ryan and me. I believed that helping him out on a business trip meant we were dating. Look, we had an amazing dinner and we chatted and shared lots of stuff and he gave me the biggest hug before I went to my room.

"And I ended up assuming the rest!

"Luckily he took me aside yesterday and reminded me he's happily married and although he's a friendly guy, he knows that I'm lonely and that I might be reading too much into the friendliness.

"I cried buckets afterwards but it was mostly out of embarrassment, as I knew he was right and I'd been such a fool.

"Please tell your friend it was a misunderstanding. I'll be leaving soon and I'd hate to think that my own silly imagination had caused any damage to such a wonderful family!"

Cassie looked down at the screen and felt nauseous.

It wasn't true. What she had said in this letter was a total lie. She was lying to protect a man who didn't deserve it, who was in all probability a serial liar, and who was still doing his utmost to string her along.

On the other hand, if Trish found out, there'd be no sympathy from her, Cassie was sure of it. Sleeping with a married man, in his marital bed, in the house where his two children lived, was unforgivable, and nobody would believe her if she said she hadn't known.

She couldn't risk this situation blowing up in her face, especially since she didn't have the correct visa to be working at all. If Trish found out that Cassie had been having an affair with her husband, she would be looking for any excuse to stick the knife in.

Cassie sensed Trish was a stickler for the rules. It was evident in her whole demeanor. If she learned that Cassie had taken this job while on a visitor visa, she wouldn't hesitate to report her.

Cassie didn't think Trish liked her much anyway, and might even instinctively suspect that things between her and Ryan were not what they seemed.

She gritted her teeth. Unfair as this was, she was going to have to do it because there was no other choice. If she didn't she would suffer the consequences and they would be harsh.

Pressing her lips together, Cassie stabbed the Send button and watched as the email disappeared.

Then she turned her phone off, not wanting to face any more incoming emails, and went to get the children ready for their day.

She checked Dylan's bedroom with nervousness uncoiling inside her, and was relieved to find he wasn't there and had already made his bed.

Cassie woke Madison, and when she was dressed, the two of them walked to the kitchen together. Pasting a fixed smile onto her face, Cassie wished she could be anywhere else. Anything was better than having to interact with the man who'd slept with her and lied to her and led her on, while pretending nothing was wrong.

"Morning!" Ryan greeted them. He was at the stove making omelets while Trish, seated at the kitchen table, was busy with a large book. Dylan, on the other side of the table, was finishing his food.

Cassie looked at Dylan uneasily, wishing he was the one who'd lied about what he had done and that it had been Ryan who'd told the truth.

Dylan glanced at her briefly and then returned his attention to his plate, without giving her any hint of the disturbing conversation they'd had last night.

"Morning," Cassie replied in a faux-cheerful tone, wondering how she would manage to survive this meal. She already felt as if she was about to snap from stress. She looked from Ryan to Trish and back again, vainly hoping to pick up signs of conflict or estrangement.

"Coffee's on the counter," Trish said. "It's a help-yourself morning. I need to keep my hands clean."

"What are you doing, Mum?" Madison asked curiously.

"I'm creating a scrapbook. One of the speakers on a recent tour talked about the importance of creating physical memories and not just digital ones. We've been bad that way because our photos are mostly digital, but I found one album in the lounge. I'll go into town later and get more recent photos printed out."

Madison looked over her shoulder, but Cassie noticed she wasn't as fascinated by the scrapbooking as she'd expected her to be. Since she loved working with her hands, Cassie assumed she'd join in and offer to help, but she didn't.

Cassie found herself fuming all over again at the mention of family memories. This was not what you did when you were getting divorced—was it?

She felt tears prickle her eyes and worried that she might lose control and burst into hysterical sobs in front of the family. She concentrated on imagining a high brick wall in her mind, where thoughts about Ryan were imprisoned, unseen and unfelt. With the wall in her mind, she tried to maintain composure as she made tea for Madison.

"Omelet?" Ryan asked. "We've got a choice of ham, mushrooms, and cheese. What's your preference, Maddie? Dylan had the works."

Madison shook her head.

"I'm not hungry, Dad."

Ryan laughed. "You're the most un-morning person I know. I'm going to make you one anyway, and when you come back from school, Cassie can heat it up for you in the microwave. Sound good?"

"OK," Madison agreed. "Ham and cheese, please."

"For you, Cassie?"

She couldn't bear to look at him, never mind speak to him.

"I'll pass, thanks," she said. "I'm feeling a bit sick this morning."

She realized it was the truth. Her nausea was worse, and the thought of an omelet made her want to throw up.

Cassie expected someone to comment on what she'd said, or offer sympathy, but Ryan was leaning over Trish's shoulder, absorbed by her project.

"I remember you in that wedding dress," he said. "Wow, it brings that day right back."

Trish laughed.

"To think how I almost chose a massive white meringue gown. Then at the last minute, my mother of all people intervened. She said, go for elegant."

"Go for stylish." Ryan stared down admiringly.

"Why thank you," Trish said.

"Weren't we married just before you got your skipper's license?" Ryan asked.

"No. I already had that. But if you remember, I was working on my MBA at that time. You joked that I'd be project managing the wedding."

Ryan smiled.

"You organized it perfectly. It was such a special day."

Cassie turned away from them, unable to deal with any further revelations about Trish's accomplishments. She guessed ten years ago, Trish would have been about the same age as Cassie was now. She had already been highly qualified in numerous skills and clearly successful. What had Cassie achieved? Nothing. All she could boast so far was that she'd been an average restaurant waitress and a catastrophically unsuccessful au pair.

How could she have thought for a moment Ryan would be serious about her?

She wasn't a highly intelligent, multi-skilled pillar of society like Trish was. How could she not have seen this entire debacle for what it was—a husband messing around with the temporary help, behind his wife's back?

She could never be the caliber of Trish or Ryan, she never had been and she never would be. When she compared herself to them, she felt ashamed of herself, and everything she'd ever strived to achieve. Her independence, her self-sufficiency, the few qualifications she had managed to earn, were pathetic compared to what these wealthy, successful people had accomplished.

She had to stop herself from slinking out of the kitchen there and then. Instead, she forced her mind back to what Madison needed, seeing the child's actual parents were both preoccupied by Wedding Appreciation Hour.

She stood up. "You should eat something before school. Can I pack you some cheese? Dried fruit? Take it with you. Eat it on the bus."

"All right," Madison agreed, and Cassie filled a lunch box with a selection of snacks.

"Talking of the bus, you two should get your bags," Ryan said, glancing at the kitchen clock.

"I'll fetch you at one," Trish said.

Cassie realized that with Trish's return, she had become redundant. Trish was taking the reins, and she had a car, whereas Cassie's was out of action for who knew how long.

She needed to find out about the car. As soon as it was fixed, she was going to leave.

For her own sanity, it was the only solution.

Cassie got her coat and walked with the children to the bus stop. It was a relief to be out of the house and to be able to pretend, for a little while, that everything was normal.

Even so, she didn't think the children were fooled. Madison wasn't herself at all, and since she wouldn't tell Cassie what was wrong, Cassie could only suspect that she'd picked up on the atmosphere in the house.

As for Dylan, she had no idea what to say to him. Normal conversation seemed impossible when every time she looked at him, she imagined him reaching into the cage, grabbing his pet, and snapping its neck with brutal force.

Suddenly, Cassie imagined doing the same to Ryan. It was what he deserved for the pain and anguish he'd put her through, and it gave her some bitter comfort to visualize clamping her fingers around Ryan's strong, smooth-skinned neck and squeezing until she throttled him. Or, better still, taking one of the sharpest knives from the expensive array in the kitchen, and stabbing it deep into his traitorous heart.

Even though she knew she could never do such a thing, fantasizing about revenge made her feel better.

There was no point in going back to the house after the children had left. What would she do there? Sit around and listen to Ryan and Trish loving each other up? Although, thinking back, Cassie realized it had been Ryan complimenting Trish and her agreeing with him.

When the bus had gone, she headed into the village, hoping to walk off some of her anger. Perhaps she could find the Seafarer's Arms and see if it looked romantic.

In the cold, gray morning, the magical charm of the village had worn off completely. It looked somber and dull, the colors muted. The few people she met along the way were unfriendly, huddled in jackets and hurrying to get out of the drizzle that had started to fall.

Cassie turned her face to the rain. The icy drops scoured her face, and she welcomed the distraction, because every word Ryan and Trish spoke, every one of his attentive gestures to her, was corroding her inside. She couldn't bear it. She felt as if an unstoppable force was building up inside her; a toxic mix of anger and guilt. Who knew what would happen when it exploded?

She randomly turned right, then left, then right again. Zigzagging through the streets, Cassie realized the homes were becoming smaller and higher, most double-story, built onto a steepening hill. Space was at a premium here, and the elevated view was the draw card.

Then she stopped, frowning.

Parked ahead of her was a car, low-slung and white, and she was sure the number plate was the one she remembered.

FZR. Now that she saw the letters in front of her, she remembered their order clearly. That was definitely the plate she had seen.

Cassie was so embroiled in her thoughts that she nearly walked on past.

Then she changed her mind.

The driver of that car had nearly killed her in that narrow lane. This was her chance to find out who the person was, and whether it had been intentional or a terrible mistake.

Cassie marched up to the white-painted front door, raised the brass knocker, and brought it down with a loud bang.

CHAPTER TWENTY THREE

Cassie banged the knocker a second time and waited outside the house, breathless from her uphill walk, feeling nervousness flooding in. She didn't have any idea what she would say when the door was opened. She wasn't great at winging it at the best of times, and thanks to the hell she'd been through since Trish arrived home, this was not the best of times.

Cassie was about to turn away when, through the stained-glass panel on the side of the door, she saw somebody approaching.

A moment later, the door opened.

Cassie found herself staring at Harriet the housekeeper.

Harriet's greeting, "Hi, can I ..." trailed off in mid-voice as she realized who was standing outside and she stared back at Cassie, horrified.

Then the housekeeper tried to slam the door in her face.

She was quick, but Cassie was quicker.

Remembering the delivery man's strategy, she got her shoe into the gap and the door bounced off the rubber sole, giving her enough impetus to shove it back and push her way inside.

Harriet stepped back, looking wary. She folded her arms protectively across the green smock she wore. Cassie noted, bemused, that she'd changed her hair color to turquoise.

"What're you doing here?" Harriet asked.

"Why did you try to slam the door on me?" she countered, feeling her ever-present anger boiling up again.

"'Cause I'm just cleaning here." Harriet sounded self-righteous. "I can't let anyone in, for security reasons. I take deliveries at the front door."

"Well, I haven't come to deliver anything."

"Why're you here then? You lost?" Harriet spat at her.

Cassie could feel her resentment, like a tangible force.

"I recognized your car."

Now Harriet's gaze slid away.

"My car? From where?"

"You tried to run me over on Saturday morning, while I was walking back home."

"Why would I do that?" Harriet asked, her voice full of outraged innocence. "Are you mad, to think I'd do that?"

"It was your car. I saw it for certain. And there's nobody else in this village who's been nasty to me except you. You have been appalling right from the start."

Harriet took a step back, nearly tripping over the lime green knotted rug on the hallway floor.

"You have been insufferable. Geez, how unprofessional can a cleaner be! Swearing at your boss, insulting people in front of young children. You even went through my trash can! What the hell was that about?"

"Look, I can explain—" Harriet began.

Cassie's rage was rising now; she couldn't stop it.

This wasn't just about how Harriet had behaved. Everything was boiling to the surface. Her anger over the unfairness of what had happened and her shattered hopes and dreams. The helpless fury that surged inside her when she thought about the way Ryan had treated her and how he had lied. Finally, she had the chance to vent it all on somebody who deserved it.

"You can't explain a thing. You're a sad, jealous, mean bitch. And you ended up hating an innocent person so much that you tampered with their car and then tried to run them over while they were walking home."

Harriet had gone pale.

"I never did that. Honest."

"You're going to deny everything now? Lie and deny, is that the route you're taking? Well, I know for sure that it was you on the road, and if you try and kill somebody and then lie about it, it makes you an even worse person than I thought you were."

Using the vicious words as weapons, Cassie could see from Harriet's face that they were finding their mark.

"And are you such an attention whore that you swerve into someone because their employer didn't want to date you? Seriously, is that how evil and egotistical you are?"

"I didn't try to kill you," Harriet muttered.

Cassie pounced on the inadvertent confession she'd made.

"So it was you. Thank you for admitting it." Her voice rose, high and sharp. She took another step forward and again, Harriet retreated.

Behind her, Cassie could see a carpeted staircase going up to the top floor, and an open door leading into a small, tidy kitchen.

"Now that you've told me you're an attempted murderer, let's get onto the topic of your behavior at the house. Parading yourself in front of your employer; staying late so you can try and flirt with him. Did you not get the memo he wasn't interested, even when he told you so? And why take it out on me, you selfish bitch?" Her voice became a scream.

"Please stop shouting," Harriet whispered.

Glaring into Harriet's stricken face, Cassie realized that there was another interpretation to the housekeeper's behavior.

The way she'd lingered in the house until Ryan came back, and rushed to meet him, wearing far too much makeup for the simple job of house cleaning. Cassie had thought, and Ryan had confirmed, that Harriet had just been flirting. Now, Cassie remembered her anger when she was ignored, the way she'd stormed out of the house, the near-deadly incident on the road. She realized Harriet's reaction had been well out of proportion to an innocent flirtation that had been cut short.

Harriet had been distraught, furious, and vengeful. Her behavior had been on par with what Cassie was feeling now. Therefore, it must be for the same reason.

"Wait a minute." She was breathing rapidly. "You did sleep with him, didn't you? I've just figured it out. Now everything makes sense. You and he—you had a fling. And when you walked in last Monday, you thought it was still on?"

She knew, watching Harriet's eyes, that she was right. She put her hands on her hips and stared her down, daring her to deny it.

"Yes," Harriet whispered. "We slept together."

Then she did something Cassie hadn't expected at all.

She burst into tears.

These weren't ordinary tears. They were sobbing, wailing hysterics, as if Harriet had been holding an ocean of misery inside herself. She buried her face in her hands, collapsed onto the carpeted stairs, and cried her heart out.

Cassie's anger melted away and she started to feel desperately sorry for Harriet.

Under the stairway was a door that led into a bathroom. There, she grabbed a handful of tissues for Harriet. Then she sat down beside her on the step and rubbed her back.

"It's OK," she soothed her. "Don't be sad. Please."

Her sympathy only made Harriet start to cry harder, and Cassie felt a chill of guilt that the cleaner had no support structure, and had endured her experience alone.

It took a few minutes for her sobs to die down and for her to regain enough control to speak.

She rubbed her face with the tissues, and Cassie handed her another bunch.

"Yes. OK, you're right. I slept with him. But you're making it sound like it was all my doing."

She turned to Cassie and stared at her through swollen, reddened eyes.

"I promise on my life it wasn't like that. That wasn't what happened at all."

"Do you want to tell me?" Cassie asked.

While Harriet was blowing her nose, Cassie brought her a glass of water from the kitchen. As she set it down on the stair beside her, she couldn't help feeling a sense of incredulity. When she knocked at the door, she'd never imagined this would happen.

"He came on to me," Harriet said.

Cassie felt cold at the words.

"Are you sure?" she asked.

"Am I sure?"

Now that she was over her tears, Harriet's spirit seemed to be returning.

"Of course I'm sure. I know when a guy comes on to me and that's what he did. He flirted with me for a couple of weeks. Suddenly he always seemed to be home when I was there, and then in the same room when I was there. Talking about how it was a marriage of convenience between him and his wife, and they were basically separated. I mean, it seemed true enough. She was hardly ever around."

Listening to Harriet's version, Cassie felt as if she'd been yanked out of reality.

How many different stories had Ryan told? It seemed he would say whatever suited his needs.

"He told me to come round for drinks on the balcony," Harriet continued. "Then he invited me down the pub. I'll tell you one thing, he knows how to make a girl fall for him. Those looks, that talk. We slept together a few times, once at his place, the rest at mine. He teased me for having green hair—it was pale green at the time. I told him I'd dye it pink and he dared me to. Then, suddenly, he wasn't there for two of my afternoons. When I arrived next time, and you were there, it was like talking to a damn stranger. It was like he'd never said, "Oh, Harriet, I'm so lonely and you're so beautiful."

She sniffed hard.

"Then I saw the way he spoke to you and I was upset. I thought you'd stolen him."

Cassie shook her head vehemently. She didn't want Harriet to believe that for a moment, although she could see why she'd thought so.

"I didn't steal him. I didn't know about any of this. He told me on the phone that he was divorced and that's why he needed help with the kids. I thought he was telling the truth. Why would he lie?"

She felt as if she was asking herself the helpless, unanswerable question, but at the same time she longed to find a logical explanation for Ryan's actions, to prove him truthful despite the weight of evidence building up against him.

Harriet shrugged. "Some people are like that, I guess. They can't help but lie."

Cassie had never thought that there were people—ordinary people—who would create a fictitious reality for no good reason when they didn't have to. She was battling to accept this truth.

Harriet sighed. "Anyway, I didn't mean to hit you with my car, just to give you a fright. I was so angry when I saw you on the road, but honest, the minute I swerved I started feeling terrible, as if I'd gone too far, as if he'd made me into a bad person and someone I wasn't."

Cassie rubbed Harriet's shoulders, understanding full well what that was all about.

"So anyway, you go for it, date him, do whatever, but you should know what he's like, and what he did to me."

"I don't want to have anything more to do with him, or even spend another night in that house," Cassie confessed. "Dating's not in the cards anyway, it's like I'm already history and nothing ever happened between us. I feel like I've been used, too. I feel completely messed up over all of this. I don't know what's true and what isn't."

Harriet's face hardened.

"Best advice I can give you? Get out of there. You don't want to be involved in that situation. He's a liar and a user. I've asked to switch shifts with one of the other cleaners, so this afternoon will be the last time I work there, and after that someone else can deal with him. I never want to walk through that door again."

Harriet climbed to her feet.

"I'd better get on. I'm really sorry about what's happened to you and I apologize again for swerving at you."

As Cassie left, she called after her.

"By the way, I meant it when I said whoever messed with your car, that wasn't me. No lies. I'd tell you if I'd done it but I didn't. That was somebody else."

CHAPTER TWENTY FOUR

A s the front door of the cozy double-story slammed behind her, Cassie felt like throwing up. Harriet's story had exposed betrayal of the worst possible kind.

She stumbled across the road and collapsed onto a concrete drain cover. It was cold and damp, and her jeans would be wet when she got up, but she didn't care.

For a few minutes she sat, staring blankly at the road, trying to take in what Harriet had said, and what it meant.

Slowly, logical thought returned.

Cassie supposed that Harriet might not have told the whole truth. For a start, Cassie thought she might be lying about having not tampered with her car. After all, swerving at someone was attempted damage, but cutting a car's wires was actual damage, and a person could get into trouble for doing it.

However, her confession about the affair, and those stormy tears, had seemed genuine. It all made sense—Harriet's instant dislike of her, competing for Ryan's attention, the way she'd snapped and stormed out when she'd realized what was going on. Cassie couldn't blame her. She knew, too, what it was like to have her world fall apart.

She had thought this home and this family to be a safe haven, after the nightmare of her previous job with Pierre Dubois.

Now she was starting to realize that Ryan's actions had actually been more damaging than Pierre's. Certainly, Ryan had been more deliberately dishonest with her than Pierre had ever been.

Cassie couldn't bear thinking about it any longer. She climbed to her feet and reluctantly turned back toward home.

Arriving back at the house, she was relieved that Ryan and Trish weren't there. She had no idea when they would be back, because they hadn't left a note, and Ryan hadn't messaged her.

Even though the house was empty, it felt filled with memories and false hopes. Each sight and smell reminded her of her dreams that she and Ryan would make it their home together.

Every time she thought about what had happened, a new wave of disbelief hit her. Her brain simply couldn't accept that everything she'd been told was a lie, and the foundation she'd built her trust on had proved to be as flimsy as a house of cards.

Thinking of cards reminded her of the magic show they'd watched on that sunny Sunday, when she'd taken the children on their first outing. She still had that damned card in her purse.

Cassie took out the paper packet the magician had given her, sealed with a sticker, and felt the shape of the card inside.

The queen of hearts, signifying love, had been gifted to her at a time when she was beginning to hope that there might be a special spark between her and Ryan.

With a sigh, she opened the packet.

Cassie stared down in consternation.

The card inside was the two of spades.

The magician hadn't given her the queen at all. His final trick had been slotting a different card inside. One that was disposable, and that he didn't need to use for his next audience.

Looking at the card, thinking of the misdirection she'd experienced right here in this house, Cassie felt sick. Harriet was right. Leaving was the only option. She didn't want to spend another night here.

She crumpled up the card and tossed it away.

With a jolt, she realized she had no idea whether Ryan had even told the truth about getting her car fixed. She'd have to hope that he had kept his word in that regard and that it was really where he'd promised to take it.

She was still worrying about the logistics of the car when Trish arrived back with the children.

"Would you look after them for the afternoon?" she asked Cassie. "I'm helping Ryan rearrange his office."

"No problem," Cassie said, giving a big fake smile that hurt her face.

Knowing that Harriet would arrive any minute for her final shift, Cassie decided that after the confessions they had shared earlier, it would be better for both of them if she wasn't home.

"Shall we go for a walk to that cake shop down the road?" she asked the children, thinking she would also take the names of the closest guesthouses, so she could plan where to go later that night.

"Good idea," Dylan agreed. "There's a bookshop inside that tearoom. They have some fun books."

Madison, however, wasn't so eager.

"I'm tired. I don't want to go out again."

Cassie bit her lip. Madison clearly had issues and Cassie was starting to worry that it was because she had worked out what Cassie and her father had been doing.

Her world would have been shattered, too. Most likely she was confused, upset, and resentful.

For all she knew, Dylan might feel the same way but was hiding it better.

"Come on Maddie," Dylan encouraged her. "The bookshop's a fun place."

Eventually, Madison agreed, and while they changed out of their school uniforms, Cassie counted her money.

She hadn't been officially paid yet, but every time Ryan had given her money for shopping, he'd told her to keep the change. There was enough to pay for lunch at the cake shop and a night at a guesthouse, and she'd be able to go into a bank tomorrow and withdraw more.

Out on the road, Cassie photographed two of the guesthouse signboards as they passed.

"It's a beautiful afternoon," she said, hoping to encourage some conversation and break through Madison's silence.

The tearoom half a mile down the hill was warm and cozy, and it had a good selection of secondhand books. Once they'd had lunch and hot chocolate, and Cassie had allowed them each a slice of carrot cake in defiance of the healthy eating rule, they spent some time sitting by the fireplace with the books they'd bought.

"What are you reading, Madison?" Cassie asked, hoping she could start up a friendly conversation.

"It's a story about a girl who goes to boarding school," Madison replied curtly.

Cassie felt at a loss. Clearly Madison was still set on the idea and she had no idea why.

"Is there a reason you want to go to boarding school?" she asked in a gentle voice.

Madison shook her head firmly.

"I can't tell you now," she said.

It was almost dark when they finally headed home. When they reached the house Cassie was relieved to find Harriet had gone.

"Glad to see you lovely people are home," Ryan called out as he heard the front door open.

"We went to the cake shop," Dylan said. "We had carrot cake and read books."

"Cake?" Trish called from the kitchen, sounding stern. "I hope it hasn't spoiled your appetite for supper. It'll be ready at six."

Cassie headed straight to her room and spent an hour packing her things. By six, she had all her bags ready and her shelves cleared. She was ready to go.

There would be only one more dinner to endure.

At the table, Madison had no appetite and Trish reprimanded her.

"You know the rules. No snacks in between meals, and no cake or sweets during the week. That's naughty, Maddie."

"It was Cassie's fault," Dylan said.

"I didn't know the rules," Cassie explained, but Trish had clearly lost interest in the discussion. With a deliberate shrug, she turned to Ryan.

"My next business trip will be finalized tomorrow. It's a European tour with a panel of scientists. They're deciding on the cities tonight. Paris, Frankfurt, and Amsterdam are definite, and it might also include Vienna, Rome, and Istanbul."

Cassie ate in silence as, once again, Trish and Ryan discussed a topic that neither she nor the children could contribute to.

She was glad when dinner was over and she could clear the plates away and head to the family room for television time. Cassie suffered through the hour, fuming with impatience for it to be over. She listened anxiously because although Ryan and Trish hadn't said they had plans to go out again, she couldn't leave the children if they did. No matter how angry she was, it would be unfair to Dylan and Madison. After all, none of this was their doing.

Cassie was reassured to hear Trish say, from the kitchen, "I'm off to bed. I have an early start tomorrow."

"I'll join you in a minute," Ryan replied.

After putting the children to bed at half past eight, it was time for Cassie to make her move. The local guesthouses didn't accept check-ins after nine p.m. and the closest one was a ten-minute walk away. It would take her longer with heavy bags in tow.

Getting the bags out of the house quietly was a major challenge. The wooden floorboards seemed to amplify the sound of luggage wheels. After wheeling her bag across the bedroom, Cassie was conscious of the unmistakable noise it made. She decided she would have to carry the bags out one by one. It would take longer, but be less risky.

Cassie opened the door and looked out.

All quiet. The hall light was off.

She grasped the heaviest bag and hefted it a few steps. It was so heavy that she had to put it down again and have a breather before doing another few steps.

Being quiet was costing her far too much time. The bag seemed to weigh more each time she picked it up, and her limbs were burning with the effort.

Eventually she was outside, and she placed the bag on the front porch, breathing hard.

She went back for the smaller bag and followed the same process.

Step by quiet step, she eased the bag out of the house.

The final journey was the easiest one, with just her purse and her shoulder bag. She paused at the bedroom door, wondering if she should leave a note, but decided not to. There would be no point. Ryan would have no difficulty in figuring out why she left. The only thing he might wonder was why she'd stayed as long as she had.

She closed the bedroom door quietly and headed down the hall for the last time.

She reached the front door, stepped through, and stood for a moment, breathing hard, watching her breath misting in the glow from the porch lantern.

The night was quiet and cloudless, with a cool, steady breeze. In the dark sky she could see stars, bright and clear. Despite the chilliness of the air, the effort of that heavy lifting had made her hot. Relieved that she could drag the bags along from here on, she pulled out their handles.

Then a click behind her made her jump. She spun round, tensing herself as the front door opened.

It was Ryan, and in that moment her carefully laid plans crumbled around her and she braced herself for the confrontation that she knew would follow.

"Cassie," he whispered. "Is everything all right? Where are you going?"

To her amazement, he didn't sound angry at all. He stared at her and all she could see in his eyes was worry and concern.

CHAPTER TWENTY FIVE

Cassie glared at Ryan, devastated that she hadn't been able to make her escape unnoticed. At the same time, she felt bitter satisfaction that she would, at least, be able to tell him what she thought of him and his lying ways.

"I'm getting the hell out of here," she whispered.

Ryan shook his head, stepping toward her.

"No, Cassie, please. Why are you going?"

He took her hand, but she couldn't bear his touch. She snatched her arm away.

"Why do you think? I'm sick of being strung along and lied to. I'm only sorry that I was stupid enough to believe you for so long."

"But..." Ryan looked at her helplessly. "I explained the situation."

"You lied to me."

Cassie stood behind her suitcase, its bulk shielding her from him. She didn't want any more of his good looks, his charming ways, or his false promises.

Ryan sighed deeply.

"Please trust me."

"Why should I?"

She shivered. It hadn't taken long for her to cool down in the chilly evening.

"Oh, Cassie."

Ryan stepped around the suitcase and the next moment, he'd wrapped his arms around her. Cassie found herself blinking tears away, because his embrace felt so strong, so familiar. It made her wish that the nightmare of the past two days had never happened, and that everything was the way it had been before.

She knew she shouldn't, but it was so easy, so safe, to lean against him and listen as he explained.

"I've been going through hell myself since Trish came back. Don't think I haven't been crippled by guilt over how this must look to you. It's a process and we are getting there. She's a difficult person and I knew if I didn't handle this right, it would turn nasty. I've been doing my best. Making her feel valued, but at the same time encouraging her to see reason, that we need to move on."

"Is that so?" Cassie wasn't sure whether to believe him.

"We have had a few chances to talk things through. She spent the afternoon at my office, rearranging things and letting me know what she wanted to take with her, because some of the furniture in the waiting area and admin rooms is hers."

"Oh, I see," Cassie said.

Relief flared inside her even though she did her best to suppress it.

"The photos, the memories, are all part of the same process. We agreed after we'd had drinks with the Robinsons that this divorce will be amicable. We have to respect what we've built and shared. For the kids, we want to do this in the least confrontational way possible."

Then Cassie remembered what she'd seen in the filing cabinet, while searching for any evidence of an upcoming divorce.

"You had a wedding anniversary and vow renewal earlier this year!" she accused him. "That's not exactly reassuring to me."

Ryan stared at her as if she was crazy.

"Cassie, who told you that?"

For a moment Cassie didn't know what to say. Now she would be the one who'd have to lie, because she couldn't tell Ryan she'd searched through his private files.

"One of the children mentioned it," she said, hoping he wouldn't ask which one or what they had said.

"That's so strange. Why would they have said that to you? Look, we did talk about it early in the year. Trish looked at venues and I think we even had invites designed. I guess, during that process, she might have told the children. When it became clear that a vow renewal wasn't on the cards, for many reasons, we canned it. If I remember, Trish was actually away over our anniversary, and I took the kids to Brighton for the day."

"Oh." Cassie felt overwhelmed by shame that she'd assumed wrong. "Perhaps I misunderstood."

"You must have done."

Then Cassie remembered what else had happened that morning.

"And what about Harriet?" She clenched her jaw and stared up at him, daring him to prove her wrong.

"What about her?"

"She said you two slept together!"

Cassie felt herself tensing in his embrace as she waited for his response. But instead of an outraged denial, Ryan started to laugh.

"No way! She never said that to you! Please, Cassie, tell me you didn't believe her."

Cassie remembered she'd doubted some of what Harriet had said, but not that.

"I believed her. She was genuinely devastated."

"Well, it seems to be her modus operandi, as I found out yesterday." Ryan's voice was hard.

"Her modus operandi? What do you mean?"

"The Robinsons also hired her for a few months. Vaughan told me over drinks that she stole a number of valuables from their home during that time. When his wife confronted her, Harriet burst into screaming hysterics and said that Vaughan had made passes at her and that she wasn't comfortable working for them any longer, and was considering pressing charges."

"Really?"

Cassie was disturbed by how plausible this sounded.

"Given that she'd already asked me out to the pub, and that Trish couldn't find her gold bracelet yesterday, I decided to nip this in the bud. I called the agency first thing today and asked if they could send someone else. Unfortunately they could only make the change from Friday, but we locked the jewelry away while she was here. I'm glad you'll no longer have to put up with her rudeness—it was unacceptable and out of line."

"Oh. Wow."

Cassie didn't know what to say. It seemed that Ryan had canceled Harriet and not the other way round.

It was a possibility. Everything he'd said made sense. Cassie felt utterly confused. It was like looking through two ends of a tunnel and seeing two completely different scenarios inside.

Ryan gently released her and smoothed her hair back from her face. The wind was getting stronger and it was becoming bitingly cold.

"Please, angel, can I help you carry your bags back inside?"

"OK," Cassie agreed.

In a couple of minutes, her bags were stowed in her bedroom again.

She thought Ryan would leave her then, but instead he reached into his jacket pocket.

"You might have wondered how I knew you had gone. It was because I came to find you. I wanted to apologize for what you've been through, and explain that it's been part of a necessary process. Also, I wanted to give you this."

To Cassie's amazement, he produced a large, square velvet box from the inner pocket of his jacket.

She opened it, and even though she'd been trying not to show any emotion or surprise, she caught her breath as she looked down.

Inside was an exquisite diamond necklace.

"I chose it for you today. I wanted you to know beyond doubt how much you mean to me. This is how much I value you. It's a gift that comes with my heartfelt apology for what you've been through, and with my commitment that we will be together soon."

Ryan spoke softly in a serious voice.

Cassie stared down at the diamonds, watching the stones flash with color where their facets reflected the hallway light.

"It's beautiful," she breathed.

"Wait till you see it in sunlight. It's magnificent. Most of all, Cassie, most importantly, it's given with my love."

Cassie stood still, holding the box tightly, unable to believe what she'd just heard, because he'd said he loved her.

"Please, will you stay awhile longer? Just so that I can prove to you that what I've said now is the truth?"

Cassie's mind was reeling. It was possible that she'd believed alternative versions, which were lies, and that Ryan had meant what he said. Didn't they say actions spoke louder than words? The gift of this exquisite piece of jewelry was proof of commitment.

"I'll stay," she promised him.

Ryan's face softened in relief. He drew her into his arms and kissed her deeply, and as Cassie responded with all the suppressed passion she'd been feeling, she realized her eyes were wet with tears.

CHAPTER TWENTY SIX

The next morning, Cassie had thought she would wake up full of hope. Instead, as soon as she raised her head, she felt nauseous. Her stomach was churning and tender, and she felt leaden with exhaustion.

"Ugh," she said. She sat on her bed and doubled over, hoping that the queasiness would subside, but even the smell of coffee and toast wafting through from the kitchen seemed to be making it worse.

What had Trish cooked last night? Could the food have been off? Cassie wondered. In that case, the whole family would feel unwell.

Then a horrific thought occurred to her, which turned her blood to ice.

She could be pregnant.

What if she was?

Cassie closed her eyes, powerless to reason with herself and to stop her imagination from running away with worst-case scenarios.

She had never felt such fear. This brought home to her, in the most brutal and inescapable way, that her actions had consequences.

She had to check as soon as possible, because she needed to know.

She decided to ride the bus to town with the children. She could stop off at the pharmacy and pick up a test, and if she was lucky she might even be able to catch another bus back.

There was no way she could join the family for breakfast. Not the way she felt now, and definitely not after what had happened last night.

She wanted to spend the rest of the day in her room, staring at the necklace Ryan had given her, thinking of the words he'd whispered to her the previous night, and trying to convince herself that everything was going to be OK. She couldn't bear anything to shatter the fragile hope she'd regained.

Slowly, Cassie got dressed, made sure there was some money in her coat pocket, and joined the children outside when it was time to catch the bus.

She hadn't thought she would see them today at all and it felt strange to be continuing as normal, when she had imagined she would be holed up in a guesthouse and planning her escape from town.

"Are you coming with us?" Madison asked curiously, as Cassie took money out of her purse when the bus approached.

"I'm going to a shop," she said.

"Who's going to pick us up from school?" Madison asked after they had boarded the bus.

"I don't know. I guess your mother will," Cassie said.

She noticed that Madison didn't brighten when she said that, as she'd expected her to. Instead she frowned.

"Mum said she was going away."

Cassie's heart leaped.

This was it, at last—the moment that Ryan had promised and that she'd been waiting for. Hope surged in her as she realized that there was an end in sight to this living hell, and that it would be sooner than she'd expected.

He hadn't lied.

That necklace had come with a proper certificate, saying that the diamonds were genuine. You didn't give genuine diamonds to somebody unless you cared. After all, diamonds were forever. They were a symbol of true love.

"Then I guess I'll pick you up," she said to Madison.

"Yay." Madison's face brightened.

Cassie felt confused, wondering if she had misinterpreted the young girl's behavior all along. Could it be that Madison was upset about her mother being home?

For now, she had bigger worries on her plate, and her nausea flooded back as she remembered why she was heading to town.

To be pregnant now would be an absolute catastrophe.

In the pharmacy, Cassie searched for a while without success before realizing that the tests were behind the counter, where she would have to ask for them. That meant she had to wait until the shop was empty of customers. Then she sidled up to the pharmacist.

"Please, could I have a pregnancy test?" she asked.

"What kind, love?"

Cassie didn't know. She wasn't aware there were different kinds. Surely pregnancy was pregnancy?

"The cheapest one will be fine," she said.

She paid for it hurriedly and stashed the box inside her coat.

The bus was only due in an hour, so Cassie walked back, feeling better after being out in the fresh, crisp air. Even so, as she approached the house, her nervousness about the pregnancy test returned.

As soon as she got into the house, she rushed to the bathroom.

From down the corridor, she heard Ryan's voice, filled with concern and understanding.

"Are you all packed up, Trish, love? You have everything?"

Hope buoyed her as she heard his words. It was happening. After a rollercoaster ride where she'd started believing her happiness was false and her reality was based on lies, it was all unfolding as Ryan had promised.

She locked herself in the bathroom and opened the box with shaking hands. This was the only thing that could still complicate the situation. Cassie prayed that it was a false alarm, and her sudden nausea had been due to stress, or else just a stomach bug.

She read the instructions carefully before squatting over the toilet, holding the test clumsily in her unsteady hand.

At that moment there was a loud knock on the bathroom door.

"Cassie?" Ryan called, sounding anxious. "You in there?"

In her fright, Cassie dropped the test stick into the toilet bowl.

She fumbled for it in a panic.

"Cassie?" Ryan called again.

"Yes, I'm here. I'll just be a moment."

What an embarrassing disaster. She dried the stick as best she could with toilet paper before trying again. The test had said wait two minutes, but she couldn't keep Ryan waiting.

Since she couldn't exactly come out holding it, she wrapped it up in more tissue and hid it in the bathroom cupboard.

Then, feeling sick with nerves and anticipation, she opened the door.

"Good morning, Cassie."

Ryan sounded as cheerful as ever, and she picked up from his formal tone that Trish was nearby.

She waited, heart pounding, for him to announce the news that Trish was leaving.

Then he looked around.

"Ah, darling, you're all set?"

Trish walked past, carrying an outsize shoulder bag—but where was her suitcase? This wasn't the departure that Cassie had expected.

Ryan caught Trish around her waist as she passed and pulled her close for a tender kiss.

Cassie felt her world shatter all over again. What the hell was happening?

Trish looked immaculate as always. Her hair was perfectly blow-dried, and she was wearing navy jeans and a crimson coat.

"See you in the car," she said, squeezing Ryan's arm as Cassie gaped in consternation. Her perfume lingered in the air as she passed.

"We're heading out to the countryside today. A combination of work and play," Ryan told her, and Cassie couldn't believe the casual way he announced it.

"We're going to visit one of the area's most famous vineyards—with a view to holding one of Trish's events there. So it's all tax-deductible research." Ryan winked at her.

"What about the children?"

"You can use Trish's car for the school run. Everything's on the timetable as usual. Here are the keys."

Ryan handed her the keys to the smart black Volvo.

He glanced behind him, and Cassie realized that he must be checking whether Trish was watching.

Then he leaned close to her and whispered in her ear.

"Everything will be OK. I promise you. This is the last hurdle. I need you to trust me, Cassie."

He hand cupped her face, and before she could summon the strength she needed to push him away, he kissed her, deep and lingering.

"My beautiful," he whispered.

Cassie could smell Trish's perfume on his skin.

As Ryan walked away, Cassie wanted to vomit. Her nausea flooded back and she swallowed hard, leaning against the wall.

She was about to run into the bathroom and try to throw up in the hope it would make her feel better, when she realized that Ryan and Trish hadn't yet left. They seemed to be having an altercation outside—or at any rate, a spirited argument.

Then she heard the click of heels, and Trish marched down the hall toward her.

"Please give me those keys," she said. "No offense, but I'm not willing to allow anyone except Ryan and me to drive the Volvo. Here are the Land Rover's keys. You can use it to fetch and carry the kids."

She held out her hand and Cassie gave her the car keys, accepting the others in return.

A moment later the front door slammed and she heard the purr of the Volvo pulling away.

In the blink of an eye, everything had changed.

Ryan's reassurances seemed worthless now. Her sense of security had evaporated and she knew that deeply, instinctively, she had never believed his version.

She was back where she'd been the previous day.

The only difference was that she now had the additional worry that she might be pregnant, which made her predicament a thousand times worse.

Cassie headed back to the bathroom and unwrapped the pregnancy test. Her hands were so shaky that she almost dropped it again.

Taking a deep breath and steeling herself for the worst, she stared down at the test.

CHAPTER TWENTY SEVEN

Peering at the window of the pregnancy test, Cassie frowned.

According to the instructions, there should be either one or two lines in the window. One would mean she was not pregnant and two would mean she was.

Instead, the window was gray and blurred and there were no lines visible at all. It shouldn't be like that, and it must mean that the test had malfunctioned.

Cassie let out a gasp of frustration.

She'd messed it up by dropping it in the toilet bowl, and now she would have to go back and buy another test. She could do it on the way to fetch the children. Probably, she should buy two, just in case, because she couldn't keep going back to the damned pharmacy. This was a small town and people would remember her. Cassie could imagine the gossip.

"The girl with the auburn waves came back three times for tests. Three times! I'm sure I've seen her in town before. Who does she work for?"

Cassie felt shredded by stress. She hadn't realized how much Ryan's support had meant until it had been torn away. Now she was entirely alone. There was nobody she could talk to or trust, and she couldn't hold back the tears.

She lay prone on the bed and sobbed. She was roused a few minutes later by the ringing of the landline.

She climbed off the bed, scrubbing her eyes as she made her way to the hall.

"Hello, Ellis residence," she said.

"Is that Mrs. Ellis?"

"No—no. She's just left. It's Cassie speaking. Can I help you?"

"It's the school secretary phoning. We've had a small fire break out in one of the classrooms, due to an electrical short. Nobody has been hurt and the fire is under control, but there's a lot of smoke in the building. We're calling to ask you to collect your children immediately. School will be closed tomorrow while we effect the repairs and ensure the air quality complies with the required standards."

"All right. I will."

"Your promptness will be appreciated. Thank you, ma'am."

Damn, Cassie thought. So much for purchasing the next pregnancy test at her leisure. She'd have to ask the children to wait in the car while she ran in and grabbed it.

She wondered if she should tell Ryan about the fire and decided to wait until the children were home. When she checked her phone as she was about to leave the house, she was astonished to find a text from him.

"We've decided to make our trip an overnight stay. You can expect us back late tomorrow. Thanks—R."

Overnight stay?

Cassie's jaw clenched so hard as she read the words, she thought her teeth might break.

This wasn't ending things. Quite the contrary. From this text it was clear that Ryan and Trish's relationship was business as usual, and the lighthearted message was just rubbing her face in it.

"Screw you, you bastard," she muttered as she put her phone away, remembering that these were the exact words that Harriet had spat at Ryan on her way out.

Cassie realized there was no worse feeling than being the victim of a serial liar. It had annihilated her self-worth and left her feeling cheap and completely disposable. She wondered if she would ever be able to trust again, after having been deceived so badly.

Outside the school's entry gate, it was organized chaos. Two traffic police had been deployed to manage the influx of cars. A fire engine was still parked outside the building, even though Cassie could see no smoke or flames.

Dylan and Madison ran over to the Land Rover and seemed pleased that she was behind the wheel.

"We had such fun, Cassie," Madison said. "We didn't get to do any lessons today. It was thrilling. It was a real fire drill, for a real fire."

"The fire started in our classroom. There was so much smoke, we could hardly see the door," Dylan added.

"That sounds exciting, but a fire is always serious so I'm glad you're OK and that you stayed calm. We're going to stop by the pharmacy on the way as I need to pick up something."

She was able to find a parking space just around the corner.

"I won't be a minute," she told the children before rushing inside.

The attendant recognized her.

"Back again?" she asked as Cassie gritted her teeth.

"The test didn't work. I messed it up. I need another, please."

"How long is it since your missed period?" the attendant asked, turning to the boxes.

"I—er." Cassie's mind whirled and for a moment she couldn't remember. "No, I haven't missed it yet. It's due in a couple of days, but I've been feeling sick and wanted to make sure."

"You want the early detection one, then. It should give results as early as five days before your period. There are two brands here—which one?"

"Whichever's cheaper," Cassie said faintly.

The woman slid the box across the counter.

To her horror, Cassie noticed that Dylan had come into the shop. He was standing nearby looking at something on the shelves and she had no idea how much he'd overheard.

She started shaking, fumbling the coins and dropping a pound coin so that she had to scrabble for it on the floor.

Dylan walked over to the counter.

"Could you buy me something for my throat? It's sore from the smoke."

"Yes, yes, of course."

Cassie turned back to the attendant, praying the woman wouldn't mention the pregnancy test, or recognize Dylan.

She saw her frown, as if she were trying to place him.

"Were you in the class with the fire? We've already had two others come in complaining of sore throats. I recommend these tablets and this syrup."

She pushed a packet and a bottle across the counter.

"They should sort you out, soothe your throat, manage the pain and any coughing, and you'll be as good as new tomorrow."

"What about that one?" Dylan asked, pointing to a product high on the shelf behind her.

"Which one?" The woman turned and, after a few false tries, found the packet Dylan was indicating.

"Oh, no, love, those are straight painkillers. The syrup I gave you actually contains painkillers, as well as chest decongestants. So the syrup is better."

"OK, thanks."

Cassie paid for the medications and left the shop, and the chatty attendant, as quickly as she could. As soon as she got to the car, she opened the lid in the central console and quickly stashed the bag with the pregnancy test inside.

She drove home, with the children still rehashing what had clearly been the most exciting school day of their lives, and decided it would be better to leave the test in the car and come back for it later in the evening. That way, the children wouldn't notice.

Cassie went straight to the kitchen and pulled together an early lunch for the children, since Dylan's medication had to be taken with food.

She felt exhausted by the stress of the day and still in utter disbelief that Ryan could have sent her that text; such a blatant confession that he'd lied, and had no intention of leaving his wife.

Cassie was starting to suspect that he'd strung her along in order that she would willingly fit in with the plans he'd already made with Trish.

The fact her car was disabled hadn't helped either. If the car had been drivable, Cassie was sure she would have left by now. She wouldn't be stranded here, needing to wait till it was fixed.

Thinking about the car, Cassie felt like kicking herself. Last night, when Ryan was giving her gifts and whispering those meaningless sweet nothings in her ear, she could have asked him about it. Instead of empty promises, she could have had actual information on the progress of her car's repairs.

"Lunch is ready," she called to the children.

She hurried to the bathroom, but as she walked in she stopped dead.

Cassie felt dizzy with confusion. She must be going mad, and starting to do things without remembering them, because right there, on the bathroom counter, was a pregnancy test.

This was insane. How could she have brought it inside and left it out in full view on the counter? She remembered putting it away in the car's cubbyhole and being careful not to open it as she hadn't wanted the children to see.

Now here it was—but looking more closely, Cassie saw it wasn't.

This was the more expensive version, the better of the two brands, the one she hadn't chosen. There was no logical way that this item should be here at all.

She jumped as behind her, Dylan spoke, his voice filled with triumph.

"I stole it for you," he said.

CHAPTER TWENTY EIGHT

Cassie dropped the test on the counter and whirled round to face Dylan, appalled.

"What? You did what? Dylan, this is insanity! How did you—"

He stood in the doorway, smiling slightly, looking completely unfazed.

"I heard you asking for it and saying that the last one hadn't worked. So I stole you another one. I've been practicing. You see, I used misdirection so that you and the attendant looked at the top shelf. Then you weren't noticing my hands, so I grabbed a test for you. It was easy, really."

Madison spoke from behind Dylan.

"Move over. I can't see. What's happening? What did you do?"

Cassie clapped her hand over her mouth as Madison pushed into the doorway next to Dylan.

"Did you steal something else?" she asked.

Her gaze focused on the pregnancy test, even as Cassie snatched it up.

"What's that?"

"Nothing. It's—" Cassie began, her voice squeaky with panic, but Dylan interrupted.

"It's a pregnancy test, Maddie. It's what you take to find out if you are going to have a baby."

Even though he'd claimed to be helping Cassie, Dylan sounded gleeful as he informed Madison of the facts.

"Why would Cassie be having a baby?"

"Well, let me see," Dylan began. "Shall I explain? I'm not sure you would understand."

Abruptly, Cassie snapped. "Stop it!" she screamed, so loud that Madison took a step back.

"Dylan, you will not behave like this. Stop taunting Madison. It's not fair and it is not kind. And I am furious with you. You know the rules on stealing. I told you, you're not allowed to. Not for me, not for anyone, not just because you can. You're going to get into so much trouble. This is putting your entire future at risk. You have to stop doing it. Now!"

Cassie felt lightheaded after her outburst—with rage, and also because she'd been hyperventilating.

Dylan's lips were clamped together and he was looking just as angry as her. Staring at his face—those blank eyes and that shut-down expression—she felt a thrill of fear.

"Go to your room," she ordered, trying not to show him how afraid she was. "I'll speak to you in a minute."

She had no idea whether he would do as she asked, or even listen to her at all, but after a pause that felt like an eternity, he turned and walked away. Cassie let out a shaky breath, bitterly regretting her outburst.

"What is that thing, Cassie?" Madison asked again. She sounded tearful but her voice was full of determination.

"It's a test women can do, to find out if they are having a baby," Cassie said, knowing that her response was pathetically incomplete, but she had no idea how much Madison knew about the facts of life and this was certainly not the time or place to enlighten her.

"How do you tell?" Madison sounded worried.

"You pee on the stick," Cassie told her. "Your pee is different if you're going to have a baby, and the stick can tell the difference."

"So why did you take the test?"

"Because I wasn't feeling well, and I wanted to check this wasn't the reason."

"Do I need to take it?" Madison looked worried. "I was feeling sick yesterday. Mum's food always makes me ill."

"No, no, feeling sick from food is different. Besides, you can only take this test when you're older," Cassie said.

"Oh."

Madison still sounded confused but Cassie thought she had managed to give her enough information for the subject to have lost its fascination.

"Maddie, you can choose supper tonight," Cassie said. "Go and have a look in the kitchen and decide what you'd like me to cook."

"OK. I will."

Brightening up, Madison turned and left the bathroom.

Cassie collapsed on the edge of the bath and buried her face in her hands.

Madison's honesty and outspokenness meant that she was like an echo chamber. The chances of her mentioning this, or repeating what Cassie had said, in front of her parents were extremely high. In fact, it was a certainty.

Never mind that she'd told Ryan she'd been single for months; Cassie knew she'd better dream up an alternative story about an ex-boyfriend she'd met up with while in London.

This bare-faced lie would be essential to prevent Trish from suspecting the truth.

The problem was that it wouldn't wash with Dylan.

He knew what the pregnancy test was and he'd seen her going to Ryan's bedroom in the night. Dylan knew exactly what was going on, and by screaming at him, Cassie had made him angry. Dylan held all the cards now, and she could only imagine what his revenge might be.

She couldn't use the threat of telling his father about this theft. Cassie was sure Dylan knew exactly why she wouldn't do that now.

When Cassie knocked on his door, hoping to smooth things over, Dylan refused to answer.

There was no lock on the inside. She could have flung the door open and marched in and demanded that they discuss this. But she decided not to, because it would only make Dylan angrier.

Instead, she said, softly, "Dylan, I'm sorry I shouted. We need to talk about this. Tell me when you're ready."

Cassie waited, hoping for an answer, but when none came she turned away, feeling cold with fear and utterly alone.

She headed to the kitchen, unable to stop thinking about the furious words she'd screamed at Dylan, and the way he had shut down; his face blank and immobile, his eyes emotionless.

She should never have snapped at him that way. His behavior had proved to her that he was not normal emotionally, and that he would make a dangerous adversary. The only reason she had lost control was that she was petrified by the consequences of a pregnancy.

Her emotions felt like a toxic melting pot, and she'd let them all out on the one person who, in his own twisted way, had been trying to help her.

She'd had one ally in this house. Now, thanks to her own actions, she had nobody.

She heard his bedroom door open a few minutes later, but he didn't speak to her or come through to the kitchen. Instead, he headed outside and when she hurried after him, she found he had set off into the darkening evening on his bicycle.

Now, worry about him was added to her emotional burden. She had no idea which direction he'd gone, and doubted whether he should be riding so late. If he wasn't back by the time it was fully dark, she'd have to go out and look for him.

In the meantime, Cassie started preparing the roast chicken that Madison had asked for, but she was so distracted that she got the oven settings totally wrong.

When she opened the oven, black smoke billowed out.

The bird was charred on top, but when she carved it, she found it was still raw and bloody inside.

"Oh, hell," she said, staring down at the inedible meat, thinking of Madison's disappointment and her own incompetence.

She should have ordered takeout. Why had she attempted to cook when she was so distracted, and when she felt actual physical pain visualizing Ryan and Trish on their overnight trip?

She knew they were together as a couple; this was no "business trip." She had seen it in their looks, their touches, how he'd kissed her, and the way they had flirted and romanced in front of her.

What were they doing now? Heading into early evening they would be inside, perhaps having a private wine tasting. She imagined them seated at a table near a roaring fire, their legs brushing, their hands clasping from time to time. She imagined how Ryan was looking at Trish, and the expression in his eyes, and how they would talk and laugh, sharing in-jokes that were part of their own private language after more than a decade of married life.

And here she was, her sanity unraveling, with a ruined meal and children who hated her and a whole world of fears pressing down on her shoulders.

Cassie collapsed onto a chair, buried her face in her hands, and sobbed.

It felt like hours later, but was probably only a few minutes, when she heard the front door slam. Knowing Dylan was back forced her to pick herself up and carry on. She sensed it would be foolish to show weakness in front of him, and worse to show fear, no matter how she was shaking inside.

"Hello, Dylan," she called out, and felt enormous relief when he called back a casual "Hi."

This small encouragement gave her the strength of will she needed.

She could not let this family destroy her.

As soon as Ryan got back, she would be free to leave, and this time, she wouldn't allow herself to be swayed by any of his lies.

The chicken was salvageable. If she cut off the burnt part and put the rest back in a lower oven, it should be edible.

Meanwhile, Cassie decided, she was going to use the gift that Dylan had given her. As it was the most reliable pregnancy test, she was going to take it right now, so that one way or another, she wouldn't have the uncertainty of not knowing.

Back in the bathroom, she held the stick carefully and this time she followed the instructions to the letter, waiting the full two minutes before looking down.

To her utter relief, the test was a clear negative.

Cassie breathed out a sigh that seemed to take all of her tension away with it. This test wouldn't be wrong, because it was the most accurate one.

Finally things were starting to move in her favor.

Cassie woke the following morning feeling confident about her decision. She would not believe another word Ryan said to her. All she was doing was annihilating her own self-esteem. No matter what he said or did, she was going to walk out as soon as they got back.

Cassie played a board game with the children before lunch, and when the rain cleared in the afternoon, they went for a walk down the path to the beach. Dylan seemed to have warmed to her again, and she hoped that he'd understood that she'd lost her temper, and had accepted her apology.

As the hours went by and there was still no sign of Ryan and Trish, she started to wonder when exactly they were planning to arrive. Ryan had said "late," but what did that mean? She'd assumed it meant late afternoon, but five o'clock came and went with no word from him. Exactly how long were they planning to extend this loving little jaunt?

Cassie fumed and fretted, repacking her bags as the evening drew in. She wanted to get her departure over and done with. No kind words, no kisses, no diamond necklaces could change her mind this time. She'd seen Ryan for what he was—a pathological liar who'd strung her along because it suited his plans.

It was only when she was finishing off her packing that she remembered the other test—the one she'd bought—was still in the Land Rover's cubbyhole. Tempting as it was to leave it there and hope that it might prove an interesting conversation point for Ryan and Trish at some future date, Cassie decided it would be better to remove it.

She headed out to the garage and opened the cubbyhole in the central console. The test had fallen right to the bottom, and when she rummaged in the cubbyhole's dark interior, the first thing she pulled out was a pair of wire cutters.

She placed them on the seat and delved into the cubbyhole again.

This time she pulled out a short knife.

Now she could feel the plastic bag containing the test—but there was something else there, as well. What was it?

Cassie pulled out the test bag and then scrabbled with her fingers, picking up the small, sharp items she could feel there.

She took them out and stared at them, dumbfounded.

They were fragments of wire.

The last time she'd seen wire of this color and size had been when she'd been staring down into her car's open hood.

Cassie felt dizzy with horrified realization.

No wonder it had been so easy for her to agree to stay on, and to accept Ryan's lies about Trish. Being stranded, and dependent on him to fix her car, had been the main reason for that.

He'd trapped her here, forcing her to rely on his helpfulness by cutting the wires in the first place. With his wife due to fly back, he'd needed a contingency plan. He must have gone out after her and driven behind her to the hardware store.

She'd left her car unlocked, but if she hadn't, she was sure he would have done something different—slashed two of the tires, perhaps.

One way or another, he'd devised a foolproof plan to force her into staying.

She'd been manipulated by him without even realizing it.

Chapter Twenty Nine

A s the reality of what Ryan had done sunk in, Cassie was filled with a fury so huge that she couldn't think straight.

He had sabotaged her car to make sure she couldn't leave. He'd been using her this entire time. Seeing she was vulnerable, he'd trapped her in a spider's web of lies and deceit, so that he could get everything he wanted from her.

With shaking hands, Cassie put the incriminating objects back in the cubbyhole and hid the unused pregnancy test in her suitcase.

She made supper for the children and even managed to eat a few bites herself. She felt far too emotionally drained for cheery conversation, but in any case, the mood at the table seemed somber. Madison didn't speak a word and Dylan paged through a cycling magazine while he ate.

Staring at the opposite wall, Cassie put the finishing touches to her exit strategy.

Both the children possessed damaging information about what had happened and they could reveal it at any time. Madison would do so innocently, but if Dylan said anything, it would be deliberate.

Let them drop the bombshells when she was safely out of here. It might even occur while they were enjoying a lively discussion about current events over the dinner table, and Ryan could lie to his heart's content as he tried to wriggle out of it.

As the evening drew on, Cassie started to wonder if they had booked at the wine farm for another night and hadn't bothered to tell her.

She even wondered briefly if they'd had an accident on the way home.

After their hour of television she put the children to bed and packed the last of her belongings away. It gave her a bitter satisfaction to see her shelves totally clear.

"Screw you, Ryan," she whispered as she zipped up her suitcase.

As the minutes ticked by, Cassie realized in frustration that she was going to be stuck here for the night, because it would be too late to book in at one of the nearby guesthouses. Her plan had been to leave immediately, but that wouldn't be possible now.

It was close to ten p.m. when she heard the front door burst open.

With a babble of laughter, Trish and Ryan entered the house.

"You are so, so, so bad," she heard Trish giggle. "Was it really necessary to stop at our pub? A bottle of champagne, yes, well and good, but the brandies? Whose idea was that?"

She giggled loudly and hiccupped. She sounded very drunk.

"The champagne was my idea, the cognac was yours. Come on, my lovely, time to get you into bed now."

Ryan didn't sound entirely sober himself.

Cassie opened her door and stepped out into the corridor.

There they were. Ryan had their bags in one hand, and was holding Trish's hand in his other. She was leaning on him and laughing.

"Hello there, Cassie. You still up? Everything good here? Kiddies all in bed?" Ryan said.

"Everything's fine."

She stared at Ryan as they passed, wondering if he had any idea how much she hated him.

He'd destroyed her emotionally, but would walk away from this debacle squeaky clean. He'd carry on with his privileged life, and his perfect family, his beautiful house and expensive cars, doing what he wanted, screwing who he wanted. Smoothing his way with lies, with no heed for the devastation he caused.

In that moment, Cassie changed her mind. She wasn't going to walk out. Before she left in the morning, she would have her say to both of them. She wordlessly reentered her room.

A few minutes later, a tap on her door made her jump.

"Hello, beautiful," Ryan whispered.

Cassie stared at him, incredulous.

How could he possibly be continuing this farce? Was he deluded?

Clearly he was—grinning at her from the doorway like nothing was wrong at all.

"Trish is asleep. Are you coming out for a nightcap?" he asked.

"No," she hissed, and turned her back on him.

Then she felt his hand on her shoulders, massaging her in a way that previously would have sent a flood of desire and happiness through her. Now his touch revolted her and she flinched away.

"Just one drink. Come on. I've missed you. I need to talk to you."

"All right," she said.

If he wanted talk, he would have it. She wouldn't be shy about what she was planning to say.

She grabbed her jacket—the gloves were packed—and followed him down the corridor.

When they were out of earshot of the bedrooms, he began to talk in a normal voice, as if nothing was wrong.

"There's a storm brewing. You can't see it from this side; it's approaching from the other way. The lightning was incredible coming back. We might only have time for one quick drink outside, but it'll be worth it for the spectacle—and the rain will be blowing over the balcony."

Cassie followed in silence as he collected a bottle and glasses from the kitchen.

Outside, the wind was starting to gust, but as he'd said, due to the storm's direction, the balcony was sheltered. The waves were crashing onto shore and in the faint ambient light she could just see the white crests of the breakers.

This would be the last time she'd sit out here. Thinking about all the other times, what he'd said to her and what she'd believed, filled her with rage all over again.

"My gorgeous, I've missed you so. Has everything been well here?"

Ryan moved his chair closer to hers and handed her a glass.

Cassie downed half of it in one gulp.

"Firstly, I'm not your gorgeous."

He stared at her, eyebrows raised, genuine puzzlement in his eyes.

"What do you mean? Is something wrong?"

How had she ever believed him? Looking at him now, Cassie couldn't comprehend how badly she'd allowed herself to be misled.

"Ryan, I've had enough of your games. It's perfectly clear you're not trying to get a divorce."

He sighed.

"Cassie, don't be like this. Please. This is difficult enough for me as it is. Do you know—"

"Oh, spare me!"

She saw his face change as he picked up the blunt sarcasm in her tone, but she continued in full tirade.

"What are you going to say? 'It's so hard for me having to nurse Trish through this divorce. Oh, Cassie, please understand.'

"Well, Ryan, I do understand. The only difficult thing for you right now is coordinating your stories, because there is no divorce. There isn't, there never was, it's all just a complete bullshit story. You're a liar, Ryan. A compulsive, dangerous liar and even your children know it. You've been stringing me along in so many ways and I believed you because I'd never met anyone like you before, and it took me a while to work out that people could actually be as blatantly two-faced as you."

"Cassie, stop it!"

Ryan's face was flushed with rage. In that moment she couldn't believe how ugly he looked, with his narrowed eyes and twisted, snarling mouth.

Cassie slammed her glass down before continuing.

"I happened to open your car's cubbyhole. What a shame you hadn't had time to move the wire cutters you used to disable my car. I should have realized what a coincidence it was that my car was sabotaged the day before your wife came back. You were making sure you'd have an on-site babysitter for your romantic jaunts. Definitely a good way to stop me from leaving in a huff—especially since you were the hero of the day and said you'd look after me. Ryan, I have the utmost contempt for you. You should seek professional help to deal with your psychological problem. Maybe they can fix you."

Cassie spat out the words.

"I'm leaving first thing tomorrow, and before I go, I'm going to bring your dear wife up to date on what's been happening here. She and I can have a chat over a nice cup of coffee so that she knows exactly what kind of a pathological liar she married."

Lightning flashed above the ocean and a thunderclap shook the whole house.

As she turned, Ryan grabbed her arm, and Cassie shrieked as he yanked her back. His fingers closed around her bicep, clamping hard, and she felt a sudden thrill of fear.

Had she thought he'd just lie down and accept this?

"You will not," he spat at her. "And I'll tell you why. If you say one word to my wife about this—if you even hint at it—I'm going to report you for child abuse."

Cassie stared at him, horrified. Report her for abuse? What was he talking about?

Ryan raised his voice, almost shouting, and Cassie realized that he was far angrier than she'd realized.

"For child abuse. I will call the social workers to come and examine the children and they will find bruises. There will be evidence for them to see, I promise you that."

She stared at him, appalled by what he was implying—that he would hurt them, and blame it on her. How could a father do such a thing to his own children? This wasn't a joke, he wasn't saying it lightly. He was stating it as fact.

Cassie didn't want to speak another word to him. If it had been her own safety at stake, she wouldn't have tried, but now that he'd threatened Dylan and Madison, she had to stand up for them.

"Ryan, please, not your own children! You can't—" she began.

Enraged, he shouted her down, with her arm still trapped in his vise-like grip.

"I can and I will. While we're about it, I'll be shocked to discover that you don't have the correct work permit. I'll tell them you lied to me and I'll cooperate fully to have you penalized, fined, and deported—after you've served your jail time for the abuse."

Cassie had no words left. The extent of his threats had silenced her. What he'd said was beyond shocking; she felt crushed by the viciousness of his intent.

Lightning flashed, brightening the scene in blue-white for an eerie moment.

Ryan continued in a quieter tone.

"You stupid little girl. If you think you are going to do anything to compromise my plans, you are wrong. Trish is loaning my business a large amount of cash, and I'm not letting anything jeopardize this. Particularly not your hysterical behavior. There will be no complaining, no doing anything except what you've been hired to do. You will shut up and grow up, and keep the children happy until I tell you that you can leave. Understand?"

She couldn't speak, but managed a nod.

"So for now, you—are going—nowhere."

Ryan gave a final wrench of her arm before releasing it so suddenly Cassie nearly fell over.

Her arm was throbbing, and all she could think of was getting away from him. She staggered back, found her balance, and fumbled her way through the glass doors and back into the safety of the family room.

Her breath was coming in sharp, ragged sobs.

She was petrified by the violent side Ryan had revealed. Under that handsome, charming façade lurked a pathological liar who was prepared to do anything—threaten, damage, and harm—to protect himself.

What had the children gone through in the past? Had Ryan hurt them before? How could she defend them when she herself was an illegal worker who was now being threatened with deportation?

Cassie knew she had to find a way to handle this situation, for the children's safety, to prevent Ryan from following through on his appalling threats, but she feared it was too late. She'd lost control of the situation, and whatever trust he'd had in her was gone.

She should have remembered Dylan's warning, that his dad got "weird" when you tried to call him out on a lie.

Weird was an understatement. Ryan had become totally sociopathic.

What an utter fool she'd been to believe him, to fall for him, and what an idiot she'd been to think she could have the last word.

All she had done was reveal her hand, and now he had her in his power.

CHAPTER THIRTY

Cassie was hiding under the bed, her hand tightly clasped in Jacqui's. They could hear her father in the room downstairs. He was on the rampage, as Jacqui called it. Cassie didn't know exactly what that meant, but she knew it sounded scary. It explained why it was important that they hide, because the word was threatening and evil, just like his actions.

Rampage.

It meant shouting, swearing, the smashing of glass, and Cassie knew the next day they would have to walk carefully, because the splinters could hide, sharp and deadly. She could be walking, or kneel down, only to find a piece of glass sliding into her skin, invisible apart from the pain and the dark welling of blood.

"We'll be OK if we can reach the sea," Cassie whispered.

"Yes," Jacqui replied.

Over the commotion, Cassie could hear the sea; the constant sighing of surf, even though she knew it was nowhere near their small apartment. The wind must be in the right direction because she could smell it, too.

She could hear something else now; the tramp of heavy footsteps that meant her father was coming upstairs, and she squeezed Jacqui's hand more tightly, shrinking back into that dark, claustrophobic place between the bed and the wall.

"He's going to hurt us this time," she whispered. Helplessness para- lyzed her as she thought about how big he was; how his angry presence would seem to fill the room as he burst inside, and how strong he could be when he was drunk.

"We need to get out," Jacqui said.

"He's coming. There's no time."

"There's time if we're quick. Follow me."

She dragged Cassie out from the bed and over to the windowsill. The room was gloomy and the footsteps sounded louder. Her father must be right outside the door, and Cassie felt exposed. The room was freezing. The window was wide open and an icy breeze was blasting through it, lashing the curtain.

"Help me," Cassie pleaded, because the drop from the window was immense. They were high up, so high she couldn't see the ground below, only hear that faraway sound of the sea, and her father's angry roar.

"I can't," Jacqui whispered, and suddenly she let go of Cassie's hand. Cassie was all alone, and Jacqui was fading away, screaming with laughter as she disappeared.

"No!" Cassie yelled, but Jacqui was gone, leaving only a trace of ghostly laughter behind.

There was no time to get back under the bed. Her father was wrenching at the door. Jacqui had lured her out from her hiding place and now the only escape was out of the high window. Cassie stared down, terrified, knowing she would have to jump.

"It's a dream, you'll be OK," she told herself. "Jump. Just jump and wake up."

But something was stopping her and she couldn't do it.

She was cold. So cold, and the grass was wet under her feet.

With a gasp, Cassie woke, to find herself outside.

Where was she? The sea was so loud.

She took a disoriented step forward and realized, to her horror, she was almost at the edge of the bluff. Another step and she would have fallen over the cliff, tumbling all the way down to where the wicked rocks waited in the darkness.

With a cry she reeled back, twisting away from the dark drop.

"How the hell?"

A light rain was still falling. Her bare feet were freezing and her pajamas were damp and cold.

She lurched back toward the house, where the outside lanterns cast a pool of light onto the paving, illuminating the icy drizzle with a golden glow.

Cassie was shuddering with cold. This hadn't felt like sleepwalking. It had been so real. She could so easily have jumped in her dream and then what?

What would have happened to her?

The front door was open and rain had blown in, spattering the hallway rug. It felt soft under her bare feet. She closed the door, thinking she should go and have a hot bath, because she was chilled to her bones.

As she closed the front door, the events of the previous night came rushing back to her. She started shivering afresh, even though she knew it was more from shock than cold this time.

She had unleashed a monster.

In her anger, she hadn't visualized the consequences. She hadn't thought about what it might mean to Ryan to be accused of being a liar, and what lengths he'd go to in order to protect himself. She visualized him grasping Madison's slim arm and crushing it with his strong hands, intent on causing visible bruises.

Would he threaten Madison into silence, or force her to say Cassie had done it? Cassie couldn't bear to think what he might be capable of.

Additionally, she hadn't realized how financially dependent he was on Trish. The story about his successful business had been another lie. It was struggling and in debt—the signs had all been there and she'd blissfully ignored them.

Ryan couldn't afford to have anything go wrong.

Cassie feared that for the next few days, she would be in actual danger now that Ryan had dropped his pretense and shown her who he really was.

Calling him a liar meant crossing a line, and when you crossed that line, you became his enemy and all bets were off.

She guessed people had learned to tread carefully around him, and even enable him, rather than face the dark side of his personality, and that was why he got away with doing what he did.

Cassie headed back to the bedroom, but as she passed the family room, she noticed the porch light was still on.

Was the glass door open or closed? It looked open, and the room was drafty.

Cassie headed out to check, glancing at the clock as she passed. It was a few minutes after three in the morning.

The door was open, and Cassie was about to close it when she stopped.

There was something—no, someone—in the chair nearest the balcony. She could see legs stretched out and a dangling arm. It was Ryan. He must have drunk himself into oblivion. She could see a second bottle standing beside the first.

Even with a jacket, he could have serious exposure by now, passed out there in the icy cold. Pushing aside the thought that he deserved it, Cassie went out to wake him up.

"Ryan," she said, shaking his shoulder.

His head lolled to the side.

It was freezing out here, and Cassie was losing patience.

"Wake up!"

She shook him again, harder. When there was no response, with a tendril of worry taking root inside her, Cassie walked around the chair to stand in front of him.

She stared down, horrified.

His face was pale and hideously bloated. His blue eyes were wide open, staring sightlessly ahead. His mouth hung slack, and she saw that he'd vomited—there was a huge crimson stain running down his chin and over the front of his shirt.

Red wine—or—?

"Ryan!" she screamed. "Wake up, wake up, please, tell me you're OK!"

Take his pulse, take his pulse, she told herself, and her shaking fingers closed around his wrist.

She couldn't feel anything, not the faintest tremor.

"He's dead," Cassie whispered.

CHAPTER THIRTY ONE

Cassie backed away into the safety of the family room, unable to take her eyes off Ryan's slumped, immobile form.

"He's dead," she repeated.

Shuddering with shock, she hugged herself, remembering how his wrist had felt when she'd tried to take his pulse. It had been clammy and icy cold, like a piece of meat and not like a wrist at all. That made her feel nauseous and she swallowed hard.

She had to get help. She should wake someone.

Cassie's brain felt sluggish with shock and fright. Doing what had to be done felt impossible. She didn't know how to call emergency services, or who should respond.

She would have to ask someone, but not the children. They couldn't know their father had died.

Trish. She should wake Trish.

Dread curdled in her stomach as she thought of what Trish's reaction might be.

Cassie stumbled down the corridor and knocked on the bedroom door.

"Trish!" she called softly, realizing she was sobbing out the word. "Trish, can I come in?"

Fearing that Trish had passed out, and that any more noise might wake the children, Cassie opened the door and stepped into the room. It smelled of perfume and sleep. She fumbled for the light switch and snapped it on, as Trish sat up, blinking.

Her hair was mussed and makeup was smudged under her eyes. Cassie guessed she'd been too drunk to remove it properly, and she still seemed groggy.

"Please come quickly. Something terrible has happened," Cassie whispered.

"What? What is it?"

"Ryan is dead. He's outside on the balcony. I just found him there."

"What?"

Trish jerked upright.

"You're kidding me!"

She glanced at the empty bed beside her as if expecting to see her husband there.

"I'm not. Please, come quick."

Trish scrambled out of bed and headed down the hall at a run, with Cassie following close behind.

"Oh, Lord," Trish said when she saw him. Her face crumpled and Cassie felt tears welling inside her as Trish stumbled forward, dropping to her knees, grasping his wrist to take his pulse just as Cassie had done.

Trish hadn't known he'd been a liar and an adulterer. Cassie had only ever seen him treat Trish like a princess.

What must she be feeling now?

Cassie couldn't look anymore. She felt consumed by guilt. She went back inside and collapsed on the couch, appalled by the prospect of breaking this news to the children.

A minute later, Trish joined her.

She seemed fully alert, the earlier grogginess had gone. She looked shocked, and although she hadn't been visibly crying, Cassie got the impression she was only managing to hold things together with a huge effort.

"I'm going to call the police. The children must stay away. Dylan's bedroom will be best, as it's biggest. Will you wait there with them? I've no idea how long it will take for the police to arrive."

"I'll do that," Cassie agreed.

She detoured to her room and pulled on the warmest clothing she could find, hoping that the extra layers might stop the shivering that seemed to come from deep inside her core. She didn't know how she would manage to console the children when she felt as if she was falling apart herself.

It took her two tries to put her top on the right way around, and she was shaking so badly she could hardly zip her fluffy boots.

When she was dressed, Cassie gently woke Madison, helped her dress in a tracksuit and trainers, and then shepherded her through to Dylan's room.

Dylan was already awake. Cassie realized he was a very light sleeper, and she felt apprehensive as she wondered how much he'd heard.

"Dylan, can you move over? Madison's tired. She needs to lie down."

"Why's she in here?"

Cassie couldn't tell him the truth.

"Your mum told me to bring her here. She'll explain everything soon. Try to go back to sleep now."

"Where's Dad?" Madison asked in sleepy, querulous tones.

Cassie looked down at her in consternation, wondering what on earth she should say.

"I think something's happened to Dad," Dylan said.

"What?" Madison sat up. "What's happened?"

Cassie fought to stop herself from breaking down. She remembered the happy family times in the kitchen, the jokes that Ryan had shared with his children and how he had cooked for them. They didn't know that he had threatened to harm them if Cassie stepped out of line. They only knew him as their dad, the center of their world.

It wasn't up to her to break this news. She wasn't even the right person to be comforting them now. They needed their mother. Why wasn't she here? How long did it take to call the police?

"I'm not sure what has happened," she said, struggling to keep her voice even, because a wobble would lead to sobs and complete loss of control.

Dylan was craning his head, peering out the window.

"I can see a car coming," he announced, and Madison joined him, kneeling on the bed and pressing her face against the glass.

"Three more cars," Dylan observed.

Cassie bit her lip. The more cars and the more police, the more time this was likely to take. She needed Trish to get here before the children started to panic, and already Dylan's guess had placed her in an impossible position.

"What are they unloading?" Madison asked anxiously.

"That's a stretcher."

"Is Dad sick? Is he hurt?"

Cassie bit her lip.

"That van says 'Coroner' on the front," Dylan said. "That means someone's died."

He turned away from the window and stared at Cassie.

"Isn't that right?" he asked. "The coroner takes a dead body away, right?"

While Cassie was still fumbling for a coherent response, Madison put two and two together.

"Dad's died. Oh, Dylan, Dad's died, hasn't he?"

With a scream of grief, she launched herself into Cassie's arms, wailing at the top of her voice.

In tears herself, Cassie hugged the young girl. She was sobbing so hard, she was incapable of saying anything that could console Madison, or even speaking at all. All she could do was hold Madison tight as she cried out her grief, her body convulsing as she wept.

CHAPTER THIRTY TWO

It seemed like hours later that Cassie heard footsteps approach the bedroom door.

She had no idea what had taken the police so long. Madison had cried herself to sleep in her arms, and Cassie had nestled against a pillow and done her best to soothe the young girl.

Cassie didn't know if Dylan was still processing the shock, or in denial. He was reading, but she didn't know how much he'd taken in, because he was only turning the pages occasionally.

As she struggled into a sitting position, Madison woke and began to sob again.

She heard Trish's voice outside and it sounded hoarse, as if she'd been crying.

"I don't want them alone with her. Please," Trish said.

Cassie felt a stab of shock. Was Trish referring to her?

The door opened and Trish rushed inside, with a plainclothes policeman following.

"My darlings, Mum's here."

She looked swollen-eyed and her face was sheet white.

"I'm going to keep you company now. It'll be OK, my precious ones, I promise."

Cassie realized that she'd never before heard Trish call her kids "darling" or "precious." As her dazed mind was taking this in, she realized the tall, balding policeman was speaking to her.

"Ma'am? Ms. Vale? Please come with us. We need you to talk us through what you saw."

Cassie struggled to her feet. Her legs had been crushed by Madison's weight and now painful pins and needles were coursing through them.

She hadn't thought that the police would want to question her, but of course they would need to take a statement since she had discovered Ryan's body. She hoped it wouldn't take too long.

As she walked to the door, she noticed that Trish cringed away from her, wrapping a protective arm around Madison, and she was puzzled to see fear in her eyes.

Outside, the balding officer introduced himself.

"I'm Detective Bruton, and this is Detective Parker."

Parker looked younger than Bruton, and more aggressive. He was short and muscular, with close-cropped blond hair, and looked as if he spent hours doing weights at the gym. The way he looked at Cassie made her more nervous. In fact, she corrected that impression. The demeanor of both detectives was making her increasingly uneasy.

"Take a seat here, ma'am."

The police had commandeered the kitchen table. It was covered in papers and official documents, and a camera bag stood on its corner.

Cassie sat with her back to the wall and waited while the detectives cleared some space.

"Your name, please?"

"Cassandra Vale."

"Permanent address?"

Cassie realized she didn't have one. She'd given up her rental apartment when she left the States. She found herself stammering out the home address where she and Jacqui had lived while her mother had been alive. Her father had moved many times since then. Nobody at that house would know her now.

She hoped the police wouldn't ask for her passport with the incriminating lack of a working visa. Even though they were here for a death, these police looked ready to tackle any infringement of the law, however minor.

"What are you doing here?"

She swallowed.

"I knew Ryan Ellis slightly. He invited me to stay for a couple of weeks."

He was dead; he couldn't contradict her story. Even so, Bruton's eyebrows rose as he wrote her explanation down.

"You're not working?"

Parker's gaze was drilling into her and in spite of the cold, Cassie felt her armpits start to sweat.

"I was helping out."

"Mr. Ellis's widow seemed to think you were hired as an au pair."

"I was helping out," Cassie repeated, doggedly sticking to her story.

"We'll have a look at your passport in a minute."

Bruton and Parker exchanged glances and Cassie felt sick.

"What day did you arrive?" Bruton continued with the questioning.

When had it been? Cassie groped back into the past, trying to remember when she'd gotten here, filled with hope that she was making a move to something better. Her memory was in pieces and it took her a while to recall the day.

"On a Saturday. Last Saturday."

"How did you get here?"

"I have a car. It's in for repair at the moment. I can find the license plate details."

"We will take those later. Now, tell me about what happened yesterday evening."

"Ryan and Trish came back late. They'd been away the previous night. I think they'd both been drinking. Trish went straight to bed. I updated Ryan that the kids were OK. We had a glass of wine out on the balcony. Then I went to bed, too."

She closed her eyes, not wanting to think about what had actually happened, and the way he'd turned on her. The moment she'd realized that hidden under his easy charm was a vicious manipulator who would stop at nothing to achieve his ends.

"I woke up at three a.m. and went to the bathroom."

She wasn't going to mention her sleepwalking either, in case it complicated things.

"I noticed the porch light was still on, so I went to check. I saw Ryan was still outside and when I went up to him I saw immediately that he was dead."

She swallowed back a sob.

"I called Trish, and she told me to go and stay with the children."

They were looking at her expectantly as if waiting for her to say more. But what more was there to say?

The silence felt uneasy.

It was Parker who spoke next. He leaned forward, placing his corded arms on the table.

"What was your relationship with the victim?"

Cassie stared at him, confused.

"Why is Ryan a victim?" she asked.

She saw Bruton glance quickly at Parker as if her question had surprised him.

Parker looked angry, scowling at her momentarily. Cassie thought he probably got angry easily and even though he had used the wrong word, he wanted to blame her for pointing it out.

But instead, he repeated it, slowly and clearly.

"Your relationship with the victim."

"Friends," Cassie said hesitantly. She worried they would know it was a lie. Trish might already have told them that Cassie was a stranger who had never met the family before.

Parker stared at her and the silence grew uncomfortable.

"Are you sure about that?"

Cassie nodded. She felt anxious about where this was all heading. Ryan's untimely death had blown all her secrets into the open. Now she was caught up in the investigation and if this line of questioning continued, Trish would find out what she and Ryan had done.

"Cassandra Vale." Parker's voice was hard and uncompromising. His gaze pinned her.

"Your statement today will form part of the official investigation into this death. Perjury is a crime, as is defeating the ends of justice."

He reached into one of the brown envelopes on the table and brought out an evidence bag.

Cassie caught her breath in horror as she saw it contained the first pregnancy test she'd taken; the one that she'd messed up by dropping into the toilet bowl.

"We discovered this while searching the house, and Mrs. Ellis has confirmed it is not hers."

How had they discovered it? Cassie was sure she'd thrown it away carefully. Had Dylan put it somewhere? Had Trish suspected something and gone searching for it? At any rate, here it was, out in the open— together with her secrets.

With a twist of her stomach, she remembered that the children knew. Madison had seen Cassie kissing Ryan and knew she hadn't slept in her own room. Dylan had seen her on the way to Ryan's bedroom, wrapped in his robe. She wouldn't have a chance if she continued to deny.

"We slept together a couple of times," she whispered, as her eyes filled with tears.

She felt like a whore, confessing this in the family's home, with Ryan's bereaved wife and children waiting down the hall.

"Please understand, I had no idea he was married. He told me he was divorced. I only found out the truth when his wife came back from a business trip overseas."

The detectives exchanged another glance.

Cassie was starting to realize there was more to this. The way that Parker had called Ryan "the victim"—even the way that Trish had looked at her so fearfully earlier, and how she'd demanded that Cassie should not be left alone with the children.

Bruton nodded at Parker, who stood up.

"Give us your passport, please."

Cassie walked with the policeman to her bedroom and took it out of her purse.

He took the passport and they all went back to the kitchen.

Cassie dreaded that they were going to seize the passport. She'd been questioned by the police at her last job, after the suspicious death at the chateau, and they had ended up taking her passport away. She remembered the trauma of feeling trapped, unable to get away, a prisoner in the house.

Cassie feared this was going to happen again.

In fact, what they did next was even worse.

The policeman took out a tape recorder and spoke briefly into it, giving the date and quoting a reference number and some other information that she couldn't make out.

Then Parker turned to her.

"Cassandra Vale, we are arresting you on suspicion of the murder of Ryan Ellis. You do not have to say anything at this time, but it may harm your defense if you do not mention, when questioned, something on which you later rely in court."

He continued to read Cassie her rights, but she couldn't hear him.

All she could hear was the panicked thoughts inside her own head.

They thought Ryan had been murdered, and suspected she had done it.

Given that she'd admitted she'd had an affair with him, and that he'd lied to her, Cassie realized she'd unwittingly given the police exactly what they wanted—a cast-iron motive for his murder.

CHAPTER THIRTY THREE

Cassie stared at the two officers in terror. Bruton looked stolidly professional but Parker seemed pleased, as if he was inwardly satisfied that this was happening.

"No!" she said loudly. When they didn't respond she tried again.

"No!" She screamed the word. "You can't do this. You have no right to arrest me. I'm innocent. You're framing me, this is a conspiracy. I refuse to allow this to happen. Get me a lawyer. Now!"

Parker grabbed her arms and forced them behind her back. She struggled with him, feeling as if she was fighting for her life, not just her freedom. This was a nightmare she had to escape from. It couldn't be happening, it wasn't real.

"This way, please, ma'am."

Shrieking at the top of her voice, straining against the tight embrace of the handcuffs, Cassie found herself half-carried, half-marched to the waiting police car.

It was only when they turned her around to force her into the car, in a practiced and efficient way, that she saw Trish and the children were standing at the front door, watching her go.

Cassie was appalled that this would be the children's last sight of her, the last impression they would have. Her hands restrained, being manhandled into the vehicle like a criminal. For a crime she didn't commit.

"I'm innocent," she called to them, sobbing out the words. "I'm being framed. Please help me!"

She hoped they might run to the car and intervene, but they simply stood, watching, and she realized that Trish must believe completely in her guilt

Cassie had never felt so helpless and alone.

The drive to the local precinct took only a few minutes but to Cassie, it felt like eternity. She was crushed by fear. These were no trumped-up charges; this was the British police system that operated like a well-oiled machine. If they had arrested her, it was because they knew they had a watertight case. She regretted struggling when they'd taken her away. Overcome by panic, she'd fought them instinctively, but it could only have cemented her guilt in their eyes.

When they arrived, the police helped her out of the car and escorted her into the police station. There, finally, they removed her handcuffs and released her aching arms.

She could not stop crying. She sobbed as the station's constable, a dark-haired woman who didn't look much older than Cassie, photographed her and took her fingerprints. She cried while they read her rights to her again, still unable to take in what they meant.

She was being framed. That was all she could cling to. Trish had found out she was sleeping with Ryan and had accused her of somehow causing his death.

The fact that this was even being allowed was terrifying. Cassie wondered whether there was corruption at work. In this close-knit community, Trish might have a connection within the police department. If that was the case, who knew how far her influence reached, and would Cassie be able to get beyond it to plead her case?

"In here, please, love."

The kind constable had stopped calling her "ma'am" after the third pack of Kleenex had been opened. Now she seemed to have adopted a motherly concern for Cassie, but the fact she cared only made Cassie cry all the harder as she was shepherded into the tiny prison cell.

The door clanged behind her and she was alone, locked into this cramped, chilly space that stank of chemical cleaner, with a sour undertone of old vomit.

She hadn't taken her meds last night—she'd been too distraught to think about it after escaping from Ryan's threats. That was probably why she'd had the nightmare and sleepwalked. Now here she was, locked in a police cell without them, for who knew how long. Would she be able to cope?

Cassie doubted it. Her mind felt as if it was on overload, with red alarm buzzers sounding on all sides. Her ability for logical thought had shut down completely. The hysterical crying had made her nauseous, and in fact, she spent some time dry retching over the metal toilet pan that was wedged in the tiny space behind the Spartan bed.

Then she collapsed on her knees next to the bed and buried her face in the coarse blue blanket.

She lay there, her sobs gradually lessening, until she slipped off the bed onto the hard linoleum floor.

Constable Aria Chandra peered worriedly through the bars.

The pretty redhead had suffered a bout of hysterics so severe that the constable had been on the point of calling the precinct's doctor, as she'd thought a tranquilizer should be administered.

Now she'd finally calmed down, but she was on the floor. The girl should at least be on the bed.

Reading through the charge sheet, Chandra learned she'd been arrested at home. She had appeared sober and not under the influence of any drugs, although she'd grown hysterical upon being arrested and had attempted to resist the officers.

Chandra sighed. This girl looked pretty, and fragile, and harmless; and it wouldn't do her any good to be lying on the floor. When the detectives came back later in the morning, she'd be taken for questioning. She needed some rest.

"Watch me, will you?" she asked her shift partner, a junior sergeant.

She made some warm, sweet tea in a paper cup and headed into the cell, with the sergeant standing by outside the locked door.

Chandra put the cup down on the shelf.

"Come on, love. Get up. You'll have a better rest on the bed. That floor's too cold for you to be spending time there."

She helped the girl up, thinking she was in a right state and wondering if she should give the doctor a call after all. She was shivering and shaking and she started crying again.

"It's a setup," she kept repeating.

"Love, you need to get some rest. Here's your tea."

She placed the cup in the girl's hand, noticing she felt icy cold, and held it steady while she drank. She'd been crying so much she needed fluids. When Chandra was sure she was able to hold it on her own, she let go.

Once the tea was finished, she helped her onto the bed and pulled the blanket over her. Then she left, hoping that she would calm down and be able to get some sleep.

An hour later, she returned to check up on Cassie, bringing her another cup of tea. She was still in two minds about whether to call the police doctor, because although the girl had finally stopped crying, she was shaking violently.

"I'm so sorry," she whispered, as some of the tea splashed onto the floor.

"It's all right. Try to be calm. Remember, nobody's out to get you. They just have to follow the processes."

Returning to the front desk, Chandra saw that Parker had returned to work.

There was no need to ask him if he'd had any sleep, because he'd obviously spent the interim at the gym. His hair was still wet from the shower and he was carrying his gym bag over his shoulder.

"Good workout?" she asked.

"The best. Keeps me sane." He grinned at her.

"Are you going to question the girl now? Don't be hard on her. She's very nervous."

Parker frowned.

"Chandra, she doesn't deserve special treatment. She's a murderer. We're going to put on the table now what she's done, and I'll be very surprised if she doesn't cave in immediately and give us a full confession."

"She says she didn't do it. She told me so; she kept repeating it."

"All the evidence points to the fact that she did. If she says differently, she's a liar."

"A liar?" Chandra asked. "You really think so?"

Chandra wished she had more experience. She'd only been with this unit a year and was still in training to be a detective. She didn't have any proof that the auburn-haired girl wasn't lying, only a gut feeling, and what use was a gut feeling when you were still a trainee?

Parker sighed heavily and leaned his arms on the front desk.

Speaking in a low voice he said, "This is personal for me, you see. Ryan Ellis was my friend. We knew each other from gym. We even trained together when my shifts allowed."

"That so?" Chandra asked. She wasn't very surprised, because in the town there was only one police station, and only one gym.

"He was a good guy, a family man, who spoke highly of his wife and children. He owned a boat hire business, I think. He trained hard, regular as clockwork, Monday to Friday—and sometimes Saturdays, from seven to eight-thirty a.m. When we got the chance to work out together, he was a fantastic weight training partner."

Parker smiled sadly. "I remember he joked to me that his family thought he went to work early every day. That was what he told them. But instead, he was at the gym."

Chandra raised her eyebrows.

"And you're calling her the liar?"

Parker scowled.

"She's alive. He's dead. I'm going to be as hard on her as I need to."

Chandra took a frustrated breath, ready to argue back, but then her phone rang, and Parker marched away.

She could only hope that the questioning didn't end up breaking this fragile, nervous young girl.

CHAPTER THIRTY FOUR

W hen Cassie heard the tramp of feet heading toward her cell door, nervousness boiled inside her and it was all she could do to stay on her feet. She felt dizzy, disoriented, and incapable of stringing even the simplest of sentences together.

How was she going to stand up to their onslaught?

The two policemen looked grim, and Parker in particular seemed hostile. He didn't even greet her, although Bruton offered her a brief "Good morning."

At least they didn't handcuff her this time, but as she walked alongside them she began to feel more lightheaded with every step.

The tiny interview room was warm and felt airless. She collapsed onto the steel chair, staring down at the table while the two officers sat across from her and switched on the recording equipment.

After stating her name and address again for the record, Parker got straight to the point.

"Tell us what happened last night. In detail, please. Leave nothing out. Give approximate times where you can."

Cassie wanted to cry. Where was he going with this? Why did he keep on asking her the same thing? Was he trying to prove that she was in some way responsible for Ryan's death? How could you be responsible for what another adult chose to do?

"I gave the children supper and put them to bed before eight thirty."

Her voice sounded weak and toneless. Would she have thought herself to be a credible witness? She didn't think so, and nor did they. She could see it in their faces.

"The Ellises arrived back at around ten. They were—well, Ryan seemed tipsy, and Trish quite drunk. Ryan put Trish to bed and then came back. I had a glass of wine outside with him and updated him on things. It didn't take long. I was in bed before eleven. He stayed out on the balcony."

"Then what happened?"

"Like I said, I woke from a bad dream. I noticed the porch light was still on. I went and found him."

Had it been the dream that had drawn her outside into the rainy garden? After her confrontation with Ryan, she'd been in a stress meltdown and perhaps she had seen, or done, something she didn't remember. That could be why the police thought she was guilty.

"Why do you keep asking me this? I didn't know he'd stay outside drinking in the cold, or that he'd finish another bottle of wine. I didn't even know people could die so easily from exposure. Why are you accusing me? I didn't lock him outside or tie him to his chair! What did you want me to do?"

Her breath was coming faster and she could feel herself starting to sob.

The officers exchanged a glance which Cassie didn't understand.

She thought that Parker looked temporarily confused, but Bruton continued impassively.

"Ryan Ellis's body was taken straight for postmortem analysis and a series of tests. The results came back an hour ago and they are as we suspected. Mr. Ellis did not die from exposure, nor of any natural or preventable causes. He died because the wine he drank was laced with a large quantity of rat poison."

His gaze drilled into her, and Cassie was without words as shock overwhelmed her.

Only now did she realize the full implications of his death.

Rat poison—the poison that she herself had bought, and then put away, because the traps were sold out.

Her mind was reeling.

Someone had poisoned Ryan. Poisoned him. How had it been done, and when?

What would it have taken to deliberately add some of that poison to a bottle of wine, knowing that he would drink it and then he would die?

Who could have callously done such a thing?

She remembered that red-stained vomit on the front of his shirt, and guessed that it must have been blood.

"I feel sick," she said suddenly, and Parker leaped from his chair. He grabbed the bucket in the corner, shoving it toward her just in time.

Cassie retched into the gray plastic bucket, unable to erase the image of the bloody vomit from her mind.

Rat poison. Someone had poisoned him, and he'd died.

She'd felt fine after the wine she had drunk; she hadn't even felt sick. Cassie guessed that made her look even guiltier.

"Can I have some water?" she asked. Her voice was wobbly and her mouth tasted terrible.

She rinsed it out with the lukewarm water they brought her, and spat it into the bucket, feeling humiliated and defenseless at having to do all of this under their unsympathetic gaze.

"You purchased the rat poison yourself, correct?"

No chance for her to recover. Cassie sensed this questioning would be relentless.

"Yes. I was supposed to get a mouse trap but there were none at the store, so the shopkeeper recommended it. Then Ryan said they didn't use poison in the house. He asked to take it back and exchange it."

"But you didn't? Why?" Parker's question sounded accusatory.

"My car broke down."

"But you had use of another car, correct?"

"Only a few days later. By then I'd forgotten about the poison. I—I didn't even think about exchanging it. I was supposed to call the store and ask them if they had the traps in stock."

"By then you'd found out that Mr. Ellis was married, and that his situation wasn't as you'd believed." Parker leaned forward.

"Yes. I was confused because he kept saying one thing to me, but acting in a different way to her. I was very miserable. I decided to leave. I would have gone last night already if they'd come back earlier, but I couldn't leave the children on their own."

"Your passport."

Now Bruton spoke and she swallowed nervously.

"Yes?"

"You don't have a work visa for the UK. You're here on a visitor's visa."

"Like I said, I was a friend."

Bruton's face was like thunder.

"We interviewed Ryan Ellis's wife again this morning. She confirmed that she has never met you, and that her husband never mentioned you."

One lie—one lie, and she was being caught out. For a moment Cassie was dazed by the irony. This could sink her. Meanwhile, Ryan had told thousands of lies, and had gone about his life with no consequences—until the end, anyway.

"All right. It's not exactly the truth."

Parker nodded in satisfaction as he noted her confession down.

Cassie sensed his antipathy toward her, although she didn't know why. It was as if he wanted her to have committed this crime and to be convicted of it. He didn't seem to have a shred of sympathy for her. Were they even considering any other suspects? Surely the spouse was always a suspect in a case like this, but it didn't seem as if they doubted Trish's version at all.

How could she convince them to consider Trish as a suspect? Was there a way to redirect their attention from her?

She stared at Parker, looked at his thickset, muscular arms crossed on the table, a frown creasing his broad forehead. He was a strong, focused guy. So maybe she needed to try to be stronger, too. Falling apart, weakness, fragility was all she'd shown and maybe, in his mind, it was painting her as the victim.

Bruton seemed more neutral, although he might just be better at hiding his feelings.

At any rate, they'd caught her out in a lie.

This was the worst thing that could have happened. Perhaps she should have admitted she'd come here to work for cash—but then she would have confessed to breaking the law and they would have gotten her on that.

Either response painted her as an unreliable witness and a criminal. There was simply no good outcome to that line of questioning. She could accuse anyone else, including Trish, of having committed this crime, but there would be no weight behind her words.

If she had lied about one thing, she could lie again. A smaller lie would lead to a bigger lie. That was why they would not believe her, and she knew they would use it against her.

That made her think about Ryan all over again, and her brain reeled as she thought about the immensity of the lies he'd told. The audacity of what he'd done, how he'd misled her, felt as shocking as it had the first moment that she'd realized.

She'd wanted to kill him.

Cassie felt a thrill of fear as she remembered the murderous thoughts she'd had about Ryan, the anger she'd had inside her. She couldn't tell the police that or they might regard it as a confession.

Nor could she tell them about the way her memory fragmented under stress, and that strange sleepwalking incident she'd had before he had died.

She swallowed hard as she wondered how much she herself remembered about that night. What if their relentless questioning triggered memories she didn't even know about?

In horror, Cassie visualized herself walking to that cupboard, opening the poison, adding it to the wine. She imagined stirring it to be sure it had dissolved and smelling it, nodding in satisfaction when all she picked up was its fruity, earthy scent. Pouring another, untainted glass for herself, and walking out to Ryan with a humble apology, telling him that she believed him after all, waiting and watching while he drank down the deadly liquid.

What if these repressed memories had caused her to sleepwalk?

Glancing at the police, Cassie saw to her relief that they were reading through their notes. Perhaps that meant questioning was over for the day. But then Parker put down his pen and picked up her passport again, paging through it carefully.

"I see here you have a French student visa, stamped in October. So you were working there. That was supposed to be a year's contract, correct? What happened?"

Cassie felt short of breath. She'd thought the information inside her passport couldn't get her into any more trouble, but now she was realizing it could, and would.

"The family I worked for didn't need me anymore," she said.

"Is that so?" Parker's voice dripped with sarcasm and she couldn't summon the nerve to look him in the eye. Instead she stared down at the table.

"Can you give us the name, all the contact details?" he pressed her. "We will need to check if there were any irregularities during the brief time you were in their employ."

Irregularities. Now it seemed as if there was no air in the room at all. She couldn't lie her way out of this, it was too serious, even though the truth would instantly incriminate her.

She thought of her ex-employer and wondered whether he was being held in prison while awaiting trial.

He had insisted, from the start, that he had been wrongfully accused of the crime.

Now Cassie was discovering exactly what that felt like.

What a twist of irony that she had ended up in the same situation— the only difference being that he had a top legal team working around the clock to exonerate him, and she had nobody.

"I was working for the Dubois family," she said. "Pierre Dubois employed me."

There was a short silence, and then, as Parker realized who she was speaking about, she saw the blaze of triumph in his eyes.

CHAPTER THIRTY FIVE

When Chandra entered the conference room after taking the redhead back to the cell, she found Parker and Bruton discussing the case. Their conversation was heated.

"It's too much of a coincidence," Parker insisted. "She works for that French family, and the fiancée ends up dead. Now she works for this family, and the husband ends up dead. What is she? I know I'm thinking a few steps ahead, but this points to serial killer methodology."

Bruton shook his head.

"As a woman, it's less likely she's a serial killer. Look, it could point to plain bad luck, but there's also a possibility that the experiences at her previous job pushed her over the edge. A young girl who's mentally unstable and who's been through the traumatic experience of a suspicious death at her workplace—that could be a trigger."

"It could," Parker agreed.

Since she was part of the team, although a junior member, Chandra was tempted to speak out in the girl's defense, but she held herself back. They were more experienced and less naïve than she was. Even though she couldn't believe what she was hearing, she had to accept that perhaps their conclusions were correct.

Bruton spoke forcefully, counting off on his neatly manicured fingers.

"First, a traumatic incident occurs in France. Second, she gets to what she thinks is a place of safety. Third, her supposed protector who's just seduced her is proved to be a liar when his wife arrives home. That's a bad hand to be dealt. She's an anxious person; look at those medications we found in the suitcase. She buckles under stress. This would have been extremely stressful."

Parker nodded, his face grim.

"That's a good alternative explanation."

"She might even misremember herself. Her testimony was shaky. I don't doubt for a moment that we could question her three days in a row, and get three different versions of events."

"You're saying she might have committed the murder and then repressed the memory?" Parker leaned forward.

"It's a possibility, given our first impressions of her, and the medication that she's on. However, it could also have nothing to do with her. We can't discount that she might be innocent. Remember that she seemed genuinely surprised that he hadn't died from exposure," Bruton said.

Now it was Chandra's turn to nod in eager agreement.

"Where's the alternative suspect?" Parker argued

"There's a family in the picture." Bruton sounded cynical.

"A close family, despite Ellis's misleading her about being married."

Chandra found it interesting that Parker didn't want to use the word "lies."

Bruton sighed impatiently. "Look, Mr. Ellis was clearly a serial liar."

Chandra felt a thrill of satisfaction that Bruton didn't share Parker's loyalties.

"You don't know that!" Parker leaped to his friend's defense. "He might have just wanted to get her into bed with him."

"Even so, they slept together, and the wife knows. Therefore, we can't rule her out as a suspect just yet."

"Bruton, she only knew about their affair when we told her. She had no idea beforehand—you saw how shocked and tearful she was."

"Ms. Vale appeared shocked and tearful, too," Bruton reminded him.

"Mrs. Ellis told us she arrived home drunk after a romantic getaway, and passed out in bed as soon as they got home. That doesn't set the scene for murder." Parker said.

"Well, where's the hard evidence pointing to Ms. Vale?" Bruton asked, and now Chandra realized that Parker was suddenly quiet.

"There is none at this point," Bruton continued. "Not enough, anyway. We can get in touch with Pierre Dubois's lawyer and his family, but any input from them would just be character evidence. It's not proof."

Parker thumped the table in frustration.

"You're right. We need proof in some form. A confession would do it. Or else, concrete, incontrovertible evidence."

Chandra was horrified that they sounded as if they were brainstorming for solutions to send her down. Did neither of them have any empathy for the girl? She'd been in floods again when Chandra had escorted her back to her cell. Worse still, she'd been gasping, "I deserve this. I brought it on myself," between her sobs.

Chandra took a deep breath and decided to have her say.

"Couldn't there be an alternative suspect who isn't part of the family? Isn't it possible that Ryan Ellis might have done this before? Slept with other girls, I mean."

Parker looked up with an irritable frown.

"It's possible, but Mrs. Ellis didn't know of any recent visitors to the home."

"Apart from the cleaner. She mentioned that they have help twice a week," Bruton added.

"We'll certainly interview the cleaner, but at this point she's not a suspect and Ms. Vale is. So we have to build a strong case against her, because we are obliged to. After all, somebody killed Mr. Ellis."

Chandra sighed. It wasn't looking good for the girl. And what did she herself know anyway? These detectives were seasoned professionals and if they believed that Cassandra Vale was a killer, then most probably she was.

"It couldn't have been suicide?" she ventured.

Parker shook his head.

"The cause of death, and the fact that there was no note, ruled that out straight away."

"Oh," Chandra said, disappointed.

"Good thinking, though," Bruton said approvingly, and Chandra felt a flicker of pride.

"Is there anyone manning the front desk?" Parker stared meaningfully at the camera screen that showed the reception area. Following his gaze, Chandra saw that a member of the public was walking in.

"I'm on my way," she said.

She hurried out of the interview room and to the reception area.

The lady waiting inside was a tall, slender brunette with hair cut in a perfect bob, and she wore a stylish suede jacket that Chandra immediately coveted, while knowing it probably cost more than her entire month's salary.

"Sorry for the delay, ma'am," Chandra said. "How can I help?"

"My name is Trish Ellis," the woman replied in a calm, authoritative voice. "I believe you're holding my au pair, Cassie Vale, as a murder suspect. I've come to bail her out."

Chandra stared at the woman in utter shock.

She couldn't believe what was happening. The victim's widow had arrived to bail out the murder suspect. Why?

All she could think, in her confusion, was that Parker was going to be furious.

CHAPTER THIRTY SIX

Cassie sat hunched on the bed with her elbows on her knees. Throughout the questioning she'd held out hope that the police would believe her, but nothing had gone her way. Now she felt a deep depression overwhelming her.

The police hadn't brought her meds along. They had been left at the house, which was a blow, because in times of severe stress, she relied on them. Without them she knew from experience that her anxiety would escalate. The panic attacks would start—the warning signs were already there and she knew she could expect one soon.

She had no idea how long she'd be kept prisoner here or what the next step was. She guessed it would be a court appearance. By tomorrow, she'd be in pieces—anxiety played havoc with her memory. There would be no way she'd be coherent on the witness stand and she might well end up giving a different version of events and contradicting what she'd said today. Her own confusion would seal her fate.

Perhaps it would be better to confess. To flesh out the scene she'd so powerfully imagined about pouring the poison carefully into the wine glass, and stirring it slowly so that no trace of the residue remained.

They'd believe her in an instant if she told them that. There would be no doubting or second-guessing her story. After all, there was nobody to contradict her version, so perhaps she had.

Tears stung her eyes as she thought about the bad choices that had landed her here.

Then a rattle at the door startled her out of her despair.

She looked up, hoping it would be the friendly constable from the front desk, because maybe there was a way she could fetch Cassie her

meds from the house—if she pleaded that they were prescribed medication, it might be possible.

Her heart plummeted as she saw it wasn't the constable.

It was Parker, and he looked livid. His jaw was clenched and she
could see a vein pulsing in his forehead.

He spoke, and it was clearly an effort for him to keep a normal tone
of voice.

"Come with me," he snapped.

Cassie wanted to ask why, but was sure he wouldn't tell her. What
could it be? Only more trouble for her, that she was sure of. Perhaps her
court date was today and they were going to take her there in a van. If so
she should probably ask to use the toilet first, but she couldn't bear to do
that in front of Parker because what if he didn't look away?

Her legs felt wobbly, and when his hand clamped around her arm she
was grateful for the support.

She did her best to keep pace as he marched along.

When Cassie reached the front desk she nearly fell over from
shock.

Trish was there.

She was busy signing a sheaf of official-looking forms, and barely
looked up when Cassie walked in.

The friendly constable gave her a sympathetic smile but Cassie was
too nervous to acknowledge it.

What was going on? Had Trish come up with more evidence that
would convict Cassie immediately?

Bruton provided the answer.

"Ms. Vale, Mrs. Ellis has kindly offered you bail. We have decided
to allow it, subject to certain terms. We are permitting bail because at
this point, we do not have sufficient evidence for a conviction. However,
we are continuing our investigation, and if or when additional evidence
comes to light, you may be rearrested. Do you understand what I am
saying to you?"

She nodded, although her head was spinning and she was starting
to wonder if this might be a realistic dream that her anxious mind was
conjuring up.

Dream or no dream, Cassie was certain that Parker had opposed the decision, but been overridden by the more senior detective. That would explain his angry demeanor.

Bruton continued. "You must remain at the Ellis family's premises. You are not to leave the premises unless accompanied at all times by at least one adult, and even when in the company of an adult, you are not allowed to leave the village. You will cooperate with further questioning at all times. Do you understand?"

"Yes," she said, realizing her voice was so faint it was almost soundless.

"You will be required to check into the police station every Friday, between the hours of four and five p.m. Starting from this Friday."

"I will," she said.

"And we are holding your passport," he concluded.

Parker stepped forward.

"Ms. Vale, breaking any of the bail conditions will be immediate grounds for your rearrest."

"I understand," she whispered.

Her hands were shaking so badly that she could hardly sign in the places where Parker was indicating.

Trish squeezed her shoulder.

"It will be all right," she said.

Cassie looked up, astounded by the unexpected kindness.

"I've parked round the back. Can we leave now, Officers? I've a lot to get done today."

"Certainly, ma'am," Bruton said.

Cassie walked with Trish, but as she rounded the corner, in her nervousness, she dropped her jacket and fumbled to pick it up.

Behind her she heard a heated conversation at the front desk.

"She's a flight risk!" Parker was almost shouting.

"We have her passport. There was no reason to deny bail," Bruton said, in a more level voice.

Then the desk constable spoke in impassioned tones.

"Parker, please. If you find she's innocent, promise me one thing. Promise that you'll try as hard to help her as you're trying to go after her now."

Cassie didn't hear any more. She hurried after Trish and out the door into the cold, fresh air.

She climbed into the car feeling numb with shock, and decided her best course of action was to keep quiet, because she didn't know what she would babble out if she started to speak. Why was Trish helping her? Was Trish even helping her, or did she plan to get her revenge and then dispose of Cassie in some untraceable way?

Cassie's mind was spinning as she considered the possibilities.

"I'm sorry you had to wait so long," Trish said as they drove away.

She glanced at Cassie as if expecting a response, but she had no idea what to say. Trish sounded normal, just the same as she always did, but Cassie still didn't understand why she'd helped her.

As the car wound its way through the village, she felt certain that she was dreaming. She'd become too stressed out in the police cell and had fallen asleep and was in the throes of what would probably turn into a nightmare.

She waited for the plush, leather-lined interior of the car to melt away, and for her to be hanging off the side of a tall building, with Jacqui screaming with laughter above her, her voice as high and sharp as the shriek of seagulls.

It didn't happen. Instead, they pulled up outside the house and Trish climbed out as if everything was normal.

"What do you want to do first?" she asked. "Bath? Sleep? Something to eat?"

Once again, Cassie felt blindsided by her kindness. She felt guilty for having considered Trish to be a suspect. While Cassie had been wondering how to convince the police to focus on Trish, she had been trying her best to exonerate Cassie and find out who the real killer was.

"I—I'd like a bath," Cassie stammered, needing to wash the feel and the smell of that claustrophobic police cell from her skin.

She noticed that there were two arrangements of lilies on the coffee table in the family room. People had already started to offer their sympathies for the death.

"Come and have a cup of coffee first. The children are with family today, and I'll pick up some fish and chips when I fetch them. We all need a treat tonight."

While Trish made the coffee, Cassie hurried to her room.

Everything was in its place. Her phone had been put onto the charger. Her luggage and drawers had clearly been searched through because her meds had been moved, but they were still there, which was all that mattered.

Cassie swallowed down her pills and gasped with relief.

Then she went to the kitchen, to find Trish had made coffee and set out a plate of cookies.

"I have to apologize for my behavior earlier," she said. "I wasn't thinking clearly and I was beside myself with grief."

"I'm so sorry about everything," Cassie began, but Trish shook her head.

"What's done is done. There was fault on both sides; it would be wrong of me to say otherwise." She lowered her head and pressed her hands over her eyes for a minute before continuing.

"However, I don't believe you killed my husband."

"You don't?" Cassie couldn't believe what she was hearing. Trish was on her side after all.

Cassie felt tears well up again, but this time they were caused by relief and gratitude.

"I can't tell you what that means to me," she whispered. "I've been feeling so bad about everything."

"It's a complicated situation, and I'm sorry you have been caught up in it," Trish sympathized. "However, the fact remains my beloved Ryan was murdered, and somebody did it. So the question is—who?"

With her meds starting to work, the coffee in front of her, in the safe familiarity of the kitchen, Cassie found herself able to think more clearly.

One person came immediately to mind.

Harriet the cleaner.

Could she have done it?

Yes, she could. Harriet had worked on Monday—it had been her last day before leaving, and she had left on bad terms, extremely angry, with a serious grudge.

She could have opened up one of the wine bottles and added the poison. She wouldn't have known who would drink the wine or when, but she could have guessed that Ryan would probably drink most of it, and might not have cared if the poison affected other people too.

Cassie hesitated. Telling Trish about Harriet would open a can of worms. For a start, she was sure that Ryan had slept with Harriet. Trish didn't know that yet, and Cassie didn't want to tell her. She didn't feel brave enough—or medicated enough—to deal with Trish's reaction.

The other suspect was even more likely, but if she spoke up, the consequences might be worse.

Cassie couldn't forget how Dylan had sat in bed, watching her, and the chilling words he'd spoken. He'd been factual, and the only emotion he'd shown had been faint amusement at her shock and disbelief.

Dylan had shown he could steal without any guilt, and that he could kill with no remorse. Did he see a moral difference between an animal and a human? She didn't know. He might be only twelve years old but she was frightened of him. She didn't know what his motive would have been for adding poison to the wine, but perhaps he hadn't needed one; or had done it for some sort of twisted revenge.

Her bail conditions meant she couldn't leave the house. If she told Trish she suspected Dylan, and he learned what she'd done, it might put her in danger.

"I have some ideas," she said. "I want to tell you but I need more time to get my head straight. Could we discuss it later?"

Trish smiled sadly.

"I had a feeling you would sense who it was. I also have strong suspicions based on what I've heard and seen, but I'll be truthful, Cassie, I am scared to share them with you, although I know I must. So yes, please take more time. This is a serious issue. Neither of us wants to make unfounded accusations, but both of us will have to be brave and honest if we are going to work together. Have something to eat, have a rest. We can speak again later."

Cassie felt a surge of relief that Trish's suspicions clearly didn't include her. It reassured her that the sleepwalking, and her fragmented memories, had simply been due to a nightmare. After all, if Trish thought she'd committed the crime, she would never have bailed her out.

"Where are the children?" Cassie asked.

"They're visiting their aunt, Ryan's older sister. She asked if they could keep each other company today and I thought it would do them good. I'm fetching them at five, and I'll bring back supper on the way home."

Trish stood up.

"I've tried to keep this as quiet as possible, but word gets out. I've already had phone calls and visits from people in the village, and some deliveries of flowers. However, please let the phone ring to voicemail, and don't speak to anybody who knocks at the door, in case they're a journalist, as you know what the gutter press in this country is like."

Trish headed out of the kitchen, and Cassie poured herself a glass of water and sat at the table. Trish had said eat, but she didn't feel hungry in the slightest. Not when she thought about telling Trish that her son had admitted to breaking the neck of his pet rabbit.

She relied on Trish's goodwill; that was what had gotten her out of jail. That goodwill might disappear if Cassie made an accusation that hurt or angered her.

Cassie knew she had to do whatever it took for Trish to be able to trust her, because she was at her mercy now.

Chapter Thirty Seven

Cassie felt uneasy being alone in the house. She couldn't bear to look at the balcony where Ryan had died. She was terrified of breaking her bail conditions and wasn't sure if they extended to the garden. It would be better to stay indoors, especially since the tabloids might be waiting with their zoom lenses ready to photograph her.

Trish would have to do all the fetching and carrying of the children. Cassie couldn't even walk them to the bus stop. It scared her to realize how useless she was, and what a burden she would quickly become. If she and Trish were going to have their discussion, then the sooner it took place, the better.

When the family arrived home, she was encouraged to hear some laughter as the children ran to the front door. She hurried to greet them.

"Hello! How are you both doing?" she asked.

She was pleased to see that Madison looked more cheerful, and hoped that her day out had distracted her from her grief. As they walked into the house, both the children became more solemn and Madison's smile disappeared.

"We're all right, thanks," Madison said.

Dylan didn't greet her at all but trudged past with his head down.

"Food's up!"

Trish, carrying the fish and chips in a large brown paper bag, closed the front door.

"Come on, everyone. It's been an exhausting day. Let's eat, and then you children need an early night."

"Can I help you get ready for bed, Madison?" Cassie asked.

Glad to have something to do, Cassie ran her bath and helped her choose her favorite pair of pink pajamas.

"Do you think I can go to boarding school soon?" Madison whispered, as Cassie folded her bath towel.

Cassie was sure that Madison must feel as if her world had fallen apart. Perhaps boarding school would be a good idea in the long term, especially given the amount of traveling Trish did.

"We can ask your mum," she said. "If you're sure you want to go then let's discuss it with her."

To her surprise, Madison grew tearful and began sniffing hard.

"I already asked her. She said no. I asked her as soon as she came back from her trip. I asked her so nicely, Cassie, and she laughed at me. She said no. She said I was going to do what I was told and that until I was top of the class in math, I can't do any more plays."

"Oh, Maddie, I'm so sorry," Cassie said, realizing why Madison had been so uncharacteristically moody for the past few days.

"I hate her, Cassie," Madison whispered. "I'm never going to be top of the class in math. Telling me I must is unfair. I wish she was dead. She told me I couldn't be Veruca Salt because I didn't get good marks, and although my dad said I could, I was still scared. I had to make sure she wasn't watching me, because she said if my marks weren't good enough, she'd come up onto stage and drag me away. I wish she'd died instead of my dad."

She burst into sobs as Cassie hugged her hard, but even as she did her best to comfort the young girl, whispering that her mother loved her and only wanted what was best for her, she felt deeply concerned about the implications of Madison's words.

Supper was a quiet affair. Cassie could do no more than pick at her food. Tension knotted her stomach as she thought about the discussion to follow, and what she would say to Trish.

Dylan was the only one with an appetite. He piled his plate with food and had a generous second helping. Trish ate sparingly and Madison, clearly still upset, refused everything except chips.

"Put the children to bed, will you? I'll clean up here," Trish said when everyone was done.

Cassie was surprised that the obligatory hour of television was being skipped, but felt grateful that she and Trish could get onto the difficult conversation they needed to have.

Madison went to bed willingly, but Dylan grumbled about having to go so early.

"This is unfair," he told Cassie as she shepherded them down the hallway.

"I'm sorry," she said.

"There was something I wanted to watch tonight."

"Perhaps we can record it and you can watch tomorrow? I'll ask your mum if you can have some extra time."

Cassie was relieved that he wasn't angry at her, because after what she was planning to say to his mother, he would have every right to be. She couldn't protect him at her own expense, and would have to voice her suspicions to Trish.

Cassie knew she'd have to make very sure that Dylan was not listening in while she did so, because he was a light sleeper, and seemed to know far more about what was going on than he should.

For a moment, she felt sick with dread.

"Good night," she said in a cheerful voice, but Dylan looked at her strangely, as if he saw right through her act and sensed her intent.

After making sure the children's bedroom doors were firmly closed, Cassie headed back to the kitchen. She was dreading this discussion with Trish, and hoped that she might lead the way and share her thoughts with Cassie first.

When she walked into the kitchen, she was surprised to see it empty.

"I'm heading outside," Trish called.

Cassie spun around.

Trish was standing at the living room door, wearing a stylish parka. She was holding a tray with a bottle of white wine and two glasses.

Cassie hadn't expected this invitation, and it made her feel deeply uneasy. She didn't want to sit on that balcony ever again. It was too full of memories. Why weren't they going to chat in the kitchen?

Then it came to her. Trish must be concerned about the children over-hearing. If they closed the balcony door—which she and Ryan had never done—it would be more private outside.

"You needn't worry," Trish said, obviously misunderstanding the reason for Cassie's hesitation. "I bought this bottle today, at the off-license in town. It won't have been tampered with."

"I didn't—" Cassie began, and then simply said, "I'll get my jacket."

She ran to her room, grabbed her jacket, and headed outside.

As she'd expected, Trish closed the balcony door behind them.

The night was very still; there was no wind whatsoever, only the faraway crash of the sea.

"What a day it's been," Trish said. "I'm glad it's over. They say after a tragedy you just have to take things hour by hour, day by day. Now I understand what they mean."

She poured two large glasses of wine and handed one to Cassie.

"It's been a waking nightmare," Cassie said. "I'm so sorry about all of this."

"It's not your fault. What a weird scenario, both of us being together out here. I know you had drinks with Ryan a few times."

Cassie felt as if she were plunging into an abyss of guilt. Remembering those carefree evenings, those kisses, how she had felt as if she were falling in love. What a betrayal the whole episode had been, for so many people, in so many ways.

"If I'd known, I never would have done it."

She couldn't meet Trish's eyes, but instead stared out at the dark sea.

"What did he say to you?"

Now she turned, regarding Trish with apprehension.

"How do you mean?"

Trish sipped her wine.

"I would like to know what he said to you. About me, about our situation. To you, about you. I've been feeling torn up about this, so much that I've been unable to sleep. I need closure. I actually visited a psychologist today and he advised that I should talk to you. He said it would help both of us to heal."

Cassie took a deep breath. She had been doing her best to forget what had been said, and what had been done. She'd never imagined having to share the details of their conversation. On the other hand, she could imagine how devastated Trish must be, knowing she'd been part of such a huge web of lies.

If the psychologist advised it, Cassie guessed she would have to go along with it and hope that the truth would indeed be cathartic.

"When I first phoned Ryan about the job, I wasn't sure if I wanted it. I think he sensed that and looked for a way to convince me. Saying he was divorced was playing the sympathy card, I guess. He did it very cleverly. He said the kids were traumatized and didn't want to talk about it and I shouldn't pressure them. So as a result I never mentioned it to them and I only figured out what was happening after you came back."

Relating the story, Cassie felt deeply ashamed by how gullible she'd been.

"So what did he tell you?"

Cassie was glad it was dark, as she found herself blushing as she remembered what he'd said.

"That you were a strong person, but that you'd become needier as the kids had grown older, and you'd grown apart emotionally. He made it sound as if you had already moved out. I asked about your clothes after I found them in the cupboard, and he said that you hadn't taken all of them. Everything was explained away."

Trish nodded.

"What about our vow renewal? Did he mention that?"

"Did you actually have it?" Cassie asked, surprised, then caught herself. Of course its cancellation must have been another of Ryan's lies.

"Oh, yes. It was a big event. We had a hundred invited guests. My colleagues, Ryan's colleagues, my parents, his sister and brother. Ryan is estranged from his parents. He hasn't seen them for many years. His father wanted him to go to the Navy and Ryan refused; that's when the conflict started."

"Oh," Cassie said, appalled by the extent of the falsehoods she'd ended up believing.

"He told me he was in the Navy and ended up as a captain."

"Pure fiction," Trish said sadly. "Anyway, the vow renewal was held, and it was a big success. I paid for it all. As I'm sure you have gathered, my substantial salary is what subsidizes our lifestyle. Ryan's boats bring in pocket money, but not enough to make a meaningful difference to our finances, and his recent purchase of the yacht put him firmly in the red."

Cassie nodded, remembering the loan agency letter, and thinking there might be some debts that even Trish didn't know about.

"Anyway, back to you," Trish continued. "When did you find out what was going on?"

"I guess the first time I knew anything was when you walked in."

Cassie's wine was finished. She'd been drinking fast, unsettled by the turn the conversation had taken. Trish leaned over and refilled it.

On an empty stomach, Cassie knew she'd better slow her drinking down, because she needed to keep her wits about her. She was already feeling lightheaded and garrulous.

"What did you think?" Trish asked.

"I assumed you'd come back to get some of your things. I never dreamed you lived here. I couldn't believe it when you walked into the bedroom and I had no idea what I should do. Then I saw Ryan had changed the bed sheets."

Cassie felt her face flaming again.

"Hiding the evidence," Trish said with a bitter sigh.

"Yes. Now I see that. The problem was, Trish, that I believed him. I really did. I trusted what he said. So for a long time I was in total shock and every new revelation, I found a way to justify somehow."

How stupid she'd been. Looking back, Cassie wished she'd given the situation more thought, instead of blindly accepting what she'd been told.

"You must have gone through a tough time during those few days," Trish remarked, and Cassie was glad to hear the sympathy in her voice.

"I've been living in hell. Before you came back, I'd been certain that Ryan and I were going to start a life together. It felt like a fairytale, but at the same time, it was happening and he seemed so genuine. He gave me gifts. He told me that he loved me."

Tears prickled her eyes and she put her glass down to wipe them away. When she looked again, she saw Trish had topped it up and it was brimful once again.

"You must have been angry?" she asked.

"I was furious. I felt completely used. I've never been so ashamed in my life. I thought I was going mad. I felt betrayed. I realized how badly I'd been lied to and how stupid I'd been, and how skillfully he had—I guess, played me—to believe whatever he wanted me to."

Trish nodded understandingly as Cassie continued.

"I could have killed him when I realized, I admit it. That's how angry I was. I imagined throttling him, or taking a kitchen knife to him. It made me feel better to think about him dead. I wasn't coping; I felt so helpless and enraged."

Cassie let out a deep breath, glad that she was managing to be honest, even though it was with the help of more than half a bottle of wine. After all, when the conversation turned to the identity of the real suspect, she would need to be able to speak openly and not be scared of how Trish might react. And Trish would need to be completely honest with her, too.

"You haven't told me everything," Trish murmured, and Cassie frowned at her, perplexed. What more was there to share?

"How do you mean?"

"What was it like when you slept together? What did he do? Did you sleep together after I came back, or only while I was away?"

Cassie took another large gulp of wine.

How could she possibly disclose this? It was private and had no bearing on anything. Why did Trish need to know?

"Trish, I don't think I should tell you that. I don't—I don't want you to be hurt. And details like that can be hurtful."

"You don't think that not knowing is the most painful of all?" Trish asked in a gentle voice.

Cassie shook her head.

"I'm not sure, but how can more information make it any better?"

She felt confused by the direction things were heading, and wondered if asking for these details had been part of the psychologist's advice.

A moment later, Trish confirmed her thoughts.

"Dr. Mills told me that it would help."

If the psychologist had recommended this, she had to try. Probably, Trish needed closure, too. Cassie hoped that her words would heal, rather than harm.

"He was a really good lover," she said quietly. "At first it felt—I don't know—a bit awkward to me because I was thirteen years younger than him and had been hired to help out. He made me feel like a princess. He knew exactly what to do."

She glanced at Trish, hoping this would be enough, but Trish was watching her expectantly.

"Carry on," she said.

"That's it, really." Cassie glanced at her appealingly but Trish shook her head.

"There must be more."

"I can't think of anything."

"You've told me what he did, but not what he said. Please share that," Trish encouraged her.

With that, Ryan's words, and his promises, came rushing back, and Cassie found she couldn't hold the memories in.

"He told me how beautiful my body was, that he could imagine waking up with me every day of his life and was looking forward to doing that. He said I was special and unique. That I turned him on in a way nobody ever had."

"Go on?" Trish said softly.

"We didn't sleep together after you got back, but he kept promising me that everything was OK."

"Did he kiss you?"

"Yes, we kissed a few times after you were back."

"How about love? Did he ever tell you that?"

"He did. When I tried to leave one night, he told me that I needed to trust him, that he loved me. He gave me a diamond necklace then. I thought that was proof that he meant what he said—diamonds are forever, right?"

Cassie was breathing hard, reliving the anxiety and dismay she'd felt.

"Oh, poor Cassie. How angry you must have been when you realized those foundations were built on clay."

"I was devastated."

"Was that when you had the pregnancy scare?"

"Yes. I found out that it was only a scare, but it made everything even worse. It showed me how serious the consequences could have been. And it made me realize how alone I was."

"So you confronted him?" Trish asked.

"By then I was furious. My car got vandalized the day before you came back. Wires were cut to disable the battery. I found out Ryan had done it and I think he was preparing for your arrival by making sure I couldn't leave. He wanted a babysitter on site so that he could spend time with you."

Trish frowned slightly.

"Vandalism? Are you sure he went that far?"

Cassie nodded miserably. "I'm certain. I found the tools he'd used, and some of the wire scraps, in the Land Rover's cubbyhole. I don't think he'd expected me to look there, but I did."

"Then you called him a liar?"

"I called him out on everything. We were out here on the balcony. It was after you came back from your getaway—you went straight to bed. I accused him outright of being a liar, and he changed completely. I've never seen him so angry. I didn't even know he could be that way. He grabbed me and made terrible threats."

Cassie cringed away from that memory. She couldn't bear to think how it had felt, when the man she had loved and trusted had become a monster, and turned on her.

"What did he say?" Trish asked softly.

"He shouted that he'd call social services and say I'd been abusing the children, and that they would find bruises when they examined them. I couldn't believe he'd hurt his own children just to make sure there was evidence. And he threatened to report me for working illegally. He told me he would force me to stay no matter what it took because he needed you to loan his business some money and everything had to go smoothly for that to happen."

Trish let out a sharp, angry breath.

"Unacceptable. You're being so brave to speak up about this," she said.

Encouraged, Cassie continued.

"Mostly, I think, he couldn't bear that I'd called him a liar and he was going to make me suffer for it in any way he could. Suddenly, it was all about his ego. Like nothing he'd said or done to me had made a difference. I saw the monster inside him for what it was. I was furious and terrified. I felt trapped. I realized what a manipulative son of a bitch he was. I hated him for what he'd done. Hated him!"

Her voice rose to a shout and suddenly, the anger boiling inside her had to have a vent. She couldn't keep it in anymore. What he'd said and done. How he'd stripped away all her self-esteem and destroyed her, just because he could.

"What a lying bastard! How dare he use me this way? How dare he manipulate, and lie, and mislead. What gave him the right to try and ruin my life? I thought this was my chance at happiness, that we had a life together. And we didn't. It was all a goddamned lie."

Cassie heard a crack.

The stem of her wineglass dropped to the floor and smashed.

She'd been gripping it so hard she'd snapped the fragile stem in two. Hastily, Cassie grabbed with both hands at the fragile bowl.

Trish leaned over and dexterously removed the empty bowl from her grasp.

"Are your hands OK?"

Cassie looked down. Her hands were shaking, and a dark bead of blood was welling from a cut on her right palm.

"I'm fine," she said. "It's just a scratch."

"Good. Please carry on."

"I went inside. I don't remember much after that. I went to bed, I think. I had a nightmare, and when I woke up I was outside, near the bluff. I haven't told anyone that—that I sleepwalked during a terrible dream. I sometimes do that when I'm very stressed, and I also have gaps in my memory. Anyway I was cold and scared and I couldn't remember how I'd gotten out there. I went back inside and that was when I saw him."

She blinked hard, remembering those lifeless, staring eyes. How Ryan had been slumped in the chair with that dreadful deep red stain spread over the front of his smart blue shirt.

"I checked his pulse," she said softly. "Then I called you. And that's what happened, Trish. That's everything there is to say."

Cassie thought she'd faint if she stood up. She forced herself to breathe deeply, to gather her thoughts. Her version was shared now—as honest as she could make it, and more than she'd expected. Now they could move on to the logical part of the discussion, and share their thoughts about who could have administered the poison, and when.

To Cassie's surprise, she saw that Trish had stood up and was rummaging in the inside pocket of her jacket.

She wore a smile of pure triumph as she drew something out.

Cassie stared. It was a smart, state-of-the-art Dictaphone recorder.

Trish looked down and carefully pressed the Stop button and as she did so, Cassie realized, in horror, that this evening hadn't been about sharing or collaborating at all. It had never been intended for that.

It had been a trap, carefully laid and artfully concealed.

She'd walked straight into it.

Cassie felt paralyzed with fear. She knew she should grab that tape recorder and fling it out over the balcony—but her reactions were far too slow. She'd only gotten as far as the thought by the time Trish placed the recorder back in her pocket and sat down again on the opposite side of the table.

"What a thorough confession," Trish said in a tone of quiet satisfaction. "I don't think anyone will doubt for a moment now that you killed my husband."

CHAPTER THIRTY EIGHT

"Trish, I didn't kill Ryan. You know I didn't. Don't you?" Cassie's voice trembled audibly.

"Why are you doing this to me? Do you hate me that much, that you want to frame me for something I'm innocent of?"

Trish stared back at her with a slight smile, and Cassie was shocked by her composed calmness. She was ice cold, showing not a trace of empathy or emotion, and Cassie wished she'd been quicker to realize who the true psychopath in the Ellis household was.

"I didn't think the police would do an effective enough job. That's why I bailed you out. Because I knew I could."

She tapped her coat pocket.

"That information was very detailed, and should hold up in a court of law. Especially the mention of the memory loss, a very helpful addition. Along with my testimony, which will fill the gaps in your story, it should be more than enough to get you convicted."

Cassie stared at her in horror. She couldn't speak. She couldn't utter anything in her own defense. She was completely blindsided by what Trish had just done.

"By the way," Trish continued, "as you know, the money in this home is mine. So the diamond necklace belongs to me. I'm sure it will play a part in the evidence. As you said, diamonds are forever—supposedly."

"Why?" Cassie got out in a breathy, terrified voice, but Trish continued.

"Now, let me explain what's going to happen next."

Next? Cassie blinked hard. There was a next? She braced herself for what it would be, because she hadn't thought there could be a bigger nightmare than she was in now.

"I will be out most of tomorrow, making the funeral arrangements and getting my nails done. The children are still off school and are going to visit their aunt again in the morning, but I will need you to look after them in the afternoon. Then when I come back, you will pack your things and go."

"What?" Cassie's voice was high and shrill. Her mind reeled at what Trish was ordering her to do.

"Trish, I can't leave. My bail conditions don't allow it. I have to stay in the house. Or go out with an adult. That's what the police told me. I mean, I signed for it and everything."

She stared at Trish pleadingly, but Trish returned her gaze, icily composed.

"That's your problem, not mine. You will leave soon as I get back. No negotiation, no second chances. If you refuse to go, I'll turn the tape over to the police. So you have the choice. You're with me, or you're against me."

She smiled at Cassie, and Cassie knew she'd never seen such an evil expression on the face of any human being.

She saw exactly what was happening here. Trish would hand the tape in regardless. And those recorded words, together with the fact Cassie had broken her bail conditions and fled the home, would hammer the final nails into the coffin of her guilt.

Trish stood up and collected the wine bottle and the glasses.

She glanced down at the shards by Cassie's feet.

"Sweep that up before you lock up for the night, will you?" she said. "And leave that necklace outside my bedroom door."

She turned and walked inside.

Cassie felt a stinging pain in her palm and realized it was wet with blood.

She'd thought it was just a scratch, but a fragment of glass had speared her skin.

Carefully she drew the bloodied shard out, aware that the sobbing of her own breath was the only sound on the quiet verandah.

She made her faltering way to the kitchen, feeling as if she was on automatic pilot as she rinsed the blood off her hand in the sink. Her mind felt bludgeoned by what had just happened and she felt sick with self-blame, because if she'd been thinking more clearly, she could have avoided it.

Blindly, she had trusted Trish, and now she would pay the price for the rest of her life.

Cassie swept up the glittering slivers of glass and tipped them into the kitchen bin and as they fell, she started to sob. Her legs gave out from under her and she sprawled onto the floor, unable to move, horrified at the calculated evil Trish had shown, and how she'd used Cassie's desperation to achieve her own ends.

She didn't know how long she'd spent in a puddle of tears on the floor before she heard a footfall behind her.

Clumsily she turned.

It was Dylan.

He looked down at her and his face registered mild surprise.

"You OK? I thought I heard something," he whispered.

Cassie struggled to her feet. She was very clearly not OK and there would be no fooling Dylan. Her face felt swollen from crying and her eyes were puffy. The cut on her palm had bled and dried again, leaving a rusty residue. She was sure her face was sheet-white.

"You want some tea?" he asked awkwardly, and that made her start crying all over again.

"I think you should have some tea," he said.

Dylan put the kettle on and for a while the sound of it boiling was the only noise in the room.

"Sweet tea for shock," he said. "We learned it in class. You look shocked."

He added two teaspoons of sugar to the cup.

"Is my bitch of a mother harassing you?" he asked in a low voice, sitting down at the table opposite her.

Cassie stared at him, appalled by his choice of words, and also the conversational way he'd said them.

What could she say back to this strange, sociopathic, twelve-year-old boy who had been at the top of her suspects list until tonight?

She gave the tiniest nod.

Dylan grimaced.

"Dad was cool. He had his issues, but he was a cool guy. I'm sorry he died. Mum is something different."

Cassie's stomach twisted with fear.

"You think so?" she whispered.

Asking the question felt like a betrayal, but at the same time, Cassie was comforted that somebody close to Trish could say such a thing.

"She's mad in the head," Dylan confided.

"Why do you say that?" Cassie could hardly breathe as she whispered the question.

"Well, look at Benjamin Bunny."

Cassie blinked. She hadn't expected Dylan to bring up that topic. She didn't want to think about it. He'd admitted to killing his own pet. What did his mother have to do with that?

"I don't understand," she said.

"I adopted him. Friends were moving, Benjy had nowhere else to go. Nobody wants rabbits, they're not popular pets anymore. I researched it. All he was going to do was stay in a cage in my room. He'd be no harm to anyone. But she freaked out."

In a high whisper, he mimicked her.

"What have you done, Dylan? You know I'm allergic to fur. I won't have a furry animal living in this house. I'm the main breadwinner, I pay the bills. This is my home and my rules and I say the rabbit goes."

"And then?" Cassie asked, fascinated and appalled by the story.

"Before she left on her recent trip, she told me that if Benjamin was home when she got back, she'd poison him. She would have done it, too."

"No!" Cassie breathed, as the implications of what Dylan was saying hit home.

Dylan nodded.

"I thought of letting him go free, but tame rabbits can't survive in the wild, especially older ones. I looked it up."

His face hardened.

"So I broke his neck. I found out how to do it online. It was painless and he died immediately. He didn't know a thing. It was better that way."

Cassie stared at him, gutted by what he'd just shared with her.

Her hands had steadied enough for her to drink some of the sweet, milky tea and Dylan nodded in approval.

"I'm so sorry about Benjamin," she said.

Dylan shrugged.

"I had to choose," he said unemotionally. "But that's what she's like. Unreasonable. And it's all about her, her, her. If you go against her, she torments you. She wouldn't let Maddie do acting. She banned her from doing the school play and said she couldn't take part unless she was top of the class in math."

Dylan laughed scornfully.

"Maddie would never be even halfway to the top. Then she told Maddie she couldn't be the drama club captain or even in the club. She wants a daughter who excels academically. That's Maddie's role and she'll force her into it. That's how she is."

"Oh, no," Cassie breathed. This revelation explained so much about Madison's behavior. That wasn't mothering, that was forcing your own demented agenda onto your children.

Cassie had a new image of Trish now, a darker one.

She was a woman who wouldn't see reason or brook any argument.

And she wasn't normal. In fact, she was the furthest thing from it.

"Thank you for coming to find me," she told Dylan. "You've helped me a lot. We should go to bed now. It's getting very late."

"OK." Dylan stood up, stretched, and yawned.

"See you in the morning."

He turned and walked quietly back down the hall.

Cassie turned off the light and made sure the outside door was locked. She took the diamond necklace from her suitcase and placed it outside Trish's door. Let her have it. With all the lies and misery surrounding it she didn't want it.

Then she headed to bed, but once there, her panic returned.

Dylan's sympathy had been comforting, but it couldn't help her out of her predicament. The taped confession had sealed her fate. She marveled at Trish's cunning in obtaining it from her before forcing her to flee the house.

The police would track her down in no time. There was no way she would be able to hide, and without a passport, she couldn't leave.

The best idea might be to go straight to the police station and turn herself in. Perhaps the sympathetic constable would be there—but she remembered, again, the hard, uncompromising face of Detective Parker, and the way he'd looked at her as if she was already a criminal.

She remembered the hardness of the bed in the jail cell, with its scratchy blue blanket, and the chemical stink of the metal toilet, and the harsh fluorescent light of the cell that had burned itself into her vision.

That was where she'd be again, and who knew for how long?

She had no money for a defense and guessed she would be allocated an overworked public defendant. Meanwhile, Trish would be mustering her resources to ensure that her version was believed.

Cassie wondered what she would do if she was a judge.

Whose testimony would carry more weight—that of the wealthy, highly qualified career woman who was a pillar of local society? Or that of the traveler who was working illegally, had confessed her desire to kill Ryan Ellis, and despite her cocktail of anxiety meds, suffered from nightmares, sleepwalking, and memory loss.

It was a no-brainer.

The situation was hopeless.

As Cassie tossed and turned on her bed, trying her best to banish her thoughts for long enough to get some rest, one fact became crystal clear to her.

Trish Ellis had killed her husband.

It was the only way her actions this evening could be explained, and Dylan had confirmed that this was who she was.

CHAPTER THIRTY NINE

Cassie was driving out of the village, heading down a dark and empty road. Rain spattered on the windscreen, and the wipers sluiced it away.

"I'm not supposed to be here," she said, as fear uncoiled inside her. "My bail conditions don't allow it. I'm out of the village and I'm all alone."

"You're not alone."

Cassie looked at the person sitting in the passenger seat. She hadn't known anyone was there, but when she turned her head, she saw her sister, Jacqui.

Jacqui was dressed as if she was going to a fancy dinner. Her hair was curled, held back by a crystal-studded pin, and her dress and jacket looked smart and new.

"I came into some money," she said. "I can help you."

"How?" Cassie asked, because she knew it was impossible. Jacqui couldn't possibly have a steady job, and in any case, money couldn't buy her way out of this predicament. She was in deep trouble, and it was getting worse with every mile that passed.

"We need to turn back," Cassie said.

"No. Stop."

They got out of the car and walked to the edge of the cliff. Far away, across the ocean, she saw twinkling lights. If she could get there, she would be free, but it seemed so far away.

"Have some wine."

Jacqui passed her a glass of red wine and Cassie lifted it to her lips, but as she was about to drink, she realized that the wine was poisoned. There was a greenish tinge on the surface of the deep red liquid and she could see it was starting to eat away at the glass, leaving it pitted and discolored.

"No!" she screamed. "We can't!"

But Jacqui had already drained her glass, and she lurched toward Cassie.

"You can," she hissed. "You must!"

Her face was changing, hardening, growing pale, and Cassie realized she'd been wrong. It wasn't her sister at all. She was trapped now, and with her back to the cliff, there was nowhere she could go.

The person stumbling toward her with a gray, bloated face and outstretched arms was Ryan Ellis.

Cassie sat up in bed, breathing rapidly. She was drenched in sweat. More nightmares. Laced with poison, they all started with her breaking her bail conditions and ended with the vision of Ryan's corpse.

She had barely slept. Checking the time, she saw it was seven in the morning. Finally, she could get up, but she dreaded what the day would bring.

When she went to the children's rooms she found that Dylan, for once, was still drowsy and she guessed their late-night conversation had tired him out.

Madison was huddled in bed, in floods of tears.

"I miss my dad," she said over and over. She clung to the duvet and it took all of Cassie's patience and persuasion to get her up and dressed.

While she was busy with Madison, she heard the click of Trish's heels on the wooden floor outside, and felt sick with fear as she remembered her threats.

During her long, desperate, and mostly sleepless night, Cassie had considered every alternative, including breaking down in front of the children, pleading innocence, and begging Trish for clemency.

Even though it was her only hope, she was sure Trish would already have anticipated this and thought of a way to counter it.

To Cassie's relief, Trish just tapped on the door and called out a cheery "Goodbye, Maddie" before heading outside.

Only now had Cassie started to notice how little affection she showed the children. She hadn't even bothered to come in, give Madison a proper hug, or comfort her. For all his faults, Ryan had been the backbone of the family. He'd been the one who showed them love, and now he was gone and they were left with her.

Cassie could understand exactly why Madison was behaving this way.

"Come on, Madison," she cajoled. "It's breakfast time, and you need to eat something before your aunt picks you up. Can I make you a pancake? A bacon sandwich? Toad in the hole?"

"Toad in the hole is supper," Madison sniffed. "Can I have a bacon sandwich, please?"

Cassie hurried to prepare it. The children had only just finished eating when she heard a car's horn outside.

She hadn't met their aunt yet. Heading to the front door while the children got their coats, she remembered that she needed to adhere to the letter of her bail conditions. If she put a foot outside the house, she would be breaking them, and she was sure the aunt knew this.

Never mind just the aunt. This was a small village where everyone would know everyone else's business soon after the fact. Cassie had no doubt that there were eyes watching her.

She opened the door.

The aunt, Ryan's sister, was a pleasant-looking woman with curly blonde hair, who looked to be a few years older than Ryan.

"Good morning," Cassie greeted her.

"Hello, I'm Nadine. Are the children ready?"

"They're just getting their coats. I'm so sorry for your loss," Cassie said in a low voice.

Nadine didn't shake her hand and barely looked her in the eye.

Cassie could feel disapproval—no, antipathy—radiating from her. She guessed that everyone in the village already knew and believed Trish's version.

"The children will be back at one," she said.

Madison trailed to the front door, still tearful, but Cassie was encouraged to see that Nadine embraced her in a huge, comforting hug and seemed genuinely concerned and loving.

Dylan followed close behind and also brightened when he saw his aunt.

"Hello, Aunty N. Can we go past the cycling shop on our way?"

"Of course, love. We can spend some time in there if you like."

Without another word to Cassie, she turned and walked with the children to the car.

Cassie closed the front door and made sure it was locked. Remembering that Trish had warned her about the possibility of journalists arriving, she closed the curtains in the family room and her bedroom, so that nobody could photograph her inside the house.

She felt increasingly desperate as she thought about the day ahead.

Trish had committed this crime. Cassie was being forced to take the blame. But maybe, somehow, she could uncover something that would prove her innocence.

After all, she had a few hours on her own now.

Trish might have hidden the Dictaphone somewhere. If Cassie could find it and destroy it, that would be first prize.

Cassie began a methodical search of the house.

She tidied the kitchen and went through every cupboard. She checked the laundry room and hunted through the garage, rummaging in every box and container on the shelves.

She searched through the family room and checked the children's rooms carefully.

She found nothing, and although she'd tried to prepare herself for the fact that nothing would be uncovered, she couldn't help feeling increasingly desperate.

There was one last place to look—the master bedroom.

At that moment, Cassie heard a knock on the front door.

Her heart accelerated, thinking that Trish might be back early and she would be forced to abandon her search before checking the most likely hiding place.

Then common sense returned. Trish wouldn't knock; she had a key.

This could be a journalist though.

Cassie opened the door a crack and peered suspiciously through it.

The gray-haired woman standing outside did a double take when she saw her.

She was holding a covered plate, and through the glass lid Cassie could see a home-baked pie.

"Hello," she said.

People were bringing food to comfort the family, and despite her stress, she couldn't help being touched by the community's kindness.

But the woman glared at her.

"You're the au pair? What are you doing here? I thought you were in prison."

"I—I got bailed out," Cassie stammered.

"Really?" The woman stared at her suspiciously.

Cassie felt her face flush. Under this woman's condemning gaze, she felt no better than a criminal.

"Yes. You can call Trish and check if you like, or she'll be home later this afternoon. Can I take that? Is it for the family?"

"No." The gray-haired woman clutched the plate. "I'm not leaving it with you. For all I know, you'll poison it. I'll stop by again when Trish is back."

Cassie stared at her, appalled that she felt entitled to speak this way to her face.

"Trish bailed me out," she tried in a small voice, but the woman was a juggernaut.

"I can't believe you were given bail. You should be in jail, where you belong. Rest assured, I'll be attending the trial. Ryan was part of our community. You had no right to seduce him and then take his life. You little whore. You deserve whatever's coming to you."

Cassie couldn't take any more of this tirade. From inside her, a tiny voice of courage started to make itself heard.

She was not going to stand here while this woman abused her for a crime she had been wrongfully accused of.

She drew herself taller and glared back at the woman.

"Shut up!" she screamed. "Just shut your mouth. You know nothing about what's happened. Nothing! And if you did, you wouldn't be speaking like this. What gives you the right to say those things to another person, another human being, when you don't even have all the facts? Go away. I don't have to listen to this and you shouldn't be saying it."

She slammed the door in her face.

Peeking through the window, she saw the woman stand, indecisive, for a moment, and Cassie thought that she looked ashamed.

She turned away and walked to the garden gate before heading down the road.

Even though she'd had her say in return, Cassie felt shattered by the woman's accusations. Her words had cut deep. This was what everyone in the village thought of her.

As the woman disappeared from sight, Cassie started weeping with humiliation. This episode had brought her to rock bottom, and she knew there was nowhere lower she could go. Her self-esteem was ruined, she felt mired in confusion and shame. She was a victim—first of Ryan, and now of Trish, and together, the couple had annihilated her own future.

There was no hope in anything.

Cassie wanted to lie sprawled on the floor and simply let the hours pass by until the inevitable happened.

Somehow, she found the strength to get up and totter to the master bedroom.

There, she checked all the drawers and the filing cabinet. She felt under the mattress and looked under the bed and pounded the pillows.

She was running out of places to look, and she was starting to realize that of course Trish would not have left the recorder behind. Even if it had been hidden well, she must have guessed that a desperate search would uncover it.

Faced with the certain prospect of failure, it took all of her will power to hold herself together. She reached deep inside herself and to her surprise, Cassie found a steely core that she'd never known was there.

Abandoning the search would mean giving up. She wasn't going to do it. No matter that the horrors she'd been through had left her at her lowest ebb, that she was emotionally shattered and drained of strength and feeling entirely broken.

She was not going to let Trish win. Even if she didn't find the recorder perhaps there might be something—anything—that she could use to prove her innocence.

Drawing a deep breath, Cassie resumed her search. She checked the wardrobes, looking in Trish's empty suitcases and under her clothes. She went through the coat hangers, checking the pockets of every jacket, because after all, that was where Trish had concealed the recorder in the first place.

There was nothing to find.

Cassie opened Ryan's cupboard and did the same.

Her search uncovered nothing except a folded note and a business card in the back pocket of a pair of his jeans.

Curious, Cassie opened the note.

She recognized the writing.

"Hello handsome," the note read. "Thought I'd surprise you by reminding you I'm thinking about you. Give me a call when you find this and let's meet up. Dinner, drinks, pink hair, pink champagne, and you know what!"

She guessed the note was Harriet's. During their affair, the cleaner must have hidden a note for Ryan. Had he found it, read it, and put it back in his pants? Or had he never seen it at all? She didn't know.

The business card was the standard card for Maids of Devon, with an office number and an email, but on the back of the card, Harriet had scribbled her cell phone number.

Cassie looked down at it and her mind started to race.

She had one friend in this village; one person who understood what she'd been through, and who would most likely believe her innocence.

How could she use this information?

Cassie remembered the magician shuffling his cards in the town square, and his expert use of misdirection.

Dylan's matter-of-fact acceptance of his mother's intent to poison his rabbit and the preemptive action he'd taken.

The angry, aggressive stance of the detective as he'd bemoaned the lack of concrete evidence to convict her.

The confession she'd made so innocently, shouting out her anger at her betrayal, not knowing that every word would be used against her.

Cassie felt the threads of a plan start spinning together. It relied on many factors she couldn't control or predict—first and most importantly, that Harriet would answer her phone and would agree to help.

It was a long shot, a desperate stab in the dark, but it was all she had, and her only hope of escaping.

Cassie picked up her cell phone and dialed.

CHAPTER FORTY

It was late afternoon when Trish finally returned.

Sitting at the kitchen table, Cassie heard the snick of the door latch, the rattle as it closed.

She felt sick with nerves. All the decisions she made now, the variables she couldn't control—they would decide her fate. Her plan was flimsy, born of last-minute desperation. There were a thousand reasons why it might not work.

Misdirection, she thought. You can do it.

Once again, she felt that steely resilience inside her, an inner strength she hadn't thought she possessed, giving her the courage she needed to see this through.

Trish's heels clicked along the wooden floor.

"Hello, kids," she called.

Then, with a sharpness in her voice, "Dylan? Madison? Are you here?"

A moment later, Trish was at the kitchen door.

She looked as immaculately made up as if she'd stepped out of the house a minute ago. She was dressed to the nines in a tailored black suit and a string of pearls.

"Where are the children?" she snapped at Cassie. "Did they stay at Nadine's place? What's going on? I want them home, and you out of here."

She rummaged in her purse for her cell phone.

"Don't bother calling Nadine," Cassie said. "She brought the children back at one."

"Where are they then?" Trish glared at her. "Why the hell aren't they here?"

"They're safe," Cassie said. "But they're not in this house."

Now Trish was looking at her with a shocked expression, as if a worm she'd been about to crush had turned into a spitting cobra.

"What's going on?"

"I thought you and I needed to talk, alone. Would you like to sit down?"

Cassie gestured to the chair and then tugged her coat closed again. She couldn't stop her hand from moving toward the inside pocket, before she quickly lowered it.

Trish was watching her intently.

"Why do we need to talk?"

Cassie forced herself to speak as calmly as she could, even though she couldn't stop her hands from shaking.

"Trish, I know you murdered Ryan. You put the rat poison in his wine. There's no doubt about it. But what I want to know is why? It can't just be because he had an affair with me. You must know what he's like. So—why?"

Trish started to laugh. The unpleasant, bell-like sound pealed through the room.

"Open your coat."

Cassie stared at her, her eyes wide, her face stricken.

"Why must I?" Now her voice shook.

"Call it a whim. Because I'm not stupid. Huddled in a coat in a warm kitchen? Really? Go on, open it."

Cassie's face crumpled.

Slowly she opened the coat.

"I can see it there. Take it out, sweetie. Don't make me come and do it for you."

Cassie's hands were shaking so badly she could hardly remove the Dictaphone from her inside pocket.

It wasn't an expensive model, like Trish's had been. It was a much cheaper one, which Harriet had picked up on the way to fetch Dylan and Madison, who were now at Harriet's house.

Cheap it had been, but Cassie had hoped it would do the job. Now she bit her lip, staring at Trish with silent appeal as she placed the item on the kitchen table.

"Let's take a look." Trish picked it up.

"Goodness me, it's recording and all. But not for long."

She turned it off.

"How cute. You were hoping to tape my confession. Well, unfortunately, I'm not playing along. In fact, I think we'll get rid of this altogether. What a shame you had to waste your money. Not that you'll have a chance to spend it in jail."

She threw the small, silver recorder onto the floor.

Then she stamped on it. Cassie watched, horrified, as Trish brought her tough, shiny boot down on the recorder over and over.

"No," she cried. "Trish, please, no."

It didn't take long for its flimsy shell to splinter. Within a minute, the recorder was lying in fragments on the floor. Cassie stared at it, and then back at Trish, and she knew that her face must be a picture of devastation.

"No," she whispered over and over.

She could only imagine what Trish thought, watching her. How pathetic, how broken she looked after her rookie effort at deception had failed.

"You needn't bother to sweep it up before you go," Trish told her sympathetically. "I'll do that while I wait for the police to arrive."

She laughed again.

"Would you like some wine?"

When Cassie shook her head, Trish shrugged.

"Well, I'm having some."

She opened a bottle and poured herself a glass.

"Cheers," she said, and the smile she gave Cassie was without any trace of warmth.

"You're right. I did kill him," she said. "I put the poison in his wine. I wasn't as drunk as I looked. And, trust me, when I heard him yelling at you on the balcony, I sobered up rather fast."

"You killed him because he yelled at me?" Cassie asked incredulously. Trish sighed.

"Try and apply some intelligence, will you? No, I killed him because of what he threatened you with. Look, screwing around was not his prerogative. My trips overseas? Trust me, darling, we had an open relationship and I didn't grudge Ryan his little flings. I didn't even care that he was a compulsive liar, or that he was bad with money, although it did get tedious having to bail him out every so often."

"What was it then?" Cassie asked. Her lips felt numb and she struggled to get the words out; her voice sounded flat, as if she no longer cared what Trish's motive was.

"He threatened to call social services. He promised the children would show evidence of abuse. You know something?"

Trish pulled out the chair opposite Cassie and sat down, leaning across the wooden table in a conspiratorial way.

"You must have really got to him, because I haven't ever seen him so angry. Clearly, you pushed all his buttons. But threatening to harm my children is unacceptable. Having social services come round and investigate would be extremely inconvenient, and it would risk damaging my reputation. My career relies on an impeccable record, as my company deals with corporates, celebrities, and politicians at the very highest level."

Cassie cleared her throat.

"You want to say something?" Trish asked. "Please, go ahead. The floor is yours. You could call this our girls' get-together."

Cassie's voice trembled audibly as she spoke.

"I think you were worried your children might tell social services about other things. Like threatening to poison Dylan's rabbit or pull Madison off the stage. That's abuse, too, I think."

Cassie watched Trish's face twist with anger.

"Oh, my word, you have been getting friendly. Well, enough of that, I'll have a word with them later about tale-telling. I'm sick of you, and your pathetic attempts to hide your affair, and your lame efforts to ingratiate yourself with my children. Now, tell me where they are."

Cassie stood up and moved round the other side of the table, keeping it between them.

Every muscle in her body felt tense. Her breath was rapid and shallow and she willed herself to be strong, to keep reaching for that inner steel, because if she buckled now, it would all be over.

She moved aside a folded dishcloth on the kitchen counter.

Next to it was her cell phone; it had been in plain sight, but yet camouflaged, because she'd drawn all Trish's attention to the hidden recorder. She picked it up and held it tight.

"The Dictaphone was a red herring," she said to Trish. "This phone has been taping you the whole time. I'm not letting your children come home until the police have listened to it and arrested you."

CHAPTER FORTY ONE

Trish's scream of rage filled the room.

Cassie saw her face darken as she realized she'd been double-crossed.

"Give me that. Now!" she cried.

Cassie backed away.

Adrenaline coursed through her. She hadn't expected Trish's anger to be so sudden.

"No," she insisted.

Trish paused, making a final attempt to regain control of the situation.

"Cassie," she spat. "The police will never believe you. But let's talk. We can work together. We never shared who else might have done it. The cleaner would be my guess, and if you and I both say so to the police, there's a strong likelihood they'll believe us. Come on."

Cassie shook her head.

Trish laughed, but it was a high, panicky sound. She began babbling out the words.

"I can see you want more. That's fine. After what you've been through, I'll be happy to compensate you. Let's sit down again and discuss it properly."

"I'm not discussing anything with you, Trish," Cassie insisted. "I've seen who you are. You deserve what's coming to you."

In the blink of an eye, Trish's reasonable demeanor evaporated. Her eyes narrowed and her lips curled back.

"You bitch. If you don't want to give me that, I'm going to make you."

She leaped at Cassie, who jumped away in terror as Trish's nails raked her face. The tall woman lunged toward her and got hold of her arm.

"No!" Cassie screamed. She twisted away, trying to dislodge her grip, but Trish was fighting with the strength of desperation. She could hear her breath, harsh in her ear, as her fingers clamped around Cassie's wrist. Inexorably she started prizing the phone out of Cassie's hand. Cassie was shocked by her wiry power.

Flailing her free arm behind her in a panic, Cassie caught hold of something and grasped it tight. She recognized the shape of the giant pepper grinder.

Clumsily, she raised it and brought it down on Trish's head with all her strength.

Trish swore violently, staggering back, and even though she didn't let go, her grip loosened enough for Cassie to twist away.

Trish made another grab for her and got hold of her jacket, pulling her back so she ricocheted against the table. The wooden table rocked and tilted, and the bottle and glasses smashed on the floor. Glass fragments exploded over the tiles, as wine sluiced across the floor like blood.

Trish swore again as she slipped on a piece of glass, and that allowed Cassie to break free once again.

She made a desperate run for it, glass crunching under her trainers, skidding over the wet floor as she headed for the door.

Behind her, Trish had the strength and speed of total desperation. Cassie heard her footsteps thudding, far too close.

Then something tore at her jacket, ripping it open, and as she glanced behind her, she screamed.

Trish had picked up one of the long, lethal kitchen knives and Cassie had come within inches of having it slice through her flesh. The shock gave her an extra burst of speed and she leaped ahead.

Where to go? She sped down the hallway, riding on the wings of her fear, knowing that Trish was taller and probably faster, and had more to lose.

She bolted into the master bedroom. Slammed the door. She twisted the key in the lock just as Trish flung her weight against it.

Gasping for breath, Cassie realized the door had bought her only a moment's respite. The latch was too flimsy, and at any moment, Trish could break through.

She ran into the bathroom, closed the door—and realized in horror that there was no key.

Cassie flung it open again and saw that the bedroom door was starting to splinter.

She slid the phone under the bed. For now, it would be a safe hiding place. Then she ran to the window and forced it open.

The latch was stiff, and the hinges had been painted over and resisted her efforts to push it wide. The bedroom door was shaking and rattling with wood splinters scattering over the floor, and she guessed that on the next attempt, Trish would be inside.

Visions spun through Cassie's head; fragments of the nightmare where the window had become a skyscraper.

Pushing the fear from her mind, she jumped.

This was less of a drop, but the impact when she landed on the paved walkway jarred every bone in her body.

She longed to flee the property, out and away, but in a car, Trish would be much faster and could also run her down.

She was out of time; she could see Trish approaching the window. She had to get out of sight at once, and in this neatly trimmed winter garden there were few options. Hugging the wall, Cassie ran around the house, hoping for a better hiding place in the back, near the sea.

The only plant that offered cover was a small, spiky-leafed bush with red berries.

She crept around it and crouched down in its shadow, crawling as deep into its cover as she could and trying to muffle the sound of her breathing, which was coming in desperate, painful gasps.

Trish would know she'd escaped through the window. There hadn't been a chance to close it. Therefore, she must know she was hiding in the garden.

It was nearly dark. Every minute that passed would make it more difficult to see her. If she could hide here for long enough, she might be safe. But she felt like a hunted animal when she thought of Trish; a hunted animal who was trying to escape the kill.

Cassie cringed lower as the powerful beam of a flashlight shone into the garden.

Trish had anticipated her. She'd left the bedroom and gone out of the back door. Now the darkness meant nothing and in fact would be Trish's friend.

The flashlight beam dazzled Cassie, and she knew that behind its blinding glare, Trish was holding the knife.

She tried to hold her breath, to contain the ragged gasps, to become one with the grass so that nothing, not even her terrified thoughts, would draw Trish's attention to her.

She watched as the flashlight danced over the flower beds. Trish was using the light, but she wasn't moving. She was letting the beam do the work for her and staying in a place where she had the best view of the whole garden.

The light moved away from the flower beds and for a moment, it flickered over the grass.

Then it was shining right at her, through the branches, and she knew that Trish had seen her.

"Come on out, Cassie. The game's over now."

Trish's voice was hoarse and breathless, but it sounded triumphant.

She didn't wait for Cassie to obey. A moment later, she was sprinting over the lawn toward her.

Breaking from her cover, Cassie ran for her life, stumbling in the dark, because the light had dazzled her and she was temporarily blinded. Her plan had been to head to the laundry room and, from there, try to scramble over the fence into the property next door.

Terrified and disoriented, she found she was heading in the same direction she had sleepwalked—out toward the bluff.

"The phone—it's in—the bedroom," she gasped, turning to face Trish.

The flashlight pinned her and she flinched away, averting her eyes as the beam bobbed toward her.

"I am not interested in the phone now," Trish spat.

Cassie dove to her right, with Trish following close behind. The thought of that knife was making Cassie's blood run cold with dread. All it would take would be one thrust of its sharp, lethal blade—and she had no doubt that Trish would put all the strength she had into that thrust.

As she was gaining some ground, disaster struck.

Her foot caught a rock and she sprawled onto the grass, falling head-long, jackknifing out of the way in case the blade came down.

But she twisted in the wrong direction.

Cassie screamed as she felt herself slip off the cliff's edge. She grabbed desperately for purchase, hoping to find something—anything. Tussocks of grass sliced at her fingers but offered no grip.

The crashing of the sea filled her ears. Below her, she knew, was a dizzying drop to the crags. The tide was in; she could hear it. She would land broken and injured, and be swept out to sea by the cold and unrelenting waves.

Then her clutching fingers found a rocky outcrop.

The sandstone was wet and slippery and, worse still, it felt as if it was about to break loose from the cliff side.

Sandstone crumbles; she'd told Dylan so. Now this fragile hold was all that was keeping her from certain death.

Cassie grabbed onto it and held with all her might, knowing that she didn't have much time, because her flailing legs could find no purchase, and her arms were already burning.

This had bought her a minute or two, at most. She couldn't climb back up and when her arms were exhausted, they would release their hold and she would fall.

Her nightmares rushed back.

She remembered Jacqui's taunting words, her face as she looked down with evil glee, ready to abandon Cassie to her fate.

Then, above her, the flashlight blinded her again.

"You're hanging on?"

Trish gave a breathy laugh, as Cassie saw the glint of the blade. "Not for long."

CHAPTER FORTY TWO

Even if she was not within arm's reach, Cassie knew she was within knife's reach.

She clenched her teeth, willing herself to keep on holding even when she felt the knife stab into her. Even though it would slice through her skin and her tendons, ripping her flesh from the bone and opening her veins, she must still hold on. She was going to keep gripping the rock until Trish cut her away from it, or until her own strength gave out.

Then, suddenly, the flashlight veered upward.

She heard Trish shriek, and the babble of voices above, and she knew that, despite all the risks, all the things that could have gone wrong, help had arrived.

Trish would be arrested now and receive the justice she deserved.

The only problem was that it was too late for her.

Her arms were shuddering and the sweat on her palms was causing her fingers to slip.

She felt them releasing and a strange peace filled her. She felt as if Jacqui was with her, offering her comfort, and she knew that as she fell, as her bones shattered, she would not be alone.

And then, another light blazed—this time a brilliant floodlight that illuminated the entire area. Even as her nerveless fingers lost their grip, she felt two strong hands clamp around her wrists, catching her as she fell, holding her in a tight, firm grasp.

"It's OK. You're safe. I won't let you go."

Cassie stared up into the intense blue eyes of Detective Parker.

It took a few minutes for Cassie to be hauled up, and it was only when she was safely on the grass, lying on a blanket because her shaking legs would not hold her, that she realized the personal risk Parker had taken to save her.

He'd dived halfway over the cliff to grab her before she fell, trusting that his team would somehow be able to hold him and stop him from falling with her.

They had managed. Bruton was looking visibly shocked by the close call, and the friendly constable, who had introduced herself as Trainee Detective Chandra, was in tears.

"I'm so glad you're OK, Cassie," she sniffed. "Parker, you're a hero. I can't believe you did that."

He shook his head.

"I couldn't stop thinking about what you said. That I should try as hard to save her as I had done to lock her up. You're the one who made me take that risk."

"But how did you know where she was? We'd planned to search the house first!"

Parker frowned.

"Did you not hear her? As soon as I got out the car, I heard her screaming."

He turned to Cassie. "You were yelling, 'Jacqui! Jacqui! Help!' I didn't know who was screaming, I just followed the sound."

"I was?" Cassie asked, amazed. She hadn't thought she'd said a word.

"She was?" Chandra asked with equal surprise. "You must have very sensitive hearing. I was only a few steps behind you and didn't pick up a thing."

Before Cassie could ask Parker anything more about this weird coincidence, she heard a whisper from behind her.

It was Trish's bitter voice, and she looked sharply around.

"How did this happen?"

Cassie was glad to see Trish was safely restrained. Her hands were secured behind her back and she was in the firm grasp of a uniformed police officer.

Cameras flashed around them, as the detectives recorded the scene. The discarded flashlight, and the kitchen knife that the police had ripped out of Trish's hands.

"I made a plan with Harriet," Cassie told her.

She couldn't tell Trish what it had taken. How Harriet had sped straight to her house, stopping only to pick up a Dictaphone on the way. They'd planned together, nervous and desperate, knowing that their entire scenario relied on multiple factors beyond their control—as well as misdirection.

"The Dictaphone was a red herring," she said. "But when I told you I was recording everything, that also wasn't true. I called Harriet as soon as I heard you arrive, and left my phone on the counter. She recorded everything on her side, and contacted the police right afterwards."

The children were still at Harriet's house. She'd reassured Cassie they were holed up in her tiny family room, with junk food and cable TV, and that they'd be safe and happy for the evening, while Harriet waited in her bedroom—where the cell phone signal was strongest—for events to unfold.

Cassie knew she owed Harriet a massive debt of gratitude.

Bruton sighed.

"Next time you ladies plan a sting operation, please inform us beforehand and not during, or after, the fact. It's always safer. But you acted with great bravery, and thanks to your actions, we can nail the perpetrator on a variety of charges. Murder, attempted murder, perjury, resisting arrest. She won't get bail, and will be in prison a very long time. A life sentence, for sure."

Cassie couldn't imagine a worse fate, or a more fitting punishment, for the woman who'd so ruthlessly orchestrated her life and reputation to suit her own needs.

Trish stared at her, stony-faced, and although she didn't speak, Cassie could see the defeat in her eyes.

"The van's here. You can take her straight into custody," Bruton told the arresting officers. "We'll be along later, as soon as we've finished interviewing Ms. Vale."

To Cassie's astonishment, Parker handed her a white envelope.

"This is yours."

Her passport was inside. Cassie stared down at it, not believing her eyes. Then she looked back at Parker.

"Are you really giving it back to me? You're sure?"

He nodded.

"But—what about my visa?"

Bruton spoke.

"Your working status is not relevant to this murder case. We don't intend to pursue the matter, since the person who supposedly hired you is now deceased. Now, we need to take your statement and do this interview."

The friendly constable cleared her throat.

"The kitchen's a disaster zone, love, but once you've walked the detectives through the scene, and we've finished photographing, we'll get a clean-up crew in so that it's all in order by tomorrow. Meanwhile, we've had an offer from the guesthouse across the road. They will allow us to use their dining room for the interview, and the proprietor invited you to stay the night in one of the rooms at no charge, if you'd be more comfortable there."

"I would," Cassie said, gratefully. "Please tell her thank you very much for the offer."

Hopefully, word had spread in the village that she'd been the innocent party all along. Even though she knew loyalties ran deep and not everyone would believe the truth, at least it meant she was no longer the local pariah.

"I'm going to go to Harriet's house now," the friendly constable said. "We've decided the children should go straight to their aunt's for the night, so I'll organize things from that side. Could you help me with a change of clothes for them, please, and I can take a bag through?"

After she'd walked the police through the fight scene in the kitchen, Cassie hurried through to the master bedroom.

There, under the bed, was her phone and she felt filled with relief that it was still working. A corner of the screen had been cracked in the melee but it was still usable.

Heading back down the hall, she packed toiletries, pajamas, and a change of clothes into a bag for the children.

At the last minute, she tore a page off the pink notebook in Madison's room.

"I love you both," she wrote. "Sleep well. I'll see you tomorrow."

She added the note to the bag.

Then, grabbing her toothbrush, her meds, and a spare shirt, she walked with the police to the guesthouse for the final interview.

Her arms were aching, her hands in agony. Her fingers felt bruised and her palms were lined with shallow cuts. Clutching at the rock had left raw grazes on her wrists. Somewhere along the line, the sleeve of her jacket had torn, and when she took it off to shake the grit out, she stared in horror at the deep slice down its back.

Trish had come within inches of opening up a lethal flesh wound.

She'd fought for her life, but she'd won. Trish might be wealthy, and have an MBA and a high-powered job, but when the chips were down, Cassie had prevailed as the stronger person.

She remembered the inner resilience she'd sensed inside her—so tough and unexpected. Where had that core of steel come from? She didn't know, but it had allowed her to keep her nerve—barely—and to hang on to the rock for longer than she'd thought physically possible.

Cassie thought about her tough upbringing and the scars she carried, the fact she'd had to survive fights and domestic violence, and fend for herself, even if it just meant doing humble waitressing jobs. Perhaps the life she'd been so ashamed of hadn't been a bad thing.

Maybe—just maybe—it had laid the foundation for what she needed to survive this.

CHAPTER FORTY THREE

The piercing ring of Cassie's phone dragged her out of an exhausted slumber, and she fumbled to answer it.

"Hello?" She sat up, turning on the light and blinking bleary-eyed at the white curtains of the luxury room she'd been allocated.

The man on the other end of the line was a stranger.

"Good morning. Am I speaking to Cassie Vale?"

"Yes, you are," Cassie said warily.

"I'm Dave Sidley from Dave's Auto Repairs. We have your car."

"My car?" Cassie's voice was high with surprise.

"Yes. Sorry for the delay fixing it. Replacing all the wires was a time-consuming job, but it's done now. I'm coming to town with my mechanic, so I can drop it off for you in an hour if you like."

"Of course. Thank you so much."

Cassie felt on top of the world—but how much would this cost?

"What do I owe you?" she asked, wondering if there would be time to head down to the bank.

"We've heard about the family tragedy. In the light of that, I can't charge you. The job's on us. Please accept our condolences and pass our good wishes on to the children."

"I will do," Cassie promised. "Thank you so much. That's incredibly kind."

The guesthouse proprietor had prepared her a lavish breakfast. Realizing how hungry she was, with her appetite flooding back, Cassie ate every bite. Then she headed across the road, where, a minute later, she was rewarded by the sight of her car arriving.

Gratefully, she accepted the keys from the mechanic, feeling elated to have her wheels in working order. With her car and her passport, the world felt hers again. Freedom flooded her, the rush as intense as wine.

Inside the house, the police had tidied the kitchen and swept up every fragment of glass. It looked ordered and homely and Cassie found it difficult to believe that such a nightmare had happened there, that she'd fought for her life, that she'd managed to trick a murderer into a confession.

Now it was time to leave.

She packed her bags into her car and waited for the children to arrive. She'd received a text from the aunt the previous night saying they were safe, and that they'd be home to pack up their belongings, by nine a.m. at the latest.

At five to nine, the aunt's car pulled up.

This time, Nadine was first out of the car to greet Cassie.

"What a nightmare," she kept repeating. "You were so brave. Thank you for what you did."

Then Dylan and Madison were hugging her.

"We're going to stay with our aunt," Madison whispered, her eyes shining. "I'm allowed to join the drama club and I can go to boarding school next year if I still want to."

Cassie felt her heart melt with happiness.

"Can you take fish tanks in your car?" Dylan asked Nadine in concern. "Because Orange and Lemon have to come with me. I've researched how to transport them."

He shook Cassie's hand.

"You were a trouper," he said. "My aunt says I can adopt another rabbit. I'm thinking about it."

Cassie smiled at him. Although she would never know who Dylan really was, she felt that she understood him better now.

"I know you'll do your best for the little guy."

Cassie waved at the children as they went into the house to pack their belongings. She planned to head into the village, draw enough cash to keep her solvent for a while, and then go past Harriet's house with a thank-you gift. There was a diamante bomber jacket she'd seen in a shop window that she thought the cleaner would love.

And then, who knew where? Cassie resolved it would be somewhere far, far away from this village.

When she got into her car, she saw she had a new message.

Quickly, while she was still within range of the home's Wi-Fi, she read it.

It was from Renee, her friend in the States.

"Hey, Cassie," the message read. "Just to let you know, that lady phoned again yesterday. I gave her your number. She sounded stressed, and said she was worried you might be in trouble. She said she'll contact you soon. Just give her time."

Cassie read the message again and again, feeling a deep contentment as she took in the words. She felt Jacqui's presence around her, even though she didn't understand the strange turn last night's events had taken.

Perhaps she'd never be able to.

Some bonds worked in inexplicable ways that were far beyond understanding.

One day, she hoped, she would see Jacqui again.

Cassie started the car and drove away, glancing in her rearview mirror so she wouldn't miss the moment when the Ellises' house disappeared from sight forever.

Now Available!

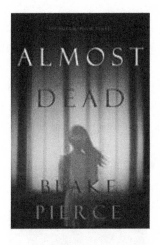

ALMOST DEAD
(The Au Pair—Book Three)

"A MASTERPIECE OF THRILLER AND MYSTERY. Blake Pierce did a magnificent job developing characters with a psychological side so well described that we feel inside their minds, follow their fears and cheer for their success. Full of twists, this book will keep you awake until the turn of the last page."

--Books and Movie Reviews, Roberto Mattos (re Once Gone)

ALMOST DEAD is book #3 in a new psychological thriller series by USA Today bestselling author Blake Pierce, whose #1 bestseller Once Gone (Book #1) (a free download) has received over 1,000 five star reviews.

After the disastrous fallout from her last placement in England, all 23-year-old Cassandra Vale wants is a chance to pick up the pieces. A high-society, divorced mother in sunny Italy seems to be the answer. But is she?

With a new family come new children, new rules, and new expectations. Cassandra's determined to make this one last - until a horrifying discovery pushes her to a breaking point.

And when the unimaginable occurs, will it be too late to pull herself back from the brink? Who, she wonders, is she becoming?

A riveting mystery replete with complex characters, layers of secrets, dramatic twists and turns and heart-pounding suspense, ALMOST DEAD is book #3 in a psychological suspense series that will have you turning pages late into the night.

Book #4 in the series will be available soon.

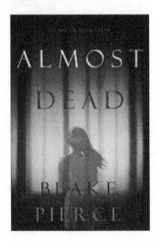

ALMOST DEAD
(The Au Pair—Book Three)

Made in the USA
Monee, IL
24 April 2022

95276364R00166